Had he truly just pledged himself to work closely with Miss Overton? Hugh wasn't sure how wise that might prove.

He'd shut himself off from more than just his emotions after the deaths of his wife and son. Grieving, angry, guilty, anguished, he'd closed out every pleasure. Including the pleasure of feminine company.

He couldn't deny, much as he'd deliberately tried not to notice, that Miss Overton...stirred something within him that he'd repressed for a long time. Forcing himself to open up to his cousin's children was necessary, whatever the pain. They were his wards, his legal responsibility, and duty required that he do everything possible to make life easier for them.

Exposing himself to the allure of feminine company was not required. After the way his marriage had ended, he didn't think he would ever risk his heart again. But presented with temptation, his body might not be so amenable to control.

He didn't see how he could avoid working with the governess—but he must take care to maintain his distance and remember she was an employee. A dependent female member of his household he had a duty to support and protect. And nothing more.

Author Note

What do you do when everything you've counted on having in your life is suddenly lost?

Heroine Olivia Overton planned on spending her life forwarding the great reform legislation under consideration by Parliament. But when her trustees' mismanagement of her inheritance leaves her virtually penniless, and unwilling to depend on a relative's charity or accept a marriage of convenience to a man she could never love, she chooses to remain independent by becoming a governess.

Hero Colonel Hugh Glendenning planned a life of service in India—until the tragic loss of his wife and child, followed by the death of his older brother, called him back to England to take over his family's badly neglected estate. Guilty and grieving, he escapes the past by burying himself in his work.

Their paths collide when Hugh's cousin dies, leaving him guardian of two little girls—who are unexpectedly deposited on his doorstep. Their presence is an agonizing reminder of the son he lost, so he hires a governess to deal with them until he can find a suitable female family member to take over their care.

As Olivia works with Hugh to try to do what is best for the girls, they both discover that sometimes what you need can be very different from what you expected. And that having the courage to seize second chances offers the possibility of joy more wondrous than you could have imagined. I hope you will enjoy their journey.

JULIA JUSTISS

The Tempting of the Governess

HISTORICAL™

**Recycling programs
for this product may
not exist in your area.**

ISBN-13: 978-1-335-50535-4

The Tempting of the Governess

Copyright © 2020 by Janet Justiss

This edition published by arrangement with Harlequin Books S.A.

For questions and comments about the quality of this book,
please contact us at CustomerService@Harlequin.com.

Harlequin Enterprises ULC
22 Adelaide St. West, 40th Floor
Toronto, Ontario M5H 4E3, Canada
www.Harlequin.com

Printed in U.S.A.

Julia Justiss wrote her first ideas for Nancy Drew stories in her third-grade notebook and has been writing ever since. After publishing poetry in college, she turned to novels. Her Regency historicals have won or placed in contests by the Romance Writers of America, *RT Book Reviews*, National Readers' Choice Awards and the Daphne du Maurier Award. She lives with her husband in Texas. For news and contests, visit juliajustiss.com.

Visit the Author Profile page
at Harlequin.com for more titles.

To my darlings Anna, Samantha and Bennett.
You prove every day what a delight
little girls can be.

Chapter One

'*I am very sorry, Miss Overton, but you have no more money.*'

Numb with shock, Olivia Overton walked slowly back down the stairs from the solicitor's office, his unexpected and horrifying news still echoing in her ears.

Reaching the pavement, she hesitated. The prospect of returning home to Upper Brook Street brought back all the unhappy memories of two weeks earlier, when she'd come in to discover her mama expired upon the drawing-room sofa.

Adding in the unpalatable fact that the home she'd occupied for more than twelve years now belonged to someone else and she knew she couldn't bring herself to cross that threshold again just yet.

She'd go visit Sara Standish and reveal her drastically changed circumstances to her best friend, the one person in London who would understand her shock, pain and distress.

Thinking with gallows humour that she'd better enjoy the luxury of travelling by hackney before her few remaining funds ran out, she walked down the street and found a jarvey to convey her to Hanover Square.

A short time later, the butler escorted her to the Standish town house's small back parlour. 'I'll send Miss Standish down immediately,' he whispered, his cautious glance towards the grand front salon letting her know that Sara's mother, who had long enjoyed being an invalid, must be reclining on her couch there, receiving friends conveying the latest *ton* gossip.

A ripple of anguish went through as she realised that the next likely topic of gossip would be her.

Have you heard? That Overton girl has lost all her money! A shame she's so odd—and plain. No chance of her getting some gentleman to rescue her with an offer of marriage.

She took a deep, steadying breath. *Ton* gossip would soon be the least of her worries. Whatever she decided to do next, she would have very little time to figure it out— before her cousin Sir Roger and the new Lady Overton arrived in London to take possession of her house.

Too restless to take a seat, she paced back and forth in front of the mantel, halting when Sara appeared on the threshold. Taking one look at Olivia's face, her quiet, gentle blonde friend came over and pulled her into a hug. 'My poor dear! Have you been missing your mama badly today?'

For a moment, Olivia clung to Sara, to the person who seemed her last safe haven in a suddenly chaotic and threatening world. 'No more than usual,' she said, releasing her to take a seat beside her on the sofa. 'Isn't it strange how you can live with a person for years, finding them an indifferent companion, sometimes even an annoyance, and yet miss them quite dreadfully when they are gone?'

Sara cast a glance towards the front parlour. 'I understand completely. And Mama isn't even much involved in my life, having taken to her couch and delegated all responsibility for me to Aunt Patterson years ago. Whereas your mother actually dined with you and took you into society with her.'

Olivia laughed wryly. 'A society I never appreciated and whose rules and expectations I could not wait to escape. Ah, how I longed to leave the Marriage Mart for good, to set out upon our independent lives and finally, finally be able to pursue what *we* feel is important.'

'Praise heaven, we won't have to wait much longer,' Sara said with feeling. 'The Season is nearly over. Soon, we'll be able to move to our house on Judd Street and begin those new, independent lives! At least, when we do, your unfortunate loss means you won't have to suffer any further tears or lamentations from your family about having made a choice that will "doom your matrimonial prospects and see you exiled from society for ever."'

Enthusiasm shining in her eyes, Sara continued, 'Only imagine, no longer being dragged out on pointless afternoon calls or having to attend endlessly boring evening entertainments! We shall be able to devote all our time to supporting Ellie Lattimar's school and working with Lady Lyndlington's Ladies' Committee. Think of all the letters we'll be able to write, urging support of the reform legislation Lord Lyndlington and his party are pushing forward in Parliament! Issues so much more important than the cut of a bonnet or the style of a sleeve, the only pressing topics being discussed by the ladies at

the Emersons' ball last night. Ah, here's our tea. Thank
you, Jameson.'

'Lady Patterson asked that I inform you that she will
join you in a few moments,' the butler said as he set
down the tray.

Sara nodded, then rolled her eyes at Olivia as the
butler walked out of the room. 'If you have something
important to say, better tell me before Aunt Doom and
Gloom arrives.'

Olivia uttered a laugh that sounded a bit hysterical,
even to her own ears. 'I'm afraid I do. Something of
rather major importance. I visited Mr Henson this morning to enquire about transferring funds for my part of the
maintenance of our Judd Street house. Only to discover
that… I have no money.'

Sara angled her head, her expression puzzled. 'You
have no money? I thought that, though the trustees retained the management of them, you could draw on your
funds at will, once you reached one-and-twenty. Indeed,
I thought you had been doing so these last two years.'

Olivia's smile turned bitter. 'So I had. Except now,
it appears, the trustees have "managed" me right out of
my inheritance. They invested both interest and capital
in a canal project that has just gone bankrupt. All I have
left in the world, apparently, is one hundred pounds in
the London bank.'

For a moment, fury consumed her that, while she, as
a single female, had not been considered competent to
manage her own funds, the supposedly wiser and more
experienced male trustees had been free to gamble her
money on a risky project.

The solicitor might be apologetic.

She was destitute.

Sara's eyes widened and her mouth opened in shock. 'That's…all? One hundred pounds?'

'Between me and penury. And to make the situation even sweeter, Mr Henson said that Sir Roger, who now owns the Upper Brook Street house, wants to take possession—immediately.'

'Oh, Olivia,' Sara whispered, taking her hand and squeezing it. 'I'm so sorry. What are you going to do?'

'That's what I must figure out. All I know for certain—and I am sorry, too, Sara—is that I will not be able to join you in the Judd Street venture.'

Sara sat silently a moment, her expression growing more and more appalled as the implications of Olivia's changed circumstances registered. 'No, of course you can no longer contribute. But perhaps all is not lost. Perhaps I could—'

'No, Sara, we discussed this. The expense of maintaining a separate establishment wouldn't be possible without an equal contribution from both of us. And even if you could manage the finances without me, I couldn't let you do that.'

'Hmmph,' said the stout dowager, entering the room. 'You'd do better if you both abandoned that foolish idea and got yourself husbands, like sensible females! As for you, missy,' she said, turning her gimlet stare upon Olivia, 'I heard you recently turned down Lord Everston. Silly girl! Don't you realise how rich he is?'

'There should be more to life than having a rich husband whose money you can spend,' Sara objected.

'You're going to give me some drivel about mutual respect and intellectual companionship?' Lady Patterson said. 'I guarantee you, a handsome income and a steady supply of fashionable gowns and bonnets is far more lasting.'

'Lord Everston is pushing fifty and only wanted a wife to watch over his household and seven children,' Olivia retorted. 'Preferably a plain, older spinster who would be grateful enough for his proposal that she'd overlook his gambling and his mistresses.'

'As long as the settlements guarantee the wife a good income, she'd probably be happy to leave intimate matters to his mistresses,' Lady Patterson said.

'That may do for some, Aunt,' Sara said in her soft, placating voice. 'But not for us.'

'The more fool, you,' Lady Patterson retorted.

'I should probably leave you…and go do some hard thinking,' Olivia said with a sigh.

Sara pressed her hand again. 'If there is anything I can do…'

Her brows creasing, Lady Patterson looked from Sara to Olivia. 'What is going on, if I may ask?'

Much as Olivia hated to confess her private tragedy to anyone but Sara, Lady Patterson had been kind to her, and in truth, a much more careful chaperone than her own mother. Nor was she a tale-teller. And in any event, gossips would get hold of the news soon enough anyway. After all her efforts on Olivia's behalf, Lady Patterson might be offended if she learned of it second-hand, rather than from Olivia herself.

'To reduce it to the bare essentials, Lady Patterson, Mr Henson informed me today that I am penniless, my inheritance lost by my trustees in a risky investment. He'd known about the bankruptcy for several weeks, but wanted to give me some time to recover from the sudden loss of my mother before he told me. However, as my cousin, Sir Roger, who now owns the Upper Brook Street house, wants to move in with his new bride immediately, I must decide in short order what to do.'

Lady Patterson stared at Olivia thoughtfully for some minutes, then nodded. 'Then I will waste no words telling you what a tragedy that is or how sorry I am, both of which are obvious. If you want my opinion, I think you should approach Lord Everston. I'm sure he'd renew his offer. Granted, marrying him isn't the solution you would have wished, but it will guarantee you a handsome income and a respectable position for the rest of your life. Perhaps even an enviable one, since Everston will almost certainly predecease you.'

'So after avoiding a marriage of convenience these last five years, I should now marry a man I neither like nor respect, hoping he will stick his spoon in the wall soon enough that I will have time left to do what *I* want with my life? That's assuming, since I no longer possess even a modest dowry to bring to the union, he would be willing to settle a "handsome sum" on me.'

'Your solicitor would insist on it and Everston would agree,' Lady Patterson replied. 'He's well enough off, even with all those offspring to fund and he's *Everston*. Since he insists on wedding a gently born lady of good family, he doesn't have many choices.'

'That's true,' Sara observed. 'Practically every female he considers worthy of bearing his name has already refused him.'

'At least you'd have a home and money of your own,' Lady Patterson argued. 'With your inheritance gone, you'll have to abandon that Judd Street scheme anyway. Marrying Everston is better than going begging to Sir Roger, leaving you always dependent on his charity. Or canvassing your distant relatives for a home, sinking you to that worst of lowly situations: an indigent, unmarried female, shuttled from household to household to care for sick children or querulous elders.'

'Couldn't she stay with us?' Sara said, looking to her aunt.

'Please, don't even ask, Sara,' Olivia said before Lady Patterson could answer, tears pricking her eyes. 'You are a darling to want me, but...but I don't want to become your dependent, any more than I wish to rely on Sir Roger or some other relative.'

'Then it must be Lord Everston,' Lady Patterson said. Her voice softening, she continued, 'I understand you have your pride, dear, and I respect you for it. But you have few alternatives.'

'If the choice is between tending snivelling brats or drooling centenarians,' Olivia said, thinking rapidly, 'I'll take the brats. And if tending them is to be my lot, I'd rather make use of my elevated education and become a governess. Oh, I know, I'd only earn a pittance—but the money would be *mine*. Not available for trustees to lose or a husband to spend on his fancy women. And I wouldn't have to become intimate with Everston to earn it.'

'Please, don't do anything hasty!' Sara said. 'Couldn't you reconcile it with your conscience to stay with us, just until Emma and Lord Theo return from Italy? I'm sure, among the three of us, we could work something out. Become a governess in some out-of-the-way manor in the back of beyond and you may be lost to us for ever.'

'It's always possible I could find a position here in London.'

'In London—where you would inevitably run into

the friends of your employers, all of them well aware of your humiliating loss of status?' Lady Patterson said.

Olivia sighed. 'Not London, then.' Having her acquaintances looking down on her with scorn and pity would be intolerable.

Her mind whirling, Olivia felt driven to halt the dizzying, out-of-control spin of her life by making a decision here and now.

It wasn't as if her options would change upon longer reflection.

A lady's only other alternative was to become some genteel female's companion. Not being much given to taking orders, it would probably be preferable to earn her pittance as a governess, where she would be giving them.

So, it appeared, a governess she would be.

She'd always longed to be independent, in charge of her own destiny, not forced to depend upon a father or brother or husband. Well, this ironic twist of fate had certainly granted that wish, she thought blackly. Just not at all in the way she'd envisaged.

'A position as a governess in an out-of-the-way manor might be preferable,' she said, pulling herself from those reflections to confirm her decision. 'Lady Patterson, do you know of an agency to which I could apply for such a position? And would you be kind enough to write me a character?'

Lady Patterson sat quietly for a moment. 'I suppose there isn't time for me to enquire among my friends and relations to discover someone in need of a governess.'

'Lady Overton could show up on the doorstep of Upper Brook Street tomorrow.'

'Surely you could stay with us long enough for my aunt to find you a position with someone she knows,'

Sara pleaded. 'Somewhere we'd be assured you would be treated with kindness and respect.'

Though touched by her friend's concern, Olivia said, 'Sara, I know you mean well. But can you even imagine how it would be? Everyone in society would know. I wouldn't be invited anywhere. I'd have no funds to borrow books or even for the paper and ink we use to write letters for the Ladies' Committee. I'd have to hide myself here just…existing. Suspended in some awful void between the life I've always known and the reality of my life now. I… I don't think I could bear it. Since the break must happen, I'd rather it be swift and clean.'

Her eyes filling with tears, Sara nodded. 'I suppose I can understand. I just…hate to lose you.'

Unable to respond without giving in to tears of her own, Olivia pulled her friend close for a hug. For a long moment, they clung together.

Pushing away the friend who, for the first time in their lives, was unable to help her solve a dilemma seemed to symbolically echo today's events in her life.

'Well, I'd best go and pack up my things. Lady Patterson, if you would be so kind as to give me the name of that agency?'

Even Sara's gruff aunt had tears in her eyes. 'I'm afraid I've forgotten. Let me go to my sitting room and ask my maid, and I'll send you a note. I am sorry, my dear.' After rising to give Olivia a quick, most unusual hug, the older woman walked out.

'Promise me one thing,' Sara insisted as she escorted Olivia to the door. 'Don't accept a contract for more than six months. You know the three of us—you, me and Emma—have always been able to solve whatever problem has arisen in our lives. I don't expect that will change just because Emma married Lord Theo. Promise me, when they return from their Grand Tour, you will come back to London and let us all re-examine your situation, together.'

Olivia knew that, unless some unknown benefactor had left her funds of which not even the family solicitor was aware, nothing about her circumstances would change in six months. Nor would she be any more able to accept charity from Emma than she could from Sara. But her friend looked so distraught, silent tears slipping down her cheeks, that Olivia didn't have the heart to refuse her.

'Very well. I'll not sign a contract for employment that lasts longer than six months and I promise to return to London and speak with all of you when Emma and Lord Theo come back from Italy.'

In the hallway, the two clung to each other, Olivia fighting back tears once more after being informed by the butler that Lady Patterson had ordered the family carriage to bear her home.

Perhaps her last journey as a well-born member of society.

'Don't you dare leave London without saying goodbye!' Sara said, giving her one last hug.

'I will let you know my situation as soon as everything is arranged,' Olivia promised. Then, as the butler held open the door for her, she walked out of her past and grimly set her face towards the future.

Chapter Two

Meanwhile, as the afternoon light faded in Somerset, Colonel Hugh Glendenning, late of his Majesty's Second Imperial Foot, sat down at his desk in the shabby library of Somers Abbey, his family's ancient home. His back ached from a long day of riding the tenant farms, occasionally dismounting to help some elderly householder with the pollarding of the willow trees that would enable him to cure the branches and weave them into the baskets that produced most of the estate's revenue.

The Abbey was still far from recovered from the shambles it had been when he inherited it from his wastrel elder brother, he thought, with a pained glance at the faded curtains and the threadbare carpet on the floor. But a year and a half of determined toil had at least built back up the estate's traditional trade in baskets and, if the apple crop were good this year, the additional income from selling cider might finally tip his finances, long tottering between solvency and disaster, firmly on to the positive side.

He was stretching out his back and thinking that a quick whisky before dinner might be just the trick when a knock came at the door, followed by the entrance of the elderly butler.

'Sorry to disturb you, Colonel, but a Mr and Mrs Allen are here, demanding to see you.'

'Mr and Mrs Allen?' Hugh repeated. After a rapid review of his memory, he shook his head. 'I don't believe I'm acquainted with a Mr Allen.' Hoping the man wasn't another of the numerous unpaid creditors his brother had left behind, he said, 'Did they indicate what they wanted to see me about, Mansfield?'

The butler shook his head. 'Only that they'd just arrived from St Kitts in the Caribbean and must see you at once on a delicate matter of grave importance.'

Hugh sighed. 'If they are from St Kitts, it must have something to do with my late cousin's estate. I thought his solicitor had already informed me of everything I needed to know, but I suppose I shall have to see them.'

'Very well, Colonel.'

Resisting the urge to jump up and help Mansfield when the old man struggled to close the slightly warped oak door, Hugh remained seated. He'd thought the butler already old when he was a boy growing up here, thirty years ago, he thought wryly. Mansfield should have long ago been put out to pasture, but Hugh's brother had been too indolent to find a replacement and, for now, Hugh couldn't spare the cash for the retirement the man's lifetime of service deserved.

Maybe next year.

Maybe next year, he'd get that door planed down and rehung—yet another project on the never-ending list of repairs and renovations needed at Somers Abbey.

A few minutes later, the butler ushered in a lady and a

tall, thin, sunburned man—trailed by two solemn-faced little girls. 'Mr and Mrs Allen, Colonel—and children.'

Hugh hastily looked away from the girls as agony lanced through him. He fought to suppress the vivid, devastating memory of a round, gamine face, the sound of childish laughter…and the sight of dusty earth raining down as a small coffin was lowered into the hard-baked Indian soil.

A surge of anger followed the pain. Why hadn't Mansfield warned him the couple had children with them? He'd have instructed him to send the youngsters off to the kitchen before he escorted the parents up.

Struggling to remain cordial, he rose and made them a bow. 'Colonel Glendenning, Mr and Mrs Allen. You come from St Kitts, my butler tells me? I hope you had a pleasant journey.'

'Tolerably pleasant, given its long duration,' Allen said. 'We're anxious to complete it, though, and be back home again in Yorkshire.'

'You are not residents in St Kitts, then? And, please, do have a seat,' he said, waving them towards the sofa in front of the hearth. 'Mansfield, bring us tea and ask Mrs Wallace to come up.' Turning back to his guests, he said, 'My housekeeper can take the children to the kitchen for some refreshment.'

'That would be most kind,' Mr Allen said, ushering his wife to the sofa, the children coming to stand stiffly behind them. 'To answer your question, I've been the export agent for a trading venture on St Kitts these last several years, but my wife has been pining for home, so I resigned my position. We will join our family as soon as we discharge our obligation to the children.'

'I see. So, how may I be of service?' Hugh asked, still

puzzled about why the Allens had come to see him. 'I assume you were acquainted with my late cousin, Robert Glendenning. Did he ask you to bring something to me?'

Mr Allen laughed. 'In a manner of speaking. Although it was, as you know, his wife who did the sending. I was given to understand that you were expecting the children.'

For a moment, stark horror froze his tongue as the import of Allen's words sank in. 'The ch-children?' he stuttered. Although he was terribly afraid he already knew the answer, he asked, 'What children?'

'Just the older ones, Mr Glendenning's two daughters by his first wife. The second Mrs Glendenning wished, of course, to keep their son and heir with her. In any event, I believe you were only named guardian for the girls, Mrs Glendenning having convinced her husband to appoint her brother in that role for their son.'

Turning back to the children standing behind him, Allen said, 'Girls, make your curtsies to your guardian. Colonel, may I present to you Miss Elizabeth Glendenning, the elder, and Miss Sophie Glendenning, the younger.'

No, this couldn't be happening.

Refusing to look at the children as they dutifully made their curtsies, Hugh stared at Mr Allen. 'My cousin's solicitor informed me that Robert had named me guardian for the girls. As their closest remaining relative, I felt obligated to accept the task and was prepared to oversee the management of their inheritance until they came of age or married—in St Kitts. There was never any mention of the children being brought to England.'

While Mrs Allen drew in a sharp breath, Mr Allen

looked at Hugh, his expression incredulous. 'You…were not expecting them?'

'Certainly not!' Hugh said. 'And had I been consulted, I would never have authorised them to leave St Kitts. Why would they wish to? That has been their home all their lives.'

'Oh, dear,' Mr Allen said, looking alarmed. 'I'm very sorry! We were given to understand that all had been arranged in advance. This is most distressing!'

'Indeed,' Hugh replied with feeling. 'I suppose there is no possibility of you returning the girls to St Kitts?'

'None at all,' Mr Allen confirmed. 'As I mentioned, we are removing to Yorkshire permanently, and have no plans to return to the islands.'

'Perhaps they could go with you to Yorkshire,' Hugh said, searching about for any solution that did not require him taking over their care. 'As I recall, my cousin left ample funds for their maintenance and upbringing. Surely they would be more comfortable in a land so foreign to them if they lived with people who know and care about them, rather than with a total stranger. A childless widower to boot.'

Although once he had been neither…

The Allens exchanged uncomfortable glances. 'The Misses Glendenning hardly know us better than they do you, Colonel. We only met them the day the ship sailed from St Kitts.'

Though he was nearly seething with fury and distaste, Hugh hadn't been a soldier for fifteen years without learning how to take responsibility for duties shirked by another—or recognising when a position was untenable. 'I suppose they shall have to stay, then.'

Looking visibly relieved, Mr Allen nodded. 'I'm sure that will be for the best.'

The butler arrived with their tea. For the next ten minutes, Hugh nodded as Mr Allen made desultory conversation. He sipped at his own tepid liquid, wishing it was his prized Scotch, all the while thinking furiously.

There was no way he could undertake the care of two little girls. After all that had happened, the idea was simply unendurable.

The housekeeper would have to look out for them until he could hire a suitable governess. With any luck, he'd be able to avoid seeing them more than once or twice a month—until they were grown and gone.

Even better, after more reflection upon the matter, he might come up with some appropriately placed female to whom he could send the children for their upbringing. After all, governess or not, the care of two small girls should be overseen by a woman, shouldn't it?

Speaking of females, the Allens were finishing their tea and making departing noises—and his housekeeper still hadn't arrived.

Very well, he could stand being alone with them for a few moments. Fortunately, they were a mannerly pair, for they had stood stock-still and silent ever since Allen introduced them.

All too soon, putting down his empty cup, Mr Allen said, 'We are much obliged for the refreshments and hospitality—especially after the shock of springing the children upon you with no advance notice! I can't imagine what happened to the correspondence from Mrs Glendenning arranging their travel.'

'Nor can I,' Hugh said drily. Though he had a pretty good idea what had happened to the 'missing' letters. His cousin's second wife obviously had no interest in caring for the children of her predecessor; sending them unannounced precluded the refusal he would have returned, had his permission been sought.

Despite his rage at having this charge foisted on him, he felt an inadvertent pang of sympathy for the two girls. They'd lost their own mother upon the younger child's birth and now, so soon after the death of their father, they'd been exiled from the only home they'd ever known.

He'd have to scour his London papers tonight and find an agency to provide him a governess with all possible speed.

By now, his guests had risen, obligating him to rise as well.

'We'll be going now, girls,' Mrs Allen said, kneeling to embrace the two in turn. 'You must be as good for your new guardian as you've been for us.'

'Yes, ma'am,' the two said in unison, while the older added, 'Thank you for watching over us on the journey, Mrs Allen.'

Walking with the Allens to the door—very conscious of the two pairs of small eyes following his movements—Hugh said, 'I wish you a safe homecoming.'

'Very kind of you, Colonel,' Mr Allen said. 'We'll be that glad to see our little stone cottage again, won't we, my dear?'

So, with a handshake and a murmured goodbye from the wife, the Allens departed.

Hugh lingered in the doorway, but there still was no sign of an approaching housekeeper. If the damned woman didn't show up in the next few minutes, he was going to have to escort the girls down to the kitchen himself.

Taking a deep breath, Hugh turned around, the wave of anguish that washed through him as he forced himself to look at the girls less sharp than the first time, when he'd been taken unawares. Every step a painful duty, he paced towards the children, who were still standing silently by the sofa.

Halfway there, it suddenly occurred to him that he should approach more slowly and put a smile on his face. A man as large as he was probably would look frightening, wearing the frown that usually furrowed his brow.

As disturbed as he was about this unwanted burden, the two little girls must be even more upset. Tired and hungry, probably still grieving for their Papa, feeling lost and possibly terrified at having been plucked from everything that was familiar, ferried across an ocean and deposited like an unwanted parcel on the doorstep of someone they'd never met.

He knew a little something about feeling tired, lost and grieving.

Halting before them, he knelt, bringing his face almost down to the level of theirs. Despite his attempt to make his movements as unthreatening as possible, the younger girl shrank back against her sister.

'Elizabeth and Sophie, isn't it?' he asked. 'Your papa used to come here and play with me when we were boys. I know it must look very different from home, but I hope to make you comfortable here.'

Until I can make alternative arrangements—the sooner, the better.

Adding another curse on the head of the still-absent housekeeper, he continued, 'Shall we go to the kitchen and get you something to eat? Then Mrs Wallace, my housekeeper, will take you up to the nursery and get you settled. It hasn't been used since my brother and I were boys, so you will have to help her make it present-able again.'

For a moment, the two simply stared at him—two pairs of large, bright blue eyes in frightened faces. Then the elder said, 'You don't want us either, do you?'

In a flash, he remembered how honest children were, spitting out exactly what they thought with no subter-fuge. Accurate as that statement was, he didn't mean to make the situation worse by confirming it.

'Well, it wasn't—ideal, sending you here unan-nounced, with no time for us to prepare for you, was it? But we shall all muddle through.'

'She didn't want us either. Madame Julienne, Papa's new wife. She was nice to us before baby Richard came. But after…' The child took a shuddering breath. 'She wouldn't even let us see Papa after he got so sick.'

His cousin had died of some tropical fever, Hugh vaguely remembered. 'Probably because she didn't want you to get sick, too.'

'Papa told us you were his best cousin. That you were a brave soldier in In-dee-yah. When Madame Julienne sent us away, she said you would w-want us.' Tears welled up in Elizabeth's eyes and little Sophie was al-ready soundlessly weeping.

Hugh knew he ought to embrace the girls—if they'd let him. Reassure them. But as much as he felt for their pain and loss, he couldn't quite force himself to touch them.

So, trying to summon soothing words, he said, 'You mustn't be afraid. I was a soldier, just like your papa told you, so I know all about protecting. You'll be safe here and we will look after you.'

He hadn't done such a wonderful job of protecting his own child, he thought, another wave of anger rolling through him. But this was England, not a hot, exotic land full of poisonous plants, reptiles and dangerous diseases that could snuff out a child's life between sunset and midnight. Though he'd sworn he'd never take responsibility for a child again, surely he could tolerate watching over them until he could turn them over to a suitable female.

At last, Mrs Wallace's tall, austere figure appeared at the door. After rapping, she walked over to peer down at where he still knelt beside the children—whom she swept with a disapproving glance.

'Mansfield said you wanted me, Colonel?'

Rising, Hugh bit back a sharp reply. No point taking his aggravation out on the housekeeper, even though he knew Mansfield would have already told her about the Allens and what had transpired in the library. Hugh had no doubt she knew full well what he wanted.

'Mrs Wallace, may I present Elizabeth and Sophie Glendenning, my late cousin's daughters. They are to be staying with us at Somers Abbey for a time. They've had a long journey and, I'm sure, could do with some bread and soup before they go up to bed. Take them to the kitchen, please, and see to them.'

The housekeeper's gaze swept from the huddled children back to Hugh. 'I don't deal with children, Colonel.'

The last of his patience unravelling, Hugh snapped, 'Well, you're going to have to, at least until I can hire a governess. See them fed and settled in, at once!'

'Very well.' Glowering, the housekeeper curtsied to him. 'Come along, children.'

Though Hugh didn't much like turning the girls over to a cold stick like Mrs Wallace, his skeleton-staffed bachelor household didn't offer many alternatives.

He'd write to a hiring agency at once. Fortunately, Robert had left ample funds for his children's care, so Hugh could demand their most superior candidate and pay extra to have her travel by private coach, so she might arrive at Somers Abbey with all possible speed.

It was the best he could do, under the circumstances. Stalking back to his desk, he flung himself into the chair, noting grimly that his hands were trembling. Doubtless from the shock of having a raw wound ripped open. Drawing in a shaky breath, he took out the bottle of Scotch and poured himself a full glass.

Chapter Three

Slightly more than a week later, as the evening shadows blurred the view from her coach window, Olivia craned her neck to catch a glimpse of her new employer's residence. 'Somers Abbey', she'd read on the note of introduction the agency had given her—and the pile of grey stone she could just perceive in the hazy distance certainly looked the part of a medieval manor wrenched from the grip of a religious community by a greedy monarch.

She had to shiver, just looking at it. Not a very welcoming appearance. Perhaps the two orphaned girls she had been sent to care for found it a place of wonders, with priest's holes to hide in and long, rambling corridors to run through.

She'd never been around children much. Stirring uneasily, she hoped they would get along.

As the carriage drew to a halt, she tried to subdue the nervous foreboding in the pit of her belly. She was no shrinking young miss, but a well-educated, intelligent, competent young woman who had managed her mother's household for years. She could handle a nursery and two little girls.

Besides, she had insisted the employment contract run for only six months. She could bear anything for six months. Although she would then return to London, as she'd promised Sara again when they exchanged their final tearful goodbyes, she didn't expect anything would happen to change her circumstances. She would still be on her own, forced to find a new position to earn her bread.

And earning about as much as, in her former life, she would have spent on a ball gown without thinking twice about it.

But reflecting on that would do no more good than giving in to her distress over leaving her home and the last close friend she had in the world. There was no possibility of going back; she could only move forward.

The hired carriage halted before the entrance. Marshalling all her resolve, she descended from the vehicle.

Her knock was answered by an elderly butler, whose livery looked as shabby as the worn carpet in the entry hall. 'Miss Overton, I presume?'

'Yes. Would you announce me to the Colonel? I should like to present my credentials before he takes me to meet the children.'

'This way, Miss Overton. I'll have your trunk conveyed to your room.'

Wondering where she would be received—probably in an office or study, not in the parlour reserved for guests, certainly—she followed the man down the hallway and into what looked to be an older section of the house, all stone walls and dark wood panelling.

He stopped before an ancient, solid oak door. After struggling to open it, he intoned, 'Miss Overton, Colonel.'

Ruthlessly quelling her nervousness, Olivia walked in to meet her new employer, who rose as she entered.

Encouraged by that gesture of respect—as he was receiving a mere employee, not a lady of the *ton*, he might well have retained his seat—she looked up at him squarely.

Tall and ash blond, with a rigidly upright bearing that proclaimed his military background, the Colonel cut an impressive figure—and was much younger than she'd expected. Having learned her employer had served his military career in India, she assumed he'd returned to England to retire. Though weariness lined his sunburned face, the man before her was in his middle thirties, at most.

Belatedly realising that she had been staring, Olivia pulled herself together. 'Good evening, Colonel,' she said, dropping him a curtsy.

'Miss Overton,' he acknowledged her with an incline of his head. 'Won't you take a seat? That will be all, Mansfield.'

Initially taken aback, she squelched the reaction, reminding herself she had been ushered into this man's presence merely to have her credentials examined and be given whatever instruction he deemed necessary prior to taking up her work. She shouldn't expect to be entertained or offered refreshment.

Yet the stark contrast with the warm hospitality she'd been offered upon her arrival at every other stately house she'd ever visited brought her close to tears.

You will accustom yourself. You must. And you're not

going to turn weak and faint-hearted at the very first hurdle.

Willing herself to calm, she walked over and handed him the documents the hiring agency had made up for her, then took the chair he indicated in front of his desk. 'These should confirm what the agency already informed you about my background.'

Scanning the papers, he nodded. 'Yes, I see that you were well educated at a private ladies' academy. You are capable of teaching English, literature, mathematics, geography, French, Italian, music and proper deportment? I see also that you have excellent references from several titled ladies.'

Who were once my mentors and friends.

'Yes.'

He nodded. 'That sounds suitable, though I can't claim to know anything about what young ladies should be taught. How much did the agency tell you about your charges' circumstances?'

'Just their ages, the fact that they had recently been orphaned and that their new guardian, a military gentleman who served in India, had requested a superior candidate be sent to Somers Abbey with utmost dispatch.'

The Colonel sighed. 'The reality is slightly more complicated. About six months ago, my cousin, who owns—owned—an estate at St Kitts in the Caribbean, wrote asking that I act as guardian to his daughters. My cousin being a young man, I had no expectation of actually having to take up that charge. Even after learning of his unexpected death, I assumed I would be required to do nothing more than manage their inheritance. Instead, with neither my knowledge nor my consent, my cousin's second wife sent the girls to England. They arrived here unannounced about a week ago.'

Olivia stared. 'You had no idea they were coming?'

'None, else I would have made other arrangements. I fear, in its present condition, Somers Abbey could hardly be less suitable as a home to shelter and raise two little girls. The estate I inherited from my elder brother had been…neglected, as I'm sure you've already noticed. In the eighteen months since returning from India, I have been doing everything I can to restore it to proper condition, which requires long hours of work and has forced economies that required me to reduce the staff to a bare minimum. I have neither wife nor mother to undertake their guidance and my household staff includes exactly four females—the cook, the housekeeper, a tweeny and one maid-of-all-work.'

'Which explains your haste to hire a governess,' Olivia said.

After giving her a sharp look—perhaps he didn't expect a mere employee to interrupt his explanation with a comment?—he continued, 'Unfortunately, I have no close female kin to whom I could send the girls, which is why they are still at Somers Abbey. I am in the process of making further enquiries, in hopes of finding them a more suitable situation. I tell you all this so you may understand that, although you were hired for a six-month period, it's quite possible the term of your employment will be much shorter. After agreeing to journey here in such haste, you will, of course, be compensated for the full six months, whether or not whoever takes over the supervision of the children decides to retain you as their governess.'

She might be free—before the end of six months.

Free to return to London with the whole of her pittance in her pocket!

Where, of course, she would simply have to secure a new position.

'So I am to do my best for them until some genteel lady agrees to supervise their care. I suppose I shall also work with the maid or nurse who accompanied them from the Caribbean.'

'They were not sent with a maid or nurse.'

Surprised, she said, 'Who cared for them during their long journey?'

'A couple returning to England—whom they had not previously met before the journey began.'

Olivia angled her head at him, frowning. 'They travelled all alone across the ocean without a single companion they knew? Those poor little mites! They must have been terrified! Surely they had a nurse at home. Why was she not sent—?'

As the Colonel raised his eyebrows, Olivia realised that, once again, she was questioning her employer as an equal, rather than merely listening, as befitted an employee. With difficulty, she pressed her lips together and went silent.

'A good question to which I doubt there is a charitable answer,' he said drily. 'You are…rather outspoken, are you not? The governesses I encountered in India all seemed to be meek, retiring creatures who barely had a word to say for themselves.'

'I'm afraid I'm not at all retiring, Colonel. I ran my mother's household until…until her recent demise and am quite used to being in charge.'

A glimmer of a smile flickered on his lips and lit his eyes before his expression turned sombre again. Unexpected—and unexpectedly engaging—that tiny spark of warmth raised her flagging spirits, like a candle illumining a dark room.

Even solemn, with a thin, care-worn face, she had to allow the Colonel was attractive. An aura of command surrounded him, subtly proclaiming this was a man used to making decisions, acting upon them and expecting others to obey. He had none of the charm or charisma of her friend Emma's handsome husband, Lord Theo, but his air of competence and absolute dependability was unexpectedly appealing.

And she had no business finding her new employer attractive or appealing. While she was reminding herself of this fact, he said, 'I'm sorry for your loss.'

Her throat gone suddenly tight, she merely nodded. His comment was too sharp of a reminder of just how much she had lost—not only her mother, but her home, position, friends and the future she'd always expected would be hers.

He stood, signifying the interview was over. 'I shall appreciate any help you can give in making the children feel more at ease during their stay at Somers Abbey. Mansfield will take you to meet Mrs Wallace, the housekeeper, who will see that you have dinner and show you to your room.'

'Are you not going to take me to meet the children?'

'Mrs Wallace will do so, if they are still awake after you've dined.'

Finding that odd, Olivia said, 'Are they not brought down to visit you in the evenings, after you return from working on the estate?'

'No. I often don't return until well after dark. Mrs Wallace believes children do better if they are kept on a regular, dependable schedule. As I am almost a total stranger to them, there really is no need for them to see me.'

'But you said you were their last remaining relative...'

The quelling look the Colonel gave her had her words trailing off. Though there was a good deal more she'd like to know on the subject, she stifled the questions. She'd meet her charges, coax out their feelings on the matter, then decide whether or not to bring it up again with their guardian.

She might now be an employee, but she was never going to be meek or retiring.

The Colonel was a military man, used to the company of rough soldiers and adventuresome officers. Like many men, he was probably not accustomed to dealing with children, especially young and female ones.

However, as she knew only too painfully, coping with the loss of your entire world was frightening and devastating—and *she* was an adult. Being the sole remaining relative of two small girls who had recently lost theirs, he should be making a greater effort to help them adjust.

A few minutes later, Mansfield arrived to conduct her to her room.

It appeared the main part of the manor was medieval, to which several additions had been added. She followed the old man around a maze of twisting corridors and up a flight of stairs, down a draughty hallway to what looked like a wing of bedchambers. At least she was to be given a proper room, rather than a garret in the attics.

The room itself was large but spartan, containing only a bed, a single dresser with a washbowl on it, and a wardrobe. Perhaps it was the approaching shadows playing over the few pieces of furniture in a room that had obviously once contained many more that gave it such a bleak air, but it was also dusty, she noted in disapproval. Since the household obviously knew of her arrival, that didn't give her a very high opinion of the housekeeper.

A knock at the door was followed by the entrance of a kitchen maid bearing a tray, which she set on the single side table beside the bed. She was followed by a tall, thin, dark-haired woman in a lace cap with a chain of keys hanging about her neck. 'Your supper, Miss Overton,' the woman said, giving her a slight curtsy, to which Olivia responded in kind. 'I am Mrs Wallace, the housekeeper.'

As if the keys worn on a chain hanging about her neck didn't identify her quite clearly, Olivia thought. 'Pleased to meet you, Mrs Wallace. Will I also meet my new charges this evening?'

'No, the Misses Glendenning have already retired. Their nursery is further down this corridor. Mary, here, will show you to it after she brings up your breakfast in the morning. Goodnight, Miss Overton.'

That was it? No welcome, no 'let me know if you need anything'? Olivia swallowed hard. Yet another reminder that she was no longer a guest to be accommodated, but simply another employee.

'Goodnight, Mrs Wallace, Mary.' She smiled at the maid who, apparently startled by her notice, smiled back—before she caught the sharp eye of the housekeeper fixed on her, dropped a quick curtsy and scurried out.

Lighting a candle—fortunately, the derelict house seemed to at least provide candles—against the gathering gloom, Olivia shivered as she sat on the bed. The stone walls seemed as chilly as her greeting.

She hoped the poor children's room was more inviting. In any event, this house needed a large infusion of light and cheer, and beginning tomorrow, she was going to provide it—regardless of what her distant employer and his stiff-necked housekeeper might want.

She could use some cheer herself. As the weariness of long travel loosened the tight grip with which she'd been containing all the devastation of loss, grief and fear for the future bottled up within her, she felt tears begin to trickle down her cheeks. Alone, with no one to witness her breakdown, she wrapped her arms around her pillow and wept.

Some time in the night, as she huddled in her bed, counterpane pulled up over her head for warmth, Olivia woke with a start, conscious of a sense of alarm. What had roused her from a deep, exhausted sleep?

Pulling the covering from over her head, she heard it again—a soft, distant, mournful noise that sounded almost like—weeping.

The hairs rose on the back of her neck. Did this near-empty house contain—ghosts?

Given its gloom, she wouldn't be surprised if the manor's halls were trod late at night by wraiths of the unfortunate monks who'd been murdered during its seizure. However, as she told herself stoutly that supernatural spirits were only a myth, the sound continued.

Might it be coming…from the nursery?

After lighting a candle and throwing on her thick dressing gown, Olivia walked out of her chamber into the hallway, where the sound grew louder. She followed its increasing volume down the hallway, to halt before a closed door, which must be the nursery. Because she was certain what she heard was the sound of a small child crying.

After rapping on the door, she walked into the night-dark room, where the wavering light from her candle fell over two small girls. The larger one had her arms wrapped around a smaller one, who was weeping piteously.

At her entrance, the sobbing stopped abruptly and both children froze. Then the older girl released her sister and jumped from the bed to stand protectively in front of her. 'It was me crying! Don't beat Sophie!'

Taken aback, Olivia said, 'Beat her? Why on earth would I beat her?'

'Because she woke you up. Mrs Wallace says we are never to disturb anyone at night, because she doesn't have enough servants to take care of this big house and they need their sleep. Most 'specially, we are not to disturb the master.'

'And she has you beaten if you do wake someone up?'

'Yes. But Sophie is so cold, she can't help crying.' Her own lip quivering, the girl added with an almost desperate defiance, 'We're both s-so cold.'

'Don't be afraid. I have no intention of striking you,' Olivia said, walking nearer. Frowning, she inspected the large room, which contained only two small beds side by side, a dresser, and a wardrobe, with a large open area that must serve as a schoolroom. Much like hers, it, too, was more sparsely furnished than its size warranted.

'I'm Miss Overton, your new governess,' she continued as she reached the girls. 'You must be—Elizabeth…' she motioned to the bigger girl '…and Sophie?'

The standing sister curtsied. 'Yes, ma'am. We're sorry we woke you up. So…you aren't going to beat us?'

'Certainly not.' Her frown deepening, Olivia fingered the thin cotton blanket on the bed. It might be June, with full summer nearly upon them, but the stone abbey walls held in the chill like an ice cellar. The girls, too, wore only thin cotton nightgowns.

'Goodness, no wonder you are frozen. Come here, both of you!'

Untying her robe, she sat on the bed. Pulling the girls into her arms, she settled one on each side of her and wrapped the thick garment around all of them.

It didn't quite meet in the middle, but the girls were small enough that she was able to almost completely cover them as they clung to her, their need for warmth obviously stronger than their fear of being so close to a stranger.

'Haven't you told Mrs Wallace that you are cold at night?'

'Oh, yes, ma'am,' Elizabeth said. 'The very first night, when Sophie woke up crying. But she said we were in England now and we would have to get used to it.'

'Used to it? You grew up on an island where it is warm all the time, didn't you?'

'Yes, ma'am.' Snuggling closer, the little girl said, 'It was always sunny, too! It's so dark here and it rains so much.'

'I've never been to your homeland, but I've read that it's beautiful. Full of exotic birds and trees and beautiful flowers. After we get you warmed up, you must go back to sleep. Then tomorrow, when we get acquainted, you must tell me all about it. Now, let's see if I can find you more blankets.'

Shrugging off her robe to leave it around them, she padded to the chest, shivering in her thin linen night rail.

She looked through all the drawers, which contained only an array of lightweight, cotton clothing. She went then to the wardrobe, but it stood empty.

She had no idea where the household linens might be kept and certainly didn't intend to rummage about the dark to try to find them. Still—she couldn't leave the girls with nothing but that worn excuse of a blanket to cover them.

Walking back to the bed, she pulled her robe from around the girls and donned it before urging them to their feet and enfolding them against her again. 'You shall just have to spend the rest of the night in my chamber. We'll find you adequate blankets tomorrow, when I can talk with Mrs Wallace.'

Sighing, the younger girl pressed closer. But Elizabeth piped up, 'Mrs Wallace won't like that. She says everything must be in its proper place. We aren't allowed to move things, or touch things, or go into any of the other rooms besides the nursery.'

'Don't worry. I'll deal with Mrs Wallace.'

If the housekeeper were such a fanatic about order, she'd do a better job of dusting, Olivia thought. Being short-staffed was no excuse for slovenliness.

She ushered the girls down the hall and into her room, then helped them climb up on the big bed. Moving them to the middle, where she could be reasonably sure they wouldn't roll off in the night, she settled the thick counterpane around them and hopped into bed herself.

She smiled as she noted that Elizabeth had arranged herself protectively on the far side of her sister, giving Sophie the warmer place next to Olivia. What a brave little champion she was.

'Go to sleep now, girls,' she said, blowing out the candle.

'Thank you, Miss Overton,' Elizabeth whispered into the dark.

'You are very welcome, sweetheart. Sleep well.'

As soon as she settled herself on the pillow, the four-year-old Sophie snuggled close to her warmth.

As she tried to recapture sleep, the unfamiliar presence of two little girls at her back, Olivia thought that perhaps she had been meant to come to Somers Abbey. She was no longer in a position to write to Members of Parliament about the great political and social causes of the day. But reduced as her circumstances had become, she could still help two small beings who were even more lost and alone than she was.

A wave of compassion displaced, for a moment, her simmering anger. After this incident, she was even less impressed with the housekeeper who ran Somers Abbey—and its deliberately distant master.

Both were going to get a piece of her mind in the morning.

Chapter Four

Despite her assurance that Elizabeth did not need to concern herself with the housekeeper, the little girl woke Olivia well before daylight. 'Miss Overton, we must go back to our room. Before Mrs Wallace comes up and finds out we came here.'

The poor child was obviously afraid of the house-keeper—and small wonder, if she were threatened with a beating for any small infraction of the woman's rules. After lighting a candle, Olivia turned to reassure her.

But the worry etched on the child's face made it quite clear she didn't trust the new governess to protect her, despite the fact that Olivia had rescued them last night. Her lack of confidence in the person appointed to look out for her was not surprising, considering that the adult who should have cared for the children had instead sent them across an ocean to live with a stranger.

A stranger who then consigned them into the charge of a woman who beat small children and was unconcerned that they were cold and lost, Olivia thought, her anger against both the housekeeper and her employer reviving.

Not wishing to increase their anxiety by keeping them

in her room, she said, 'Very well, I'll take you back to the nursery. But I'm bringing the counterpane with us, so you may stay warm until I can obtain suitable clothing and bedding.'

Elizabeth's eyes went wider. 'But Mrs Wallace will see your blanket! She will know right away it isn't ours.'

'I'll tell her I came to check on you in the night and found the nursery too cold for you to sleep in with just a cotton blanket. Since I didn't know where more blankets were kept, I brought you mine. And please believe me, I am quite capable of dealing with any objections Mrs Wallace might raise. So, ready? Let's get you back down the hallway before your toes freeze!'

After hurrying the little girls back to the nursery and draping the counterpane over their two beds, Olivia brought the candle over to the dresser and once again inspected its contents. Though the cotton undergarments and dresses were all of excellent quality, they had obviously been intended for wearing in a tropical climate. She didn't discover anything made of wool or even linen. 'We shall have to get you heavier clothing, too, at least until the weather is sufficiently warm.'

'Does it ever get warm in England?' Elizabeth asked.

Compared to what she knew of weather in the tropics, the child had a point. 'Probably never as warm as you were accustomed to at home, but we do have pretty, sunny summer days sometimes. Now, wrap up tight! I'll get dressed and be back before Mrs Wallace arrives.'

Sophie gave her sister an anxious look, but both obediently huddled down in their beds. Girding herself for the confrontation to come, Olivia paced back to her chamber, threw on her garments and returned to the nursery.

* * *

Just as dawn was lighting the sky, Olivia heard the maid's footfalls in the hallway. Stepping into the corridor, she said, 'Good morning, Mary. Bring my breakfast tray in here, won't you? I will eat with the girls.'

'If you please, miss,' the maid said. Her eyes widened as she entered, no doubt noting the forbidden counterpane draped across the beds. 'I'll bring the girls' tray up in a trice.'

'Thank you. And would you tell Mrs Wallace I would like to speak with her at her earliest convenience?'

Mary's gaze travelled from Olivia to the counterpane covering the girls' beds and back. Setting down Olivia's tray, she gave her a nervous smile. 'Yes, miss. I can take that coverlet back to your room on my way.'

Olivia returned the smile. 'That's kind of you, but it shall remain here until the children are provided with adequate blankets of their own.'

The maid stared. 'Are you sure about that, miss?'

Evidently it wasn't just her two charges who feared the housekeeper. 'Quite sure. Indeed, that is what I wish to speak with Mrs Wallace about.'

The maid hesitated, as if she meant to say something, then shook her head. 'As you wish, miss.'

After the maid walked out, Elizabeth whispered, 'Mrs Wallace is not going to be happy with you.'

'Probably not. But that's all right, because I am not happy with her, either.'

Olivia was able to finish her coffee, toast and cheese and assist the girls to dress before she heard the housekeeper's light step in the hallway. No doubt Mrs Wallace had deliberately delayed responding to her summons, intent upon putting the new employee in her place.

However, a governess occupied a unique position within a noble household. Being gently born, she was not part of the staff below stairs or under the housekeeper's authority. A fact Olivia suspected she was about to have to prove.

Which was fine with her. After the way the children had been treated, and the slovenly condition of her chamber, she was quite prepared for a confrontation.

Mrs Wallace walked into the nursery, spied the coverlet over the beds and frowned. 'Miss Overton, what is the counterpane from your bedchamber doing here?'

'The girls were cold when I came in to check on them this morning. Not knowing where the linens are kept, I brought in my own coverlet to keep them warm until I could have you bring them thicker blankets.'

Anger flaring in the woman's eyes, she turned her gaze accusingly on the girls. With a whimper, Sophie cowered behind her sister.

Looking back at Olivia, she said, 'As I'm sure you've noticed, Miss Overton, the household is living in... reduced straits. The children are newcomers to England, and will soon become adjusted to our climate. I have no household funds to spare for such frivolities as extra blankets.'

Though Elizabeth remained protectively in front of her sister, she looked nearly as scared as Sophie. The fear on their faces raised Olivia's simmering anger several more degrees.

One of us is going to yield and it won't be me, she thought. *But no point terrifying the children by hav-*

ing them witness what promises to be an unpleasant exchange.

'Perhaps you will accompany me to my chamber so we may discuss this further.'

Mrs Wallace opened her lips, obviously intending to refuse. Olivia fixed on her the hard, unwavering stare that had, in the past, reduced impudent housemaids and a few insolent footmen to silence. 'Very well,' she said at last. 'I wouldn't wish to embarrass you in front of the children.'

'Nor I, you. Shall we?'

As soon as they reached Olivia's room, Mrs Wallace said, 'Let me put some things straight right away. The household, and all household supplies, are my responsibility and I won't have you interfering in my realm. Besides, it's ridiculous, indulging a pair of orphans like that.'

'The welfare of girls is my realm, and I shall "interfere" wherever necessary to ensure it. I'm not demanding you provide them satin quilts and eiderdown pillows. Just thick woollen blankets of sufficient warmth to make comfortable two small children brought up in the tropics and unused to English weather.'

'Cotton blankets are what have always been used in the nursery.'

'Well, now it shall be using woollen ones.'

Pausing, the housekeeper scanned Olivia up and down, her gaze scornful. 'I understand you grew up in a fine house before your…change in circumstances. You should realise at a glance, having seen something of Somers Abbey, that I don't have a fraction of the funds or servants necessary to properly maintain a dwelling of this size. We all have to make do.'

'I should think there are enough servants to make sure that the few rooms that are occupied—like this one—are in clean and orderly condition.'

Mrs Wallace gave her a thin smile. 'At Somers Abbey, servants clean their own rooms.'

Olivia gritted her teeth against the sharp reply she wanted to make. If the woman thought she could cow or embarrass her over her loss of status, she was in for a disappointment. 'If you will supply me with the requisite supplies, I shall bring this chamber up to the standard I expect. I shall still need woollen blankets for the girls, of course. Or must I take up that matter with the Colonel?'

'I would certainly not disturb him over such a trifling matter,' she retorted—and then stopped abruptly. Her smile broadening, the housekeeper continued, 'If *you* think the matter important enough, by all means discuss it with him. Good day, Miss Overton.'

'It certainly is important enough for *me* to "disturb" him,' Olivia snapped furiously as she strode past the housekeeper and down the passageway. Hoping she wouldn't get lost in the maze of hallways, she retraced her steps to the front hallway and found the door leading down to the kitchens.

'Mansfield!' she called as she walked into the servants' hall. 'Where are you? You must convey me to the master at once!'

Eight years of running an aristocratic household must have rung in her voice, for when the butler popped out of the pantry, he didn't offer even a token protest. 'This way, Miss Overton.'

Carefully, Hugh walked over to his desk and lowered himself in the chair, his mouth as dry as road dust. A quick sideways glance towards the nearly empty whisky bottle on the desk set off the hammer-on-anvil throbbing in his head again. His stomach roiling, he sank his head into his hands.

He hadn't intended to drink that much whisky last night—or to spend the night on the sofa in his library. But then, in the early evening after he'd returned to the manor, Mansfield had pleaded with him to come up to the west bedchamber wing and inspect the outermost room, where he feared a leak had begun around the chimney. Reaching that room meant that Hugh was forced to walk right past the nursery.

He'd tried to shut his ears, but he'd heard it anyway— the soft murmur of a childish voice emanating from within the schoolroom. The timbre of the voice, the remembered blue, blue eyes of his cousin's girls, brought the vision back with searing clarity.

Drew, chattering to his ayah in the nursery of the cantonment house...jumping up with a shout and coming to the doorway for a hug as Hugh looked in on him before leaving for duty.

Though he'd immediately fought to suppress the memories, the flashback had beat against the doors behind which he bottled up all his still-unresolved guilt and grief. Memories made even harder to suppress after he met with the girls' new governess—the managing Miss Overton, who was not at all meek and mild. Who had not hesitated to interrupt or question him.

He'd initially been amused by her admission of her controlling nature, before its implications registered. For the last week, he'd done a fair job of avoiding his wards, even at times forgetting they occupied the schoolroom. He had a feeling that Miss Overton was going to question him every time she thought there was a problem with her charges.

Hell and damnation, that was why he'd hired a governess—to assume oversight of the girls so he would have to deal with them as little as possible. If Miss Overton expected to continually plague him with her opinions or question him over the girls' treatment, he would have to disabuse her of that notion as soon as possible.

A knock at the door reverberated through his head, eliciting another wave of pain. Pressing his fingers against his aching temples, he looked up as Mansfield entered.

'What is it?'

'Miss Overton to see you, Colonel.'

For once, Hugh didn't appreciate being right. He felt wretched enough this morning without having to deal with a managing female. 'Tell her to come back later. And ask Cook to send up some strong coffee.'

To his infinite irritation, the blasted woman walked in anyway, dropping a curtsy that was long on graceful form and very short on deference. 'I'm sorry to disturb you, Colonel, but the matter can't wait. I need to see you now.'

'You've been here less than twenty-four hours. What could be so important that it cannot wait until later?'

She drew in a deep breath, as if preparing to speak—and then hesitated. Wrinkling her nose, she scanned the room, her gaze coming to rest on the whisky bottle. She frowned.

Doubtless the room reeked of spirits. Apparently she disapproved of drinking, too.

'Are you sober enough to understand what I'm saying, Colonel?'

He stared at her in disbelief. Had a man uttered such a remark, Hugh would have struck him.

Meanwhile, his eyes widening in alarm, Mansfield hastened to the door. 'I'll bring your coffee shortly, Colonel,' he called out before disappearing.

Refraining with difficulty from delivering the sharp reprimand that sprang to mind, Hugh said stiffly, 'I am quite capable of comprehension, Miss Overton. You do realise you are addressing your employer?'

'I realise I am addressing the guardian of two small girls who, since he chose to accept that responsibility, ought to concern himself with their well-being.'

You should have been more concerned with his well-being!

The echo of that long-ago accusation lanced through him, sparking irritation into anger.

'And just what is it that you think I'm neglecting?' he asked hotly.

'As for that, I shall have more to say later. But for the moment, the issue is blankets.'

That seemed so trifling, Hugh wasn't quite sure he'd heard her correctly. 'Blankets?' he repeated.

'Yes. The girls have only thin cotton blankets. Obviously, being from a much warmer climate, they are cold at night.'

'Good——' Hugh swallowed the curse and tried to rein in his anger. 'You barged into my library at the crack of dawn to complain about *blankets*? Do I look like a housemaid? Take that up with Mrs Wallace.'

'I already have. She was decidedly unhelpful. The girls need woollen blankets—and warmer clothing, too. Doubtless they will acclimate to English weather in due time, but a week is hardly sufficient. Surely the household has woollen blankets somewhere that could be given to them. You must tell Mrs Wallace to place some in the nursery, or, if there truly aren't any in the house, authorise their purchase.'

How dared she accuse him of negligence over a matter of *housekeeping*? Incensed, he said, 'You are outspoken indeed, Miss Overton. Take care that you don't *speak* yourself right out of your position.'

Her cheeks flushed at that. But, fire sparking in her eyes, she retorted, 'If you mean that as a threat, I'm not worried. Should you discharge me, I can find someone else who will pay me a pittance to watch their children.'

'Not unless I write you a character,' he shot back.

'At least I *have* character!' she cried, her voice growing strident. 'I'm not so neglectful of the welfare of two poor little girls put into my care that I would condemn them to being cold and miserable!'

How could you be so neglectful...

'Enough!' Hugh shouted, head pounding as his own voice rose to block out the memory of that devastating accusation. 'Get. Out.'

And when she hesitated, looking as if she meant to speak further, he roared, 'Get out now!'

Her face rosy, looking as angry as he felt, Miss Overton picked up her skirts and swept from the room.

Chapter Five

Late that afternoon, Olivia settled her two tired charges back in the nursery to rest before dinner. She'd just gone to her own room to tidy up when Mansfield knocked at her door and informed her that the Colonel wished to see her at once.

Sighing, Olivia nodded. 'Inform him that I shall be down directly.'

Most likely, after their acrimonious exchange this morning, her irate employer intended to formally discharge her. When, as furiously angry as she could ever remember being, she'd stalked from Colonel Glendenning's library that morning, she'd been single-mindedly focused on providing for the children the warm blankets and clothing the caretakers of Somers Abbey were unprepared to furnish. Once that task was performed, she had resolved to resign—if the Colonel didn't discharge her first.

But over the course of the day, her anger had cooled and her compassion kindled. Who would look after brave little Elizabeth and silent Sophie, who had yet to speak a word to her, if she left Somers Abbey?

Knowing how they were situated, she couldn't just walk away—not until the Colonel found some kind female relation to take over their care—someone who showed a willingness to actually *care* for them.

So, as little stomach as she had for the idea, she was going to have to apologise to the Colonel. In terms humble and contrite enough to persuade him to keep her on.

She would have to be—how had he described the governesses in India?—*meek and retiring.*

If she kept before her the vision of the fear in little Sophie's face when Mrs Wallace had looked at her accusingly this morning, maybe she wouldn't gag on the words.

Her face washed and her hair and gown straightened, Olivia took a deep breath and took herself to the library.

Looking stern and contained, but much better than he had in the early morning light, when he'd been unshaven, bleary-eyed and obviously the worse for a night of hard drinking, the Colonel nodded to her as she entered. 'Take a chair, please, Miss Overton.'

He wanted her to sit? Perhaps he intended to berate her at length before dismissing her. Wanting to head him off, Olivia said, 'I'd rather stand, sir, if you don't mind.'

Quirking his lip, the Colonel shook his head. 'Are you always contrary?'

Belatedly realising she'd once again failed to be an obedient servant, Olivia said hastily, 'Sorry, sir. I don't mean to be.'

'I don't suppose you do. However, I'd like to inform you—'

'Please, Colonel, if I might speak first?' Without waiting for permission, she rushed on. 'I… I must apologise for my conduct this morning. It was not my place to criticise the way you are discharging the responsibilities you generously agreed to shoulder in the raising of your cousin's children, especially when you are already burdened with the heavy task of restoring your own estate, and have no wife or sister to assist you with their care. I let my…distress over their situation lead me into being much too impetuous and outspoken. I hope you will forgive me and let me begin again anew.' Not at all sure she could make good on the promise, she made herself add, 'It will not happen again.'

For a moment he stared at her unsmilingly. 'Are you sure?'

Innate honesty warred with her determination to remain the girls' protector. 'I shall do my utmost to prevent it,' she said at last.

She thought she saw the tiniest hint of a smile on his face. But surely she was mistaken, for he said, 'I understand you were…*impetuous and outspoken* with my head groom this morning. Commandeering a vehicle? Taking the girls with you to Bristol?'

She swallowed hard. 'Yes, sir. Since…since you referred me to Mrs Wallace to obtain necessities for the girls, necessities she had already refused to provide, I felt compelled to go to the city and buy them myself. As the day was warm and fair and the girls have seldom been allowed to leave the nursery, I decided to take them with me. After all, how can they come to love their homeland if all they know of it is a rainy field seen from the nursery window? And you had not given any orders that the children and I were specifically *forbidden* to venture away from Somers Abbey.'

'No, I had not expressly forbidden it, Miss Overton. But I am not in the habit of having those in my care taken away without my knowledge. Nor did you think to take a groom along to protect them, should anything have happened on the road.'

'I… I know the house is short-staffed, sir. I didn't want to pull any of the other servants from their tasks. I can manage a team quite competently, the road is well travelled and, in broad daylight, I didn't expect to encounter any malcontent who couldn't, if necessary, be discouraged by the use of my driving whip.'

'Deciding and managing once again, Miss Overton?'

Her cheeks heating, her eyes flew up to meet his gaze. *It was for their good!* she wanted to insist. But rather than voice the protest hovering on her lips, she made herself lower her eyes and say, in the most penitent tones she could manage, 'Yes, I suppose I was. I'm sorry, sir.'

'And you promise not to do that again, either?'

Eating humble pie was harder than she'd imagined. Keeping the image of Sophie's face firmly in mind, she said, 'I will earnestly try not to, Colonel.'

She heard something that sounded like a choked laugh. Surprised, she looked up—to find the Colonel *chuckling*.

She wasn't sure what was more shocking—his sudden mirth, or how the smile made his blue eyes sparkle and transformed his stern features into something unexpectedly appealing—and undeniably handsome.

She was still trying to make sense of those startling observations when he said, 'I've tortured you enough, Miss Overton. I can only imagine how difficult it was for you to hold your tongue and abase yourself to apologise, especially knowing you were right.'

'I—I was right?' she repeated, caught off guard.

'Yes. Actually, I'd summoned you here so that *I* might

apologise to *you*. I am not normally so churlish, but you caught me with the devil's own headache—and, yes, I'd indulged far too much, so you needn't add that scold.'

Then, as understanding dawned, she said indignantly, 'You were going to apologise to *me*? And yet you led me on...'

'True.' He nodded. 'It wasn't well done of me, but I think we both have a...managing bent. As I know only too well, it isn't easy for a person of that nature to apologise—especially when one knows one was in the right. I'm afraid I couldn't resist encouraging you to go through with it. You were hoping a display of penitence would dissuade me from firing you, I suppose. Because you felt you must stay on and protect the girls from their evil, uncaring guardian.'

'Not evil. But you did seem rather...uncaring.'

Some sort of anguish briefly crossed his face, gone before she could even be sure she'd actually seen it. 'I shall have to do better. Once I'd calmed down after our confrontation—and some strong coffee and beefsteak had made me feel human again—I went up to the nursery and found it just as you described. I don't recall what was on the beds when my brother and I were boys, but those threadbare cotton rags wouldn't warm a flea. Somers Abbey's finances may still be recovering, but we can certainly stand the cost of clothing and blankets, and so I informed Mrs Wallace.'

She must have grimaced, for the Colonel nodded. 'Dreadful woman. I try to have as little to do with her as possible.'

'Would that I might!' Olivia said feelingly.

The Colonel frowned. 'Do you fear she will try to

exact retribution for your having come to me after she refused your requests?'

Now that she knew she had her employer's support, Olivia was quite sure of holding her own. 'I can deal with Mrs Wallace.'

He smiled slightly and once again she was caught unawares by the strength of his sheer masculine appeal. Goodness, what a transformation when he smiled! He should do it much more often.

'I'm sure you can, my Managing Miss Overton,' he was saying. 'But if she does give you any trouble, you are to inform me. Also if she baulks at providing any other supplies you feel the girls need.'

'If she is so unpleasant, why do you not discharge her?' Olivia asked—and then remembered that, as an employee, she had no business asking such a question.

Instead of putting her in her place, though, the Colonel sighed. 'After reducing the staff to a skeleton level and spending most of my time away from the house, I had to leave someone in charge. Why my brother hired the woman, I have no idea. Once things are in better order and finances improve, I intend to replace her.'

'Providing her with a good character so you may pass your problem along to another household?'

'You are impertinent, you know,' he said, giving her a reproving glance.

'I, too, have managed a household,' she reminded him. 'To be charitable, perhaps she would be happier in a larger household with more staff to manage.'

'And to underscore her importance,' the Colonel said. 'Precisely.'

To her surprise, the Colonel chuckled again. 'I should like to have been a fly on the stable wall when you commandeered that pony cart. What exactly did you say to John Coachman?'

Feeling a little embarrassed, she confessed, 'I used my "Mistress of the Household" voice and simply ordered him to prepare it.'

'Ah, yes. Behaving as if one has the authority to command something generally gets results—whether or not one actually has that authority.'

'To be fair, he was hesitant at first. But a governess does have charge of the children, and once I demonstrated my driving ability, he was content to see us go.' She smiled. 'He probably reasoned that, if anything untoward transpired, since he'd not had orders to refuse me, I would mostly likely bear the blame of it.'

'I imagine he did.' The Colonel shook his head. 'You are the most insubordinate subordinate I've ever encountered.'

'Well, sir, you may be a colonel, but this is not the army and I am not your corporal.'

'What are you then, I wonder?'

She looked at him…and something flashed between them. An odd sense of being kindred spirits, underlain with a strong physical attraction that sent a wave of warmth through her. The feeling of connection was gone almost before she was aware of it, but the simmering heat remained, exciting, energising…and dangerous.

Before she could pull her shaken senses together, he looked away. 'We still have the matter of your purchases,' he said, all business again. 'By the way, how did you pay for them? Petty larceny from the household funds?'

'Certainly not. Besides, I wouldn't be surprised if Mrs Wallace carried the precious "household funds" around on her person. I used my own funds.'

The Colonel cocked his head at her. 'Have I paid you anything yet?'

'No, sir. I… I have a small amount of my own laid by.'

'Then I shall see you reimbursed at once. Can't have you drawing down your pin money buying necessities for the children.'

Her light mood faded as she recalled just how little money she had left. 'No, that would not be wise.'

'Very well. What was the total?'

After naming the sum, she tried to rally her suddenly sagging spirits. After all, she wasn't going to be discharged, she would have important work to do, making her charges feel comfortable in their new home—and maybe, if the Colonel really wanted to do better by them, she might figure out a way to coax him to interact more with them.

The orphaned girls so desperately needed a permanent, protective presence in their lives. She could only sympathise, as she yearned for one, too—but at least she had Sara in London to turn to, should matters become truly dire.

After counting out what he owed her, the Colonel closed the desk drawer. 'Very well, Miss Overton. You will let me know if you encounter any difficulties with Mrs Wallace—or if you feel the girls are in need of anything else.'

Might as well start now. 'There is…one more thing. You are their last remaining close relation, you told me. I'm sure they would adjust more quickly, feel less frightened, lost and alone, if they could get to know you better.'

Immediately, that forbidding look came over his face, the same look she'd noticed before when she'd mentioned him seeing more of the children. 'As I believe I already told you,' he said, his tone noticeably cooler, 'I'm busy and away from the house on estate business all day, almost every day.'

'Do you know what Elizabeth said to me in Bristol? What convinced me I would have to apologise and try to retain my position?'

The increasing grimness of his expression warned she was once again risking an abrupt dismissal. Too certain he needed to hear the child's comment to back down, she met his gaze unflinchingly.

For another fraught moment, she thought he meant to tell her he had no interest in childish confidences and send her away. Instead, with a wry grimace, he said, 'I suppose you are going to tell me, whether I want to hear it or not.'

After biting her tongue to keep herself from responding to that provocation, she said, 'Once we had made our purchases and were preparing to leave town, Elizabeth asked if I would be taking them back to Somers Abbey— or if I was going to leave them in Bristol with someone else. Please, Colonel, if you could just let me bring them in to see you occasionally, so they might start to feel they can rely on you and be reassured that you won't simply pass them along to—'

'Enough, Miss Overton,' he interrupted, a sharp look of—surely it wasn't *pain*?—crossing his face. Standing abruptly, he walked to the bookcase and halted there, his back to her. Though she ached to say more, she made herself remain silent and waited.

Finally, he turned back to her, his expression tightly controlled. 'I will do as much as I can. I rely on *you* to reassure them.'

She knew better than to press him further. At least he

hadn't ordered her out of the room this time. 'Very well. Thank you, Colonel.'

'No, thank you, Miss Overton. For helping me "discharge my responsibilities".'

So he did feel he should do more for them. She had the grace to feel a little ashamed at pushing him so hard. 'That was unfair. I am sure you are quite capable.'

He sighed. 'This time, I sincerely hope to be.'

With that enigmatic utterance, he nodded a dismissal. Giving him a curtsy, she left the room.

Late that night, Olivia tiptoed into the quiet nursery to check on the girls. As she'd hoped, her two charges slept peacefully, their small bodies covered from head to toe in thick flannel nightgowns and tucked in under heavy woollen blankets.

She smiled, remembering Elizabeth's awe when she'd first donned the nightgown. 'Oh, miss, it's so soft!' she cried, rubbing her small hands down the material. 'Sophie, we shall finally be warm!' Giggling, she'd hugged her little sister, then looked back to Olivia. 'Thank you so much, Miss Overton!'

'I may coax you into liking England after all,' she'd said, then settled them into bed and told them a story— having discovered, when she'd given the schoolroom a closer inspection that evening, that its cupboards contained neither toys, nor slates for writing, nor books she could read to them.

Predictably, when she'd asked Mrs Wallace about it, the woman had replied icily that until last week, the schoolroom at Somers Abbey had been unoccupied for the whole of her tenure as housekeeper, so she had no idea if the household possessed such items. 'Since you have such good rapport with Colonel Glendenning, perhaps you should ask him,' she'd said snidely, obviously not at all happy that Olivia's earlier talk with the master hadn't resulted in the rebuke the housekeeper had expected.

Biting back the reply she would like to have given, Olivia hung on to her temper. Much as she'd like to give as good as she got with the woman, it would make life more pleasant, especially for the children, if she could find a way to establish a more cordial relationship. 'Perhaps I shall do just that,' she'd said brightly and left it at that.

Though it was now a bit later than she'd intended, the task of putting away the supplies she'd obtained in Bristol and the storytelling having taken longer than anticipated, she still had time to visit the library. Encouraged by her employer's friendlier reception this afternoon—he hadn't entirely retreated, even when she'd pleaded with him to see more of the girls—she'd decided to ask him about the schoolroom supplies. Most likely, once the Colonel and his brother were grown, all such items had been packed away, perhaps consigned to the attic. If the Colonel had some idea where they might be located, she could go in search of them first thing tomorrow.

Thinking it best to be cautious, she went quietly to the library on her own, without asking Mansfield to announce her. She'd heard that army officers serving in India were hard drinkers and the Colonel's appearance this morning certainly seemed to confirm that. It probably wouldn't be prudent to approach him about anything this evening if he were already in his cups.

The problem of how she would manage to open that heavy oak door without announcing her presence was solved by her finding it had been left ajar. Peeping inside, she saw the room was unoccupied.

Before she could turn away, disappointed, she noticed that the desk chair was pushed back and the desk itself boasted a fully lit brace of candles, a book and a whisky bottle sitting beside a half-filled glass. All of which suggested that the Colonel had only stepped out of the room for a moment and meant to return shortly.

She'd wait for him.

She walked in, intending to take the chair in front of the desk to which he'd invited her earlier. But just as she was about to seat herself, she noted one more object on the desk, sitting in the spot most brightly illuminated by the candelabra. Curious, she bent over it to take a closer look.

It was a miniature portrait in a gilded frame, she realised. Without thinking, she picked it up and angled it so that, from her position in front of the desk, the candlelight fell fully upon it.

A small boy with ash-blond hair and brilliant blue eyes smiled up at her. A small boy whose features reminded her strongly of—

'What the *hell* do you think you are doing?' an angry voice demanded.

Startled as much by the voice's ferocity as the profanity, she looked up from the miniature to the incensed face of the Colonel pacing towards her, back to the portrait and up again. 'You—you have a *son*?' she gasped.

Reaching her, he ripped the small frame from her hand. '*Had* a son,' he spat back. 'Quite legitimate, I assure you, so you needn't go all faint and maidenly on me. How dare you creep in here and snoop among my private things?'

'I was not *snooping*!' she cried indignantly. 'I wished to speak with you, the door was open and the room appeared as if you'd only left it for a moment. I intended just to wait for you.'

'Isn't it anguish enough that he lies thousands of miles away, his little body trapped underground in a small wooden box with nothing but a stone angel to keep him company? Must I tolerate having indifferent strangers gazing upon his face?'

As he looked down at the portrait, his breathing went ragged, his jaw worked and tears sheened his eyes. 'His beloved face,' he whispered.

Horrified by what she'd inadvertently discovered, agonised by his agony, Olivia stood speechless, her mouth open in shock.

Before she could dredge up a reply, with his eyes still locked on the portrait, the Colonel made a swishing motion with his free hand. 'Leave,' he said, his voice raw. 'Please, just leave me.'

Picking up her skirts, she ran from the room.

Chapter Six

Not until she halted halfway down the hallway to catch her breath did Olivia hear it. The short, harsh sound of a strangled sob.

Hardly daring to breathe, she hurried further away. A man as commanding as her employer would hate having anyone—especially an outsider—overhear behaviour he would surely consider 'weak'.

Though she'd discovered very little beyond the fact that he'd lost a child—and obviously also a wife—as she walked back to her chamber, her heart ached for him.

Suddenly, his reluctance to have any closer contact with his wards made perfect sense. She couldn't imagine the depth of grief one would suffer upon losing a child. But she did know having other children occupy the house couldn't make up for that loss—and might well make it worse.

Now that she thought back on it, there had been other clues. Rather than dismiss children as tedious and beneath his notice, and simply order her to take charge of them, as a military man might, he'd said he would 'do as much as he could' for them. Then there was the way his expression grew shuttered each time she'd suggested he involve himself more with them. The distressed look on his face when she'd called him 'uncaring'.

No matter how or when his death had happened, the Colonel obviously still grieved for his lost son—a grief that caused immense pain. While she had in her charge two small girls, also grieving, who desperately needed the affection of a faithful, dependable protector.

If she could somehow bring them together, would that not be helpful for both guardian and wards?

Sara would tell her that reconciling the two wasn't within the scope of her position and, knowing so little about either party, her interference might do more harm than good. Emma would say that, once again, she was going to stick her nose uninvited into a place where it wasn't wanted. But she knew herself too well.

As she'd confessed to the Colonel, she was 'managing'. Perhaps because she'd had to take over running her own household at such a young age, when her mother had become immobilised after the death of her father, she also felt a deep need to 'fix' things—houses, situations, people. That strong desire had driven her intention to forgo marriage and work with Sara on forwarding the great political reform measures that would bring more justice and fairer government to all of England.

The children were probably young enough to embrace any warmth or affection offered them. The Colonel, however, was a man grown, and a soldier at that. She doubted he would appreciate anyone directly acknowledging, or intruding upon, his private pain. She would have to proceed cautiously.

But after recognising so clear a need, in both him and

the children, it simply wasn't in her nature to stand by and do nothing.

First, she'd probably need to apologise again for her supposed 'snooping'. But how to do that without dredging up again the whole distressing scene?

She was pondering that dilemma when she arrived back in her room, only then remembering that she'd not accomplished the mission that had prompted her to leave it—finding out the location of the nursery supplies.

Her shocking discoveries having left her too agitated to try to sleep, she might as well use the last few minutes of the workday to search out the butler and see if he might be able to assist her.

In the process, perhaps he might shed more light on his employer's devastating losses.

Expecting that Mansfield would not yet have retired for the night, Olivia went first to the servants' hall. The cook and the tweeny were still in the kitchen, washing and polishing pots and, thankfully, Mrs Wallace was nowhere to be seen. Hoping her impatience to learn more about furnishing the nursery would not have to wait until morning, she walked down the hallway and knocked at the door to the butler's private quarters.

'What is it now, Mrs Wallace?' he asked, a hint of exasperation in his voice as he opened the door. Seeing her upon the threshold, he checked. 'Miss Overton?'

'Yes, Mansfield. I apologise for troubling you so late, but might I impose upon you to answer a question? I'm searching for items that would be of great assistance to me in seeing the Colonel's wards are properly cared for.'

She noted with interest that he did not immediately recommend that she take up that matter with Mrs Wallace, as she'd half-feared he might. 'I'll help if I can. Would you have a seat? By this time of night, these old bones need a rest.'

She walked past him into his small sitting room and took the chair he indicated before the hearth. 'Thank you for seeing me, sir. Am I correct in assuming that you have served Somers Abbey for many years?'

He nodded. 'Since I was a lad.'

'So you have known the Colonel since *he* was a lad. Perhaps you *can* help me, then! I need to locate supplies for the nursery—reading books, toys, perhaps some additional furniture. There is almost nothing in the schoolroom now. It's possible the items were discarded after the Colonel and his brother grew up, but it's more likely they were only stored somewhere. If you don't know what became of them, perhaps one of the female staff might?'

The butler shook his head. 'I'm afraid I have no idea. Cook wouldn't know, either, and the housemaid and the tweeny didn't start working here until well after the young masters left the nursery. There is one other servant remaining from years past—a day worker, who doesn't live in any more. Travers was lady's maid to my late mistress. She stayed on as the interim housekeeper after Mrs Jeffers retired upon the mistress's death, until Mr Charles, the Colonel's brother, hired Mrs Wallace.' Mansfield sniffed. 'Mrs Wallace didn't like Travers and forced her out of the house, but she still does the fine hand laundry and sewing work for the household. She didn't deal directly with the boys when they were children, but she was close to my late mistress and might remember where the nursery supplies were put up.'

'That would be excellent! She doesn't live in, you said. Where might I find her?'

'She has a little house down near Somers village. Brookside Cottage. Mrs Wallace tried to get her out of that, too, but for all his faults, Mr Charles wouldn't have it. He knew how much Travers had meant to his mother. And now I've said more than I meant to.' He shook his head. 'The failings of an old man—gossipy as an old maid sitting round the fire!'

Not quite gossipy enough, she thought. He'd let nothing slip about his master. 'Not at all! I appreciate the information so much. Now, I'll leave you to your rest. Goodnight, Mansfield.'

'Goodnight, Miss Overton. And—good luck finding the supplies.'

She was terribly tempted to ask what he knew about his master's son, but as a long-term retainer, he probably felt a protective loyalty to the family and would baulk at revealing the Colonel's private affairs to an outsider.

But, she thought, brightening as she walked to the door, he'd told her that the retired lady's maid had been quite close to her mistress. Perhaps, while Olivia enquired about nursery articles, *that lady* might volunteer more information about the Colonel's child.

Olivia certainly hoped so. Her employer's anguished reaction tonight indicated he was unlikely to reveal anything further to her.

Though he obviously felt a deep responsibility towards his wards, she could understand that it might be terribly painful for him to be around them, serving as they would as a constant reminder of the son he'd lost. In the course of her duties of caring for the girls, she would inevitably have to consult him. If she knew more about the circumstances surrounding his loss, she would be better able to talk with him about his wards while avoiding topics that might cause him further distress.

She would have to arrange to pay a visit to the village as soon as possible. But tomorrow, she needed to gather her courage and approach her employer one more time about the supplies for the schoolroom.

Rather than begin by apologising and open anew what was obviously an agonising memory, maybe it would be better to pretend their confrontation hadn't happened. She hoped, when he was less upset, the Colonel would realise he'd accused her unfairly and wouldn't take her to task again.

Although, she acknowledged, squirming a little at admitting the truth, she hadn't *intended* to snoop, she really hadn't had any right to pick up the portrait on his desk. And much as she longed to have more answers, she didn't dare ask anything further about his son, unless he himself brought up the subject.

Which, she admitted, wasn't very likely.

The next morning, Hugh rose early, feeling drained but calm. For the first time in a long time, he'd spent an entire evening without imbibing too much whisky. He had forced himself instead to live through a night of remembrance and anguish.

But Miss Overton, blast the woman, had been right. When his cousin had named him guardian of his precious children, he would have expected his boyhood friend to do more than simply oversee the girls' finances. With their father no longer there to care for them, he would expect Hugh to step in and try to make them feel once more as safe and sheltered as they'd been before Robert's untimely death.

No matter how painful it would be for him.

Nothing and no one could replace Drew. But it wasn't fair for him to avoid his wards, just because the very sight of them brought back the searing agony of his son's death. The girls had suffered losses just as great as his.

To make them feel safe and valued, as Robert would want him to, he would have to spend time with them. And to tolerate spending time with them, he had forced himself to finally face the loss of his son, a heartbreak he'd buried under long hours of work and large quantities of whisky for more than three years.

In the process of facing it, though, he shouldn't have let his anguish lead him into losing his temper with Miss Overton, an unintentional witness to the scene. Scraping a hand across his face, he acknowledged the uncomfortable fact that he owed her an apology.

Could he think of a way to word it that would allow him to avoid mentioning Drew? However he expressed it, apologise he must and before the day was over.

Their confrontation had pushed him forward in carrying out his resolve. After the governess's departure, he'd made himself inspect that portrait of Andrew, painted just a month before his son's death. Forced himself to continue gazing upon that beloved face until the anguish boiled out, leaving him helpless as it unmanned him, making him want to howl with pain and sending a flood of womanish tears coursing down his face.

Those who said acknowledging grief and loss made it easier to bear were idiots. Afterwards, he hadn't felt any less as though his heart had been ripped from his chest.

But he knew now he would be able to face his wards without worrying that the feelings he'd worked so hard to repress would suddenly emerge to confound him. He might still find himself weeping at night, in the privacy of his library, but he'd be able to tolerate the pain until he was alone.

It still wouldn't be easy to see the girls—each meeting being a stark reminder of the child he had lost. He'd start with small steps. Maybe, as the Managing Miss Overton suggested—would he ever see her now without thinking of her as the 'Managing Miss Overton'?—he would have her bring the girls to see him briefly each night, if he returned to Somers Abbey before they were put to bed.

He'd forbid himself to continue working as he had been, staying away from Somers Abbey until it was so late, he was fairly certain of missing them.

When he brought Miss Overton in to deliver his apology, he'd tell her of this change in her instructions.

He realised that he was lucky, and should be grateful, that the governess the hiring agency had dispatched had bonded with her charges so quickly and fiercely.

As an outspoken champion of their well-being, she would make a good buffer. He could ease himself into spending time with them gradually, confident that in the interim she would help him discharge his responsibilities by watching over them fiercely and faithfully.

Maybe, in time, seeing them in the place he'd once dreamed of bringing his son wouldn't hurt so much.

Taking a deep breath, he rang the bell for Mansfield and instructed the butler to summon the governess. And then set his mind to considering how to phrase his apology.

Only then did the oddity of it strike him. Here he was, the man who almost never allowed his private feelings to show, being forced to apologise twice for revealing them in the space of just two days.

All because of the new governess. Shaking his head ruefully, he acknowledged that in the very short time she had been at Somers Abbey, Miss Overton had certainly disrupted the quiet, monotone tenor of his days—and prompted him to face something he should have confronted long ago.

He wasn't sure whether he appreciated that or not.

Like a fresh breeze, a few minutes later, she entered briskly and dropped him a quick curtsy. 'You wished to see me, sir? Which is fortunate, as there is something I wanted to speak with you about, too.'

'Please, take a seat,' he said, gesturing. 'This time, I insist upon speaking first.'

Slipping gracefully into the chair, she nodded. Hugh was relieved to note that she wore her customary calm, seeming neither upset nor nervous about meeting him again after the episode last night.

A fact that struck him as being rather exceptional. Had he bellowed at any of the other female staff members as he had at Miss Overton, they would have sulked, in the case of Cook—wept, in the case of the tweeny— or cowered, in the case of the maid—the next handful of times he met them.

Grateful anew for her calm, sensible, self-possessed nature, he said, 'Once again, I fear I owe you an apology. I'm afraid last night that I wasn't…quite myself. In my distress, I lashed out at you, which was unjust and unfair. I hope you will forgive me.'

For several heartbeats, she remained silent, studying him, as if she hoped he might volunteer something more. And though she might *deserve* to hear more, he couldn't bring himself to explain about Drew.

Finally, she nodded. 'Apology accepted. I'm just glad that you realise that when I came into the library to wait for you, I didn't mean to pry.'

'Shall we move on, then?' he asked, relieved—and grateful to her for her graciousness in making the difficult business of that apology easier. 'You mentioned there was something you wished to ask me about?'

'Yes, sir. I wondered if you might know where the books and supplies that were once in the schoolroom might have been stored. You may have noticed when you visited the nursery yesterday that the room contains little furniture and nothing in the way of school supplies. The girls should have slates on which to write and do sums, story books to practise their reading and I should like books to read to them, as well. As you can imagine, Mrs Wallace has been of no help whatsoever in locating these materials.'

As he watched her speak, he realised he hadn't really ever *looked* at Miss Overton. Though she had none of the fragile beauty that had made every man who saw his wife want to shelter and protect Lydia, there was something subtly attractive about the governess's energetic, no-nonsense manner. Her hair, what of it he could see that wasn't tucked up under a cap, was a nondescript brown, her figure taller than average but well formed, her face lively and her eyes positively glowing with intelligence and purpose. A dervish, people might have termed her back in India. Single-minded as a monk and whirling about his house.

She'd certainly stirred things up in his life.

'I'm not surprised that Mrs Wallace was unhelpful. Though to be fair, the nursery has been empty since well before she arrived. Actually, I didn't notice much about the schoolroom, my mind being occupied by the matter of blankets. I don't recall seeing any books or toys on the shelves, though, and the old table and the student desks that used to be in there have gone missing. I can't imagine that my mother would have discarded them. I expect all of it is stored in the attics somewhere.'

She sighed. 'But you don't know where.'

'No.'

'I suppose I shall have to organise an expedition. Perhaps make it into a sort of treasure hunt for the girls. That is—the attic is safe for them to wander around in, isn't it? It's floored, with a few windows to offer some light and adequate ventilation?'

'I believe so. I haven't been up there since I was a boy.'

'Thank you, sir. I suppose I should just poke around and see what I discover. I'll make a list of anything we can't locate that I believe is necessary for the schoolroom. A good day to you, Colonel.'

She curtsied again, obviously intending to leave. 'One more thing, if you please, Miss Overton,' he said, raising a hand to stay her.

About to turn to the door, she looked over her shoulder. 'Yes, sir?'

'I… I will not be going out around the estate all day today. The squire and some of the other landowners are dropping by later in the afternoon to discuss who among us might stand as a representative for the next Parliament. So… I will be available in the early afternoon, if you wish to bring the girls in to see me.'

Surprise, gratification—and then something he couldn't quite identify, something that looked almost like remorse, passed over her face. 'Thank you for reconsidering, sir. It will be wonderful for the girls.'

He smiled wryly. 'Much as it pains me to admit it—again—you were right. I should let my wards get to know me better, so they will feel more at home in this unfamiliar land. Less abandoned and alone. I can't make it up to them for their losing their father, but I can do a better job of trying to make them feel secure and welcome.'

For a moment she hesitated. Then, as if resolved to speak whether it was wise or not, she said, 'And *I* owe *you* an apology, this time a sincere one. Until last night, I had no idea you had lost a child. I won't pretend to comprehend how devastating that must be, but I do assure you, I wouldn't have been quite so…strident about insisting you involve yourself in the girls' lives had I known. I am sorry for being so belligerent! I only ask that you do what you can, as much as you feel you can bear, to help them adjust to their loss of home and father.'

He appreciated her admission, her offer and the delicate phrasing of her apology that did not require him to discuss his loss. 'Understood. My discomfort doesn't matter. Their comfort does. With your help, I hope to give them the support my cousin would expect me to provide.'

'If there is anything I can do to make dealing with them easier for you, please tell me. And if my…my *impetuous* and *managing* nature leads me into a course of action with which you are not comfortable, you have my permission to stop me.'

He had to smile. 'A handsome concession. We will do our best, then, to work together for their good.'

'Yes, sir. I would like that.'

'Until this afternoon, then.'

'Until this afternoon.' With another curtsy, she walked out, leaving him gazing thoughtfully after her.

Had he truly just pledged himself to work closely with Miss Overton? He wasn't sure how wise that might prove.

He'd shut himself off from more than just his emotions after the deaths of his wife and son. Grieving, angry, guilty, anguished, he'd closed out every pleasure. Including the pleasure of feminine company.

He couldn't deny, much as he'd deliberately tried not to notice, that Miss Overton...stirred something within him that he'd repressed for a long time. Forcing himself to be more open with his cousin's children was necessary, whatever the pain. They were his wards, his legal responsibility, and duty required that he do everything possible to make life easier for them.

Exposing himself to the allure of feminine company was not required. After the way his marriage to Lydia had ended, he didn't think he would ever risk his heart again. But presented with temptation, his body might not be so amenable to control.

He didn't see how he could avoid working with the governess—but he must take care to maintain his distance and remember she was an employee. A dependent female member of his household he had a duty to support and protect. And nothing more.

Don't think about Drew, think about Robert, Hugh told himself that afternoon as he returned to his library to await a visit from his wards. If he kept his cousin's face and memory in mind and concentrated on what Robert would have wanted for his girls, meeting with them might be easier.

Thank heaven they *were* girls! The skills they needed to master and duties they needed to be able to perform as adults would be taught to them by their governess or, once he'd found the right candidate, the genteel lady who would take over their care. He wouldn't be required to do much more than visit with them. Whereas if they had been male…having to teach them to ride, shoot, hunt and manage an estate, all things he would have done for Drew, would have been agonising.

He heard Miss Overton's soft tones and the muffled tramp of approaching footsteps in the hallway. He tensed, clenching his jaw and armouring himself for the interview to come.

There was a rap at the door, followed by Miss Overton's voice. 'Is it convenient for us to see you now, Colonel?'

You can do this. You will do this.

Taking a deep breath, he said, 'Yes. Please come in, ladies.'

He rose as they entered, the girls and Miss Overton offering him curtsies, to which he responded with a bow. Though he sucked in a breath as the inevitable wave of grief and pain washed through him, he made himself look at them.

In his shock upon meeting the children ten days ago, he hadn't noticed much about how they were dressed, but he noted now that they wore sturdy deep blue wool spencers over their pale pastel embroidered—and obviously very lightweight—cotton frocks.

He also noted that the smaller girl—Sophie, he remembered—was clutching her sister's arm, her expression apprehensive. When he looked at her and smiled, she hurriedly looked away and sidled closer to her sister.

Though her expression was nearly as wary as Sophie's, at a nod from their governess, Elizabeth said, 'Thank you, Colonel, for letting Miss Overton buy us new clothes. We are ever so much warmer now, aren't we, Sophie?'

Not daring to look at him, Sophie bobbed her lowered head.

A pang of compassion went through him. The girls were surely grieving—but they were obviously also frightened. He couldn't do much to help them with the first emotion, but he could certainly do something about the latter.

So, moving out from behind his big desk, where he'd intended to remain for this short first visit, he walked over to the wing chair by the hearth. 'Won't you ladies have a seat?' he said, gesturing to the sofa. 'I'm glad to hear you are more comfortable. I remember your papa writing to me about how difficult he'd found it to adjust to the heat, when he first went out to St Kitts. I'm sure, in time, you'll grow used to our English weather, too.'

Once the girls had seated themselves, he leaned closer, bending down so that his head was more on a level with theirs.

As he always had when he'd talked with Drew.

Pain slashed through him at the memory.

Think of Robert, not of Drew.

Then he realised he must have grimaced, for both girls drew back. Cursing himself for the lapse, he made himself smile again.

'I understand you took a wagon ride to Bristol yesterday. Did you enjoy it?'

Once again, the girls were silent until Miss Overton gave Elizabeth a nod. 'Yes, sir,' the older girl said. 'It was so nice to ride in the sun! Even though the sun here isn't very warm. The city had so many ships in it!' Her face brightening, she continued, 'Papa used to take us to the city at home sometimes. It was on the sea and had lots of big ships, too. Only the water at home is very, very blue and clear, not like the grey water here.'

'Perhaps, if the Colonel allows, we can drive to Bristol again soon,' Miss Overton said. 'We may need to get more supplies for the schoolroom. By the way, Colonel, I did a bit of looking late this morning, only to discover there isn't "an" attic, but rather several attics, none of them connected to the other.'

'You're correct. The original part of Somers Abbey is medieval and the brothers who established the priory added other buildings through several centuries before the property was sold to one of my ancestors after the dissolution of the monasteries.'

'Have you any idea which attic contains the household items?'

'The one I remember exploring as a child was over the kitchen wing—probably closest to the staff quarters, which made it more convenient for them to access.'

'I don't think I found that one. Exactly how do you get to it?'

'There's a narrow staircase leading from the kitchen to an upstairs hallway and then a small door at the end of it, with an even narrower and steeper stair that goes to the attic.'

Smiling, she shook her head. 'Maybe you could draw me a map.'

'Mansfield could show you, but I'd rather not have him climbing those steep stairs. Perhaps…perhaps I could lead you up.'

'That would be very helpful, but are you sure, Colonel? I know how busy you are and I would like to determine as soon as possible whether there are sufficient supplies in storage, or whether I need to make that trip to Bristol.'

Though Robert had left funds for the girls' upbringing, Hugh didn't intend to touch them unless absolutely necessary. He was responsible for his household and restricted finances be damned, he would provide them.

Still, if the items Miss Overton needed could be located in the attics, he'd be spared the expense of purchasing them. He was stuck here at the manor today anyway, so making a quick detour to the attic wouldn't take him away from his work.

'I don't expect my meeting to last the whole of the afternoon and we should have daylight until fairly late. I'll have Mansfield let you know when it's concluded and I can take you up then.'

'Thank you, Colonel, that would be most helpful. Very well, girls, we should leave the Colonel to prepare for his meeting. By the way, are you looking to support a reform candidate, Colonel?'

He angled his head at her. 'Do you have an interest in politics, Miss Overton?'

'Oh, yes. So much wonderful legislation has been enacted recently! A bill limiting child labour in factories, the abolition of slavery! Have you an interest in politics, Colonel?'

'If you are asking whether or not I'd be willing to stand for Parliament, the answer is no—not at this time. I've still got too much work here to restore Somers Abbey. Besides, having been in India so long, I'm afraid I don't know much about what's been going on in England.'

'Oh, but you must learn! The Factory Bill was a start in limiting hours for child workers, but there remains the matter of enacting adequate enforcement provisions and the need for more formal schooling for the children. My friends and I...' Abruptly her voice trailed off and tears pooled at the corners of her eyes.

He'd watched, fascinated, as her face had grown animated, her cheeks rosy, her eyes—they were a deep brown, he realised—sparkling with passion. Until she suddenly went silent, the enthusiasm vanishing as abruptly as if she'd been slapped.

A bleak expression passed over her face before she swiped away the tears and said quietly, 'Excuse me, sir. I didn't mean to prose on. Thank you for letting us stop by. Make your curtsies now, girls. Let's go back to the schoolroom and make a list of what I need to look for.'

The girls dipped their curtsies, Miss Overton rising from hers to square her shoulders and pace towards the door, as stiffly upright as if she were shouldering a heavy burden.

'I'll send for you when my meeting concludes,' he said to her retreating form.

'Yes, sir,' she said in that same toneless voice, not looking back at him.

As he watched her go out, curious about that dramatic transformation, it occurred to him that he knew very little about her, beyond the fact that she had run her mother's household—obviously a genteel one—and upon that lady's death had sought employment as a governess. Which indicated that this must be her first such position—and that she had once lived in much more affluent circumstances.

Which was consistent with her behaviour since her arrival. Both her self-confidence and lack of deference indicated she was accustomed to being treated as a lady of breeding—a person of a status equal to his own. She was clearly not used to being treated—or behaving—as an inferior.

How had she ended up at Somers Abbey?

But even as the question formed, he squelched the curiosity. He didn't need to think of Miss Overton as a gently bred lady, someone who might be invited into his parlour, dined or danced or flirted with. All he needed to know about her background was that she was competent to discharge her duties.

It would be much better for his peace of mind if he thought of her only as another female staff member, like Cook or the housemaid or the tweeny.

No matter how much her intelligence and passion argued otherwise.

Chapter Seven

Struggling to keep up a smile on her face for her charges, Olivia had to force herself to concentrate on settling the girls back in the nursery, telling them to rest for dinner, before she escaped to her own room to regain her composure.

Since leaving London, she'd been like the Colonel, she reflected as she sat on the side of her bed. Concentrating on filling her days with work and trying to go to her bed too tired to do anything but fall asleep. Deliberately putting her changed circumstances out of mind and refusing to think any further ahead than the next several days.

At the Colonel's announcement that he and his neighbours would discuss filling a seat in Parliament, her thoughts had automatically returned to her friends, the Ladies' Committee and the causes around which she'd centred her life. She'd begun to speak of them before the reality of her current life came crashing back—the friends far away, her involvement in the great issues of politics no longer possible.

Having never faced her losses, she hadn't developed any armour against the onslaught of memories and the resulting tidal wave of loneliness and grief. Swept away and foundering, it had taken all her will and resolve to halt the tears, finish the interview with the Colonel and manage to leave the room with a modicum of dignity.

Sober reflection told her she probably ought to come to terms with the changes in her life, but she simply didn't want to—yet. Though she couldn't see how her circumstances would improve in six months, she still clung to the knowledge that after that time elapsed, she would return to London, see her dear friends and be once again surrounded by their love and support. Somers Abbey was temporary and, whether it was wise or not, she knew while she remained here, she would simply mark time.

But mark time with a purpose. Rather than brood over her uncertain future, she would focus on the present and accomplish as much as she could for the girls— and their guardian.

After a short time spent restoring her spirits in the privacy of her room, she returned to the nursery with writing paper—some of the last of her personal stationery. She'd brought it so she might write to Sara, but though she knew her friend would be anxiously awaiting news from her, she hadn't yet been able to make herself undertake the task. Describing her circumstances would only reinforce the fact that her closest friend was far away and the two of them now occupied different worlds.

After talking with the girls as she made a comprehensive list of what she hoped to find in the attics, she had intended to have them practise their letters. But her enquiries about the extent of the studies they'd had in St Kitts revealed that not even the elder had yet begun to learn to read or write. Distressing as it was to her, Olivia wasn't surprised; many still felt that educating women to do anything outside the domestic realm was unnecessary.

She gave them the paper and pencils with instructions instead to draw her pictures of their favourite things. By the time Mansfield came to the nursery to inform her that the master was ready to escort her to the attic, she had regained her usual equilibrium. She followed Mansfield out, knowing that obtaining books for teaching the girls how to read was now a priority.

The Colonel was already in the kitchen, speaking with the Cook, when she arrived. Evidently, the woman had been giving him a litany of complaints, for he was saying, 'Believe me, Mrs Potter, I'm fully aware of the difficulties of labouring in a space so much in need of repair and improvement. I appreciate the good work you do, preparing meals for the household almost as fine as those you made for my mother, when your staff and supplies were much greater. I've hopes that we may be able to replace the stove next year. I shall certainly ask your advice on the size and kind at that time.'

'That's kind of you to say, Colonel, but I know standards have slipped. I'm sorry to be complaining, only it chafes me, it truly does, not be sending you up the sort of meals you would remember having as a young man, before you left for India. And you in such need of fattening up!'

'Many's the time I thought longingly of your cooking while I was over there,' he said, treating her to one of his rare smiles—and my, how attractive he was when he smiled! No wonder Cook was charmed.

'If that's your custard tarts I'm smelling,' he was saying, 'after I take Miss Overton through the attics, I might need to steal one—just as I used to when I was a lad.'

'You know I'd do anything to help. Your dear mama, God rest her soul, would say you work too hard!'

Another long-time employee who remembered him fondly from his youth, Olivia thought. Who seemed to serve him with the same fierce loyalty as the butler. Which spoke well for the Colonel's character.

'One of your custard tarts will surely revive me. Ah, Miss Overton,' he said, belatedly noting her arrival. 'Ready to go exploring?'

'Yes, Colonel, and I've brought along a list of the items I'd like to find.'

'Let's hope, then, that my guess about them being stored in this attic was correct. We start this way.'

After lighting a lantern he'd picked up in preparation, he led her up the servants' stairs to the next floor, then down a hallway flanked by a number of doorways. 'These were once cells for the monks, then used for storage as other structures were added on. The stairs to the attic are here,' he said, opening a door at the end of the corridor. 'Quite steep and narrow, so watch your step. Those wide skirts aren't very practical on stairs like these.'

'Fashion is rarely practical, Colonel,' she said, lifting her voluminous skirts in one hand and grasping the iron handrail to steady herself.

Holding the lantern aloft, he preceded her up the steep stairs. Her skirts were not the only things almost too wide for the stairwell. As she couldn't help noting, the Colonel's broad shoulders filled the space as well, nearly blocking the light from the lantern as he ascended.

Thankfully, when they reached the attic itself, illumination from garret windows at the two opposite ends provided some light, which, with the addition of the lantern, allowed her to see tolerably well. She scanned the large, open floor, the whole expanse filled with boxes, trunks and the shadowy forms of items draped in Holland cloths.

'Well, here it is,' he said, moving the lantern to paint an arc of brighter light around the space. 'I'm afraid leading you here is about as much use as I can be. I have no idea where the items you're looking for are to be found, if they are indeed up here.'

'If they are, it stands to reason that all the nursery items were probably stored together. If you can identify the table you said used to be in the schoolroom, we might find other articles nearby.'

'That would be logical. Let me check.' One by one, he went to the cloth-swathed furniture items and pulled aside the drapery, while Olivia occupied herself inspecting the contents of the nearby boxes. She'd discovered several sets of china in one crate and a trunk of clothing that appeared to have been left from the previous century before the Colonel called out, 'I've found the table!'

She picked her way around the crates and boxes to where he stood. Having set the lantern on the table he'd bared, he was pulling aside the swathing on several nearby items. 'Yes, these are the desks, too.'

'Are there boxes or trunks with them?'

'Three trunks and several boxes. Why don't you sit here,' he said, using one of the Holland cloths to dust off a trunk, 'and we'll open them.'

She dutifully took a seat and unlatched the nearest trunk. 'Definitely from the schoolroom,' she said as she began pulling out items. 'Toys, it appears. I've got two sets of cup-and-ball, a bag of marbles and several tops.'

'There should be a large box of toy soldiers somewhere.'

'So you knew even as a boy that you wanted to go into the army?'

'Oh, yes. For birthdays and Christmases and whenever I could wheedle treats out of Father or my aunts, I collected soldiers. By the end, I had enough to stage a respectable re-enactment of the Battle of Waterloo. My brother Charles wasn't as keen as I was, but could usually be prevailed upon to take part.'

'I hope you won't be offended, but I expect the girls will be less enthused,' she said. 'Did your brother have a special interest?'

After opening another box, he held up a miniature carriage. 'Horses and vehicles were his delight. Not to speak ill of the dead, but about the only part of Somers Abbey that wasn't in a shambles when I returned to England was the stables. Sadly, Charles never had any interest in the land or the duties required to properly manage it.' He sighed. 'Now it's my duty to try to repair years of neglect.' He gave a gruff laugh. 'Charles would have been furious to learn the first step I took was to sell off almost all his expensive hunters and thoroughbreds.'

'You do love the land.'

'I do, though I never expected to end up with it. Like many a younger son, I thought to make the army my career. But apparently fate had other plans.'

'What shocking reversals it sometimes throws at us,' she said with feeling. But that observation cutting too close to her own circumstances, she continued quickly, 'This is a humming top, isn't it? The girls might enjoy that and the two spinning ones.'

'Yes, I hope there will be a few things they want to

play with. I'm afraid we won't find any dolls or samplers or needlework.'

'Ah, and here is a wonderful set of spillikins. That was my game, more than the tops or the cup-in-ball.'

'Dexterous, were you, Miss Overton?'

'Very. I could always manage to slip one more slender stick from the pile without toppling the whole.'

'Whereas cup-and-ball was my game.'

'Have you maintained your skill? Although I suppose that wasn't a pastime much indulged in by the army.'

'Not at all. Cards, sometimes, but mainly riding, shooting and drinking.' He grimaced. 'Lots of drinking.'

'Could you still land it, do you think?'

'Probably.' Raising a brow at her, he reached over to take one of the sets she'd laid on the chest. After a few swings, he guided the ball expertly into the cup.

'Well done!' Olivia said approvingly. 'You definitely haven't lost your skill.'

Nodding, he laid the toy back on the chest. 'Charles and I used to challenge each other, to see who could land the ball the most times in a row. We were pretty evenly matched.'

Olivia continued to open the boxes as they talked. 'Aha, books!' she said triumphantly. 'I knew there must be some here.'

Looking up from the trunk he was opening, the Colonel said, 'Are there the reading books you were hoping for?'

'Yes, several of them. And books of nursery rhymes. Here's *Tom Thumb's Folio* and an *Aesop's Fables*, too shall love to read those to the girls.'

'Are there any educational materials in with the

'Such as?'

'Geographical puzzles. We had quite a few and used to race to see who could put theirs together faster. I remember being so disappointed, years later, to discover the one of India was highly inaccurate. The English one was quite good and Europe was pretty close to the mark as well.'

'Was there one of the whole world? I would love to show the girls their island and how it looks in relation to England and the rest of the nations.'

'I don't remember one, but there should be a globe. Probably about as accurate as the India puzzle.'

Opening the last box beside him, the Colonel said, 'Here are your slates. I'm not sure there is any chalk— you may have to obtain that in Bristol.'

'You haven't turned up any paper, have you? For sketching and watercolours? Although after all this time, I expect any remaining paints would have to be replaced anyway.'

'Put paints, brushes and paper on your Bristol list. Well, that's all in these boxes. Have you found anything else?'

'Looks like another bag of marbles and several more sets of cards at the bottom. I haven't found the toy soldiers.'

'Since it's doubtful the girls would want to play with them, we don't need to waste time searching for them. Let's move the boxes and trunks with the materials you want over by the door. I'll have two of the grooms come over later and bring them and the furniture down and back up to the schoolroom.'

'I could probably carry a box with me now.'

The Colonel frowned as he stacked two boxes on a trunk, preparing to ferry them to the door. 'Please don't.

Those stairs are dangerous enough in skirts, even without you carrying anything. Your good intentions to provide materials for your charges aren't worth the risk of breaking an arm or an ankle.'

'Impatient as I am to get started, I suppose you're right,' she admitted. 'However, I can at least bring the *Aesop's Fables*. Although I have no trouble making up bedtime stories, I should love to read to them, too.'

'Very well, but I insist on carrying it for you.'

She shook her head. He certainly acted the commanding officer! 'If you *insist*…'

For the next few minutes, they were occupied carrying the assorted boxes and trunks to the side of the room near the stairs, the Colonel once again intervening to forbid her to carry any but the lighter boxes, while he hefted the trunks.

They grouped all the materials together and then counted the number of containers, so the grooms would know how many they needed to fetch. Pausing by the door to the stairs, where they both had to bend a bit to avoid knocking their heads on the roof beams, the Colonel offered Olivia his handkerchief. 'This may get the worst of the dust off, although I imagine you'll want to give your hands a thorough washing when you get back to your room.'

Nodding her thanks, she took it and began wiping off her fingers. 'Yes, and I imagine the gown will need a thorough brushing, too. But I don't mind a little dust. I'm very grateful to have supplies to begin lessons for the girls. Thank you, Colonel, for taking the time to find them for me.'

Nodding, the Colonel remained beside her, book under his arm. 'Thank you, Miss Overton, for being so diligent in your care of them. They are lucky to have you as their governess—and so am I.'

Olivia couldn't help pinking with pleasure at the compliment. 'Thank you again, sir. I hope to be.'

'And something else.' He paused, looking thoughtful, before continuing, 'When I returned from India to Somers Abbey, all I could see was how much everything had deteriorated. Practically every waking hour since has been spent working to restore the place and, at times, my thoughts towards my brother have not been charitable. But going through the nursery things this afternoon reminded of what a good companion he was growing up, before we went our separate ways. Thank you for giving me back those happier memories.'

She shook her head deprecatingly. 'You are welcome, but it was the task, not me.'

He chuckled. 'A task I would never have undertaken had you not spurred me to it.' He motioned towards the stairs. 'Let me go down ahead of you—so I can catch you if you trip on those skirts.'

The idea of falling into his arms sent a little shock of awareness through her. She looked up quickly, catching one of the strands of her braided coiffure on the beam overhead. The Colonel reached up to free it for her—and halted, his hand on the beam, his gaze focused on Olivia.

His stance, half-bent over her, might have been intimidating. Instead, Olivia found the proximity of his powerful frame reassuring—but also oddly disturbing, in a way that made her skin prickle and set off flutters in the pit of her stomach. Supremely conscious of the breadth and strength of the shoulders so near to her, she was captivated by the masculine force of the face gazing down at her—high brow, straight nose, finely chiselled lips—and mesmerised by the intensity of his gaze.

Her rational mind stuttered to a halt, freezing in her brain a single coherent thought.

What would it be like to kiss him?

She should move away, but she couldn't seem to get her limbs to function. Neither could she force herself to break his gaze. Though she had virtually no experience in the matter, his intense concentration on her made it seem like maybe…he might want to kiss her, too.

And wasn't he bending lower, bringing his lips closer to hers?

Every nerve tensing, her eyes drifted closed…before she heard his harsh intake of breath—and heard him move away, setting every feminine instinct protesting.

'We'd better be getting back.' Opening the attic door, he raised the lantern and started down the stairs.

This time, Olivia was glad of the broad back that blocked the light—leaving in shadow the cheeks she could feel flaming as dispassionate reason returned.

Goodness, what had come over her, to imagine anything so nonsensical?

She was a tall, plain, brown-haired woman who'd never inspired any gentleman with passion—which was one of the reasons she'd intended to devote her life to causes, rather than settle for marriage to a man who wanted her to run his household while he pursued prettier mistresses. Her plain friend Emma had had the good fortune to find her Lord Theo, but there had never been a *ton* gentleman who attracted her—or one who pursued her that she'd had any desire to encourage.

If she were still a lady of the *ton* and the Colonel were to pursue her…

But she was not and would never be again. Besides, the Colonel was a powerful, virile, very attractive man. Even if she were not his employee, it was beyond ridiculous to imagine he might want to kiss *her*.

She *was* his employee and it was past time for her to put a stop to this fanciful imagining and behave as though she understood her place. And if she were weak enough to sometimes fall into longing over what might have been, better that she avoid as much as possible placing herself in situations where she would be alone with him.

No more leisurely explorations of the attic.

For he hadn't been the only one fondly tripping down memory lane. The toys and books and puzzles recalled her own childhood, happy times spent reading with her governess and occasionally playing with her older brother, before the tragedy of the illness that had carried him away while she was still in short skirts.

No point remembering that old grief. No point dwelling on the knowledge that had Frederick reached manhood and inherited the Overton estate, *he* would have been trustee of her inheritance and it probably wouldn't have been lost in a risky investment scheme. Or if her brother had been responsible for its loss, he would have made it up out of income from the estate—the one that now belonged to her cousin. She would not have been left homeless and virtually penniless.

Those grim reflections were enough to cool the last of the warmth the Colonel's nearness had evoked. Following him down the stairs, she felt again the desolation of loneliness and near despair that had brought her to tears when he'd mentioned politics.

Would she have done better to marry Everston? She

might have remained in London, surrounded by her friends, involved in the causes she loved.

But visiting her friends and continuing her favourite activities would not have been assured. She would have had her husband's household and his numerous offspring to manage, no guarantee of any funds of her own—and Everston in her bed.

Better that she remain where she was, no matter how lonely—or how easily her attractive employer seemed able to evoke a bitter longing for a different life.

Chapter Eight

The next afternoon, Hugh was supervising the draining of some fields in the northern sector of the estate, when a groom rode up with the news that a visitor from India had arrived at Somers Abbey.

Conflicting emotions filled him at the news. On the one hand, Stephen Saulter had been his closest friend on the subcontinent. Having started in the army and then transferred to the civilian administration, Stephen knew India well and had been extremely helpful in acclimating Hugh to that foreign world and inspiring him with a deep appreciation of its ancient culture.

On the other hand, his good friend had been a witness to the bleakest, most devastating events in his life, tragedies he had no desire to be reminded of or discuss.

But as he'd left India he'd given Stephen a blanket invitation to visit, if it proved convenient when he was on home leave, so Hugh could hardly send him packing.

Besides, his friend was intelligent and compassionate. He would no doubt sense the topics Hugh would rather not address and avoid them.

* * *

So, little more than half an hour later, he was striding into his library, where he found his friend seated on the sofa, scanning a book. Hearing Hugh enter, Saulter hopped up and came over to meet him.

'Stephen, how good it is to see you!' Hugh said, shaking the hand his friend extended. 'You're looking very well. I actually didn't expect you until next month. Has Mansfield made you comfortable? After coming so far, you must stay a few days.'

'He has and, if it will not interfere too much with your work, I will make a short stay. Yes, I'd not thought to travel until next month, but there was a ship leaving sooner, so I took it. I must say, I'd been savouring the idea of home leave. It's been far too long since I was back in England.'

'How goes the civil service?'

Stephen shrugged. 'As slowly as ever. But at least I'm not being shot at, like when we were in the army. Unlike you, I didn't end up inheriting land in England, so I must make my fortune where I can.'

'And have you made your fortune?'

'I'm no nabob, but I'm doing well enough.'

'Excellent. Then you're faring better than I am.'

Stephen nodded. 'You wrote that you'd found the estate in rather bad order. You must have been working your fingers to the bone, for it appears much more prosperous than you led me to believe.'

'The fields and farms are recovering. But as a cursory glance at the house has undoubtedly shown you, there's still so much to be done, I'm rather embarrassed to have you visit now. If only you could see Somers Abbey the way it was when I was a boy!'

'I know you'll bring it back. You were always the cleverest and hardest worker among us. But you *are* looking a bit grim. Do you ever get out, see neighbours, attend parties? Life shouldn't be all nose-to-the-grindstone, you know. I wouldn't have you turning into a hermit.'

Hugh smiled wryly. 'I'm not that bad. I spend a lot of time among the tenants, but I don't visit much with neighbouring landowners. My bachelor establishment isn't really set up for entertaining, and I don't like to accept invitations I am not able to reciprocate.'

He braced himself, but thankfully Stephen did not come back with the usual riposte about a single gentleman of property being welcome everywhere. Having confirmed that his friend would be discreet enough not to press him about his widower status, some of his inner tension relaxed.

But that didn't mean he'd cleared every fence of possible obstacles from the past. He paused, knowing it would be better to tell his friend of his new responsibilities before Stephen stumbled, perhaps literally, over his wards. Mentioning them might open a topic he was as eager to avoid as the subject of marriage, but it needed to be done.

Finally, trying to summon a light tone, he said, 'I recently had a new obligation laid on my plate. I believe I wrote you that I'd accepted the guardianship of my cousin's girls.'

'Yes, you did. I thought, under the circumstances, it was very handsome of you to agree to take up that charge.'

He grimaced ruefully. 'One should be careful what good deeds one undertakes. My cousin died unexpectedly about six months ago, activating my guardianship.'

'My condolences on your loss. You were close, were you not?'

'When we were boys, yes. But with him in St Kitts and me in India, we'd drifted apart.'

'At least your wards are far away.'

'They were. Until about two weeks ago, when they showed up on my doorstep. My cousin's second wife, who had a child of her own, apparently didn't want to bother with them, and shipped them across the Atlantic with a couple returning to England. With, I might add, neither my knowledge nor my consent.'

Stephen stated at him in astonishment. 'She sent them abroad without asking their guardian's permission?'

'She did. I had to scramble to find them a governess. I'm still in the process of searching through the family tree to turn up some respectable female who might oversee raising them.'

Hugh held his breath, but Stephen merely looked at him thoughtfully. 'I'm...sorry you had to take this on. It must be difficult for you.'

'It is,' Hugh admitted, relieved that Stephen hadn't initiated a discussion of the events around Drew's death. 'But it was past time for me to acknowledge my own losses and move on to deal with theirs. As my wards' governess brought home to me quite pointedly.'

'Did she!' Stephen exclaimed. 'How impertinent! I trust you put her in her place.'

'To be fair, when she was taking me to task for avoiding my wards, she didn't know about...about Drew.' Envisioning Miss Overton, his lips quirked in a smile. 'And the governess is not a female one can easily put in her place.'

'An old dragon, is she?'

'Not at all. She's rather young, actually—but a fervent champion of her charges and not shy about giving her opinion. Quite an intelligent and capable female. I know nothing of her circumstances, but her behaviour makes it quite clear that she was accustomed to moving in genteel circles. I suspect some sudden reversal of the family fortunes must have sent her into service.'

'So she's gently bred?'

'Absolutely.'

'She has something to say for herself—she's not meek and mealy-mouthed like the governesses who occasionally dined with us in India?'

'Definitely not.'

'Then you must invite her to dine with us tonight! Come now, admit it, I doubt you have even set foot in your dining room since returning home. I expect you eat on a tray in your library.'

Stephen knew him too well. 'Most nights,' he admitted. 'But in my defence, most nights I don't return to the Abbey until quite late.'

'Well, we'll return at the proper hour for dinner tonight. Is Mrs Potter still your cook? I remember you singing her praises in India! I imagine she can whip up something suitable even on short notice. Take at least one night to have a proper dinner in a proper dining room with a properly well-bred female at your table.'

When he hesitated, Stephen declared, 'Come now, I'm not proposing you make a habit of it! But as long as the governess is suitably well bred, most families include her on occasion. For holidays, or when they need to make the numbers even. Surely your dear friend's visit counts as a holiday.'

'She does take excellent care of the girls, which takes

the burden of assuring their welfare off me, for which I am grateful. I imagine she used to be accustomed to dining in company, so I don't think it would make her uncomfortable.'

'Good. Send her a note and tell her we'll expect her. In the meantime, you can give me a tour of the estate. After the arid dust of the Indian plains, how nice it is to ride through the beautiful green, green England countryside!'

'Very well, I'll invite her. We'll see if she deigns to attend.'

'*Deigns* to attend? Granted it's a request, not a command, but you are her employer, aren't you? Merely inviting her should be sufficient to expect an acceptance.'

Hugh smiled. 'You don't know Miss Overton.'

Stephen smiled back at him. 'You make me very curious to meet her. So, write that note and let's head for the stables.'

As his friend settled back with his book, Hugh went to his desk. But as he prepared to write, his smile faded.

He'd tried not to think of his inappropriate reaction to Miss Overton in the attic yesterday. When he'd tugged her curl free of the beam and gazed down at her, the energy and sheer feminine essence of her had wrapped itself around him like an enchantment. He'd so lost his grip on where he was and what he was supposed to do that he'd actually bent down to kiss her.

Fortunately, his watchful brain recognised the outrage his eager body was leading him into and halted him before he committed so dreadful a misstep.

He really needed to keep her at a safe distance.

Apparently it was not enough to remind himself she was his employee. Or to tell himself that she was tall, rather plain and quite opinionated. Despite these facts, there was something about her—a strength of personality, her zeal, her vibrant intelligence—that illumined her undistinguished features and made her far more attractive than her mere physical attributes might have suggested.

She tempted him far more than he wanted to be tempted.

But he could see no way to refuse to ask her to dine without seeming churlish—or inviting a closer scrutiny of his feelings for her than he'd want Stephen to undertake.

She probably *would* enjoy attending a dinner more like the ones to which she was formerly accustomed. Suspended in a social void, neither a member of the staff below stairs nor truly belonging with her employer above stairs, she must eat alone, or with her charges, he suddenly realised. What a lonely existence for such a vibrant spirit!

Besides, with Stephen present to entertain her, he probably wouldn't have to say much. Having spent his manhood in India, where society ladies were scarce enough that even the plainest were charmed, flattered and flirted with, his friend would be delighted to engage the intelligent and well-spoken Miss Overton in conversation.

He might even tease out something about her background—a matter about which Hugh was much more curious than he should be.

Meanwhile, after having decided the warm, sunny day practically obligated her to spirit her charges from the chilly nursery to explore out of doors, Olivia spent the morning taking the girls on a long, rambling walk.

They'd returned tired and happily burdened with leaf treasures, a few bird feathers, some interesting rocks and thoroughly muddy hems.

Although her expedition to the attic with the Colonel had removed the need to consult the former lady's maid Mansfield had mentioned on the location of schoolroom material, she probably ought to visit that lady anyway. Mansfield had told her Travers did the laundering of the household's fine work. The girls' cotton dresses boasted elaborate embroidery around the hems and cuffs and safely removing the mud of this morning's excursion from the delicate stitching was going to require a good bit of work.

Along with introducing herself and delivering the gowns, amid apologies for their excessively soiled condition, she might just discover a bit more about her intriguing employer.

After all, if she wished to have the best chance to successfully manage the delicate process of bringing about a rapprochement between guardian and wards, she needed to know as much as possible about the Colonel's life before, and especially during, his sojourn abroad. The woman who'd been his mother's close companion might well know a great deal about the Colonel's time in India—and the tragedies that had befallen him there. Olivia didn't intend to pry, but if the lady felt like imparting something about that, she certainly wouldn't stop her.

So, after settling the girls, exhausted from their lengthy stroll after so many weeks cooped up in ships, carriages and the nursery, she bundled up the soiled dresses, tracked down the butler for directions and to ask that the tweeny be sent up to keep watch over the girls until her return, then set off for Somers village.

The mile walk was pleasant, the road bordered alternately by apple orchards, stands of willow trees, broad meadows and fields of crops in new, green growth. She hadn't been able to observe too much from the carriage window upon her arrival and her trip to Bristol had taken her in the opposite direction, but it appeared the acreage owned by the Somers Abbey estate was extensive.

The girls had loved their explorations today and she would enjoy taking them still further afield. She knew she must not ask the understaffed house for a guide, but perhaps she could request the Colonel to draw, or lend her, a map of the estate.

Even better, if she phrased the proposition carefully enough, perhaps she could persuade him to take them all on a drive around the property. Perhaps coax him to point out favourite areas from his growing-up years?

Cheered by that thought, she soon reached the village, where an obliging shop owner gave her more explicit directions to Brookside Cottage. A few minutes later, she found the small dwelling situated in a pretty grove near a babbling stream.

Her knock was answered by a small, slim, neatly dressed lady whose silver hair was pinned up under a cap. 'Mrs Travers?' Olivia asked.

Inspecting her with obvious curiosity, the lady said, 'Yes. How may I help you?'

'I'm Miss Overton, governess to the wards recently come to live with Colonel Glendenning at Somers Abbey. Whom I'm sure you've heard about, staff and village gossip being what it is!' Holding out her bundle, she continued, 'I could have sent these over with the other laundry from the Abbey, but I thought I'd bring them myself, with apologies. After crossing an ocean and then coming from

London by carriage, the two girls have had so little time out in the fresh air that I'm afraid I was a bit too indulgent. While exploring the woods and streams and collecting treasures, they also collected an unaccountable amount of mud on their skirts. I fear it will take rather more time than normally required to launder the gowns without damaging the fine embroidery.'

Travers could have simply accepted the bundle and bid her good day, but as Olivia had hoped, the opportunity to obtain a first-hand account about recent events at the manor where she'd spent so much of her life was too enticing for the former lady's maid to resist. Pulling her door open wider, she said, 'Why don't you come in while I take a closer look?'

'Thank you, I would like that.'

'Will you take some refreshment after your long walk? I could fix us some tea.'

'That would be lovely also.'

'Have a seat by the hearth and I'll put the kettle on.'

The cottage was small, but immaculately clean and well furnished, with comfortable chairs by the hearth, rag rugs on the floor, a dining table and chairs near the tiny kitchen and a door leading to what must be a bedchamber beyond. All in all, a fine place of retirement for an employee who had given a lifetime of service to Somers Abbey.

She hoped Mansfield would have a similar cottage when he gave up his post.

A few minutes later, Travers returned with a tray full of tea things and sat down beside her. As she fixed cups and poured, she said, 'So, it's true, then! I had heard that the Colonel had recently taken charge of his cousin's little girls. So sad, them losing their papa at such a young age. What a fine young man he was!'

'You were acquainted with the girls' father?'

'Oh, yes! Young Master Robert visited Somers Abbey often as a boy. He and Master Hugh were particularly close, so I wasn't surprised to hear he'd made the Colonel guardian to his children.' She paused. 'Though I was somewhat surprised to learn the Colonel had accepted the responsibility. And beyond shocked to discover the girls had been sent over willy-nilly from St Kitts! How... how has the Colonel been handling it, having them at Somers Abbey?'

'It has been...difficult for him,' Olivia replied. 'I'm afraid I inadvertently made things worse, initially. You see, I had no idea when I arrived to take charge of the girls that he had lost his wife and child. The hiring agency told me only that the children's guardian was a military man who'd returned to England from India.'

She took a deep breath, choosing her words with care. 'Now that I do know, I should like to make the task of discharging that duty as easy on him as I can. I'd appreciate any advice you might offer that would help me do that.'

Travers nodded. 'It's kind of you to wish to make such an effort. How much do you know about the Colonel?'

'Only that he lost his wife and child in India.'

'What a sad business that was! Especially when one considers how excited he was when he went to India with his new wife, seven years ago. Although, even then, there was somewhat of a dust-up about their leaving.'

'Did his family not wish him to go?'

'It wasn't *his* family that opposed it, it was his wife's parents. Miss Lydia grew up not far from Somers Abbey and, as children, the two were boon companions. Then, when Master Hugh returned after his years at Eton and Oxford and found Miss Lydia grown into a beautiful young lady, they fell in love and planned to marry. All was well until Miss Lydia's parents learned Master Hugh meant to take a commission and go out to India. They tried to talk their daughter out of marrying him and, when that failed, pleaded with her to stay in England and let him go alone, arguing her delicate constitution couldn't withstand the rigours of such a climate. She wouldn't hear of it, of course, so eventually her parents relented, they married and off they went together.'

'How romantic.'

'It was,' Travers confirmed, smiling, a faraway look in her eyes. 'What a beautiful bride she made, so small and blonde and delicate, Master Hugh so tall and commanding in his regimentals, and both of them just aglow with happiness.' Her smile fading, she sighed. 'But it appears her parents knew her better than Master Hugh. From her son's letters, my mistress learned that Miss Lydia wasn't happy in India. We'd hoped that after the baby came, she might be more content, but having a child seemed to make her even more anxious and eager to return home. And then…' Her words trailed off and she sighed again.

'She lost her child,' Olivia filled in.

'The letter my mistress received about it was the shortest, saddest account one could imagine,' the woman continued, tears sheening her eyes. 'Just "Drew's gone. A fever. Slipped away between sunset and midnight." Broke my poor mistress's heart as surely as it did his mama's and papa's. Miss Lydia passed the very next month and my mistress two months later.'

'How awful for everyone,' Olivia said, her heart aching for the whole family, but most especially for the Colonel. She'd found it devastating, losing just one person dear to her. She couldn't imagine losing your entire family.

Shaking her head, Travers continued, 'After all her parents' insistence that Miss Lydia was not suited to live in India, I fear that Master Hugh blamed himself for her death. And for his son's. He's been kind enough to visit me several times, but he is so different from the happy, optimistic young soldier who left here seven years ago, I can scarcely believe it's the same man. He looks so weary and heavy-laden. Almost...haunted.'

'The poor man,' Olivia whispered, the woman's observations underscoring what she'd already noted about the Colonel's behaviour. 'What a terrible burden to carry—and how unfair! His wife accompanied him of her own free will. Surely he knows he has no control over life and death.'

'Ah, but who of us can resist, when tragedy strikes, rethinking every decision and wondering *If only I hadn't...*'

'I suppose you're right.'

'After my mistress died, our housekeeper retired. I promised Master Charles I'd stay on until he hired a replacement. Then, after he did, the whole household changed.' Her manner turning suddenly guarded, Travers said, 'Do you...have many dealings with Mrs Wallace?'

Olivia grimaced. 'As few as possible. We...do not get on.'

'Then I can speak plainly about her. I... I wouldn't normally repeat gossip, but as you are living in the Abbey, you need to be especially watchful. Though I'd never meant to stay on permanently in the household, after Mrs Wallace arrived, she made it quite clear that she didn't want me at the Abbey. I can't confirm for certain, but it was rumoured that she had a...more intimate relationship with the master than was proper. In any event, she did her best to rid the Abbey of any females to whom Master Charles might feel some attachment or loyalty. I was thrilled to be able to retire here and escape her! Then, after Master Charles's sudden passing, when the Colonel returned from India, I heard she tried to make up to him, too, wanting to achieve the same... position with the new master that she'd reportedly held for his late brother.'

Travers gave a short laugh. 'Not that there was much chance he'd be tempted to respond to her inducements, even if he weren't still grieving! What an ethereal, golden-haired angel Miss Lydia was! The Colonel adored her. I doubt he'll ever allow anyone to take her place.'

So much for her foolish imaginings, Olivia thought, embarrassed and angry at herself for her silly illusions. Imagining that the Colonel wished to kiss *her*, indeed! Thank heaven their respective positions as employer and employee had restrained her from giving any indication that she would welcome his advances.

It made her ill to think of putting herself on the same level as the devious Mrs Wallace.

'In any event,' Travers was saying, 'I'd be wary around Mrs Wallace, especially if she suspects the Colonel is coming to value you—which he well might, with you helping to ease the burden of caring for his wards. She'll do whatever she can to undermine you.'

She'd already had evidence of that, Olivia thought, suddenly remembering how the woman had subtly *encouraged* her to confront the Colonel over his wards. Knowing well how her master's loss would make any discussion of the children who'd been foisted on him acutely painful, she'd expected the governess to be given precisely the furious dressing-down she initially received. Only Olivia's persistence—and the Colonel's innate sense of fairness—had righted a relationship that would otherwise have gone awry from the very beginning.

'I suspected as much, but thanks for the warning,' Olivia said at last. 'I'm willing to keep the peace between us, as long as she does not interfere with the children's proper care.'

'Just be careful around her,' Travers said. 'Well, I expect you must be getting back. Thank you so much for stopping by! It's been such a treat to talk with someone from the Abbey who has some sense. That maid, Mary, usually brings me the fine work, but she's afraid of her own shadow and hardly utters a syllable the whole time she's here. I learn more about what's going on at the Abbey when I visit the village shopkeepers who supply them meat and consumables!'

'Perhaps I could bring the girls to visit one day,' Olivia said as she walked to the door. 'I know they would love any tales you could relate about their papa or their guardian when they were boys.'

'I would love to see them,' Travers said, beaming. 'How I enjoyed watching the young masters grow up! Nothing brightens an old lady's day so much as the chatter of children. Their observations are so entertaining!'

'They certainly can be,' Olivia said, smiling as she recalled Elizabeth's eager questions and commentary during their walk this morning. How attached she was becoming to the girls already!

'Thank you again for sharing what you learned about the Colonel's sad loss. I'll know not to inform him every time one of the girls takes a tumble or develops some trifling ailment.'

'Goodness, I should hope not. What awful memories that would stir!'

After bidding the woman goodbye, Olivia walked back to the manor in a pensive mood. She should be glad that Travers's depiction of the Colonel's adoration for his late wife must bring to a halt any further speculation about an attraction between them—an attraction the woman's revelations demonstrated must have been entirely one-sided. The idea that a tall, plain, managing woman might appear enticing to a man who'd loved 'an ethereal, golden angel' was ludicrous.

So why did she feel so…dispirited?

She must be fatigued from her second long walk of the day, she concluded. Surely she was too intelligent and practical to mourn the loss of a connection that had never really existed. Even if the illusion of it had made her feel so…feminine and desirable.

But a governess neither needed nor should wish to be found 'feminine and desirable' by the man who employed her. Such an appeal in a female who possessed neither the dowry nor the family connections to make her marriageable could lead only to dishonourable offers and disgrace.

She could establish a better, more honourable and lasting relationship with the Colonel by working with him and for him on behalf of his wards, she reminded herself. After all, what few daydreams of suitors and wedlock she'd not given up years ago should have been extinguished for good once she chose a life in service over a marriage of convenience.

Feeling more positive and resolute about the way

going forward, she entered the manor and walked up to her bedchamber, intending to tidy herself before meeting the girls for dinner. She'd just poured fresh water into the washbasin on her dresser when she noticed a note propped against the candle on her bedside table.

Wondering what it could be, she opened the missive. And discovered, to her astonishment, that her employer had invited her to join him and a visiting guest for dinner.

Later that evening, after seeing her charges to bed, Olivia returned to her room to dress for a meal in the formal dining room.

She'd been halfway tempted to refuse her employer's invitation. Despite what she'd learned from Travers about the Colonel's abiding love for his late wife, with her proven susceptibility to the man's appeal, it was probably the height of folly to meet him at a social occasion on which she would be, if not truly his equal, at least an invited guest. Not quite the lady of stature she used to be, but not simply an employee either.

But to refuse might give offence and, if she wanted to continue to nudge the guardian into a closer relationship with his wards, she needed to be on good terms with him.

There was also the allure of dining in company again. Olivia had never thought of herself as particularly gregarious, but in all her life, she'd only dined alone in her chamber on the rare occasions when she was ill. There was something especially depressing about taking the evening meal, which had always been an event shared with friends and family, without any companionship whatsoever. She'd decided that, in future, she would share all her meals in the schoolroom with her charges.

Then, too, the Colonel had written that she would

be doing him a favour if she would attend and help him brighten the evening for his visitor in a house that provided few opportunities for entertainment.

So she'd capitulated and sent back an acceptance.

She gazed at herself in the glass, thinking she ought to simply freshen her dull black gown. But when she'd been preparing to leave Overton House, her tearful maid, upset at the prospect of losing her long-term mistress and perhaps not entirely understanding the drastic change in Olivia's circumstances, had packed not just the new black mourning gowns, but several of her dinner dresses.

When she'd discovered them upon arrival, she'd consigned them to the back of her wardrobe, certain she would not have any opportunity to wear them and thinking perhaps at some point she might sell them for the little extra money they would bring.

Now she hesitated, knowing it would be wiser to wear sober black… Were she in London, it would be too soon after her mother's death to appear in anything but mourning attire. Somehow, her radical change of circumstance made that unhappy event, and everything else about her life that no longer was, seem as if it had happened to someone else, wholly unconnected to who she was now. Besides, there was no one from London society here to be scandalised if she failed to always go about in black.

The copper-hued gown, with its off-the-shoulder bodice trimmed with lace, had been her most flattering. Foolish as it was, some inner feminine sense craved the chance to let the Colonel see her in it.

Which should be all the evidence she needed to leave the gown in the back of the wardrobe.

And yet… What harm would it do? This might be her only opportunity for the next six months to wear something that brought her back a tiny piece of that vanished life.

The Colonel's friend had also served in India, he'd written—a land about which she'd read extensively, fuelled by the enthusiasm of Emma's good friend, Temperance. Being gowned like a lady rather than a sober governess, a servant designed to fade unnoticed into the background, would boost her confidence. Make it easier for her to engage the guest in conversation, as the Colonel clearly wished her to. She had to admit she was curious to have the visitor describe his experiences, so she might see how they matched with the accounts she'd read.

His friend's reminiscences might even lure the Colonel into sharing some of his own. One part of her brain warned that it would be wiser not to get to know any better a man who, she had to acknowledge, still attracted her far more than she should allow. But another part countered that the more she knew of his time in India, the better she would be able to navigate around the shoals of his private grief, gradually involving him in the lives of his wards while awakening as few unhappy memories as possible.

Wasn't her primary duty to see to the needs of his wards? And wasn't the greatest of their needs to once again have the security of knowing a close family member was fully committed to looking after them?

Besides, it would only be one night. After the shocks and loss of the last month, surely she could allow herself one night of pleasure. One night to escape from the reality of her new life and savour a small taste of what life had once been.

Prudence fought against the strength of that longing and lost handily. Pulling the gown out and laying it on her bed, Olivia went in search of the maid to help her into it.

Chapter Nine

Standing before the hearth in the parlour, only half-listening to his friend's comments as they awaited the arrival of Miss Overton, Hugh glanced at his image in the mirror over the side table. He probably shouldn't have dragged out his old regimentals.

But having Stephen here, a witness to how much still needed to be done to restore Somers Abbey, and fighting, as always, the familiar downward spiral of grief, anger and loss—along with the temptation posed by Miss Overton—he'd craved the reassurance of donning garb that reminded him of the time when he'd first met his friend. Newly arrived in India and so sure of himself, eager to be challenged, convinced he was capable of mastering any circumstance.

Of course, he'd still been wearing this uniform when later events proved he wasn't capable of controlling *everything*.

Even so, tonight he wanted to look more like the confident young officer he'd been than the overworked, always weary master of a struggling estate he'd become.

And it was impossible to look less than commanding and accomplished in this brilliant, gold-braided red coat.

He wondered what Miss Overton would make of him in it. With a wisp of a smile, he recalled her tart reply during a previous conversation—*'You may be a colonel, but this is not the army and I am not your corporal.'*

She still wasn't his corporal. Would his wearing this symbol of military authority provoke her to challenge him?

Or would the appeal of the uniform—the ladies in India always assured him every man looked more handsome in a uniform—attract her and deepen the sensual connection between them?

He was warning himself that was not a result to be wished for when, a rare smile brightening his face, Mansfield opened the door. 'Gentlemen, Miss Overton.'

The woman who stood on the threshold made his eyes widen as shock pulsed through him. If he hadn't heard her name announced, he wasn't sure he would have recognised this elegant creature as Somers Abbey's dowdy, black-gowned governess.

Miss Overton glided into the room in a shimmering bronze gown that bared her shoulders, moulded over voluptuous breasts and narrowed to a small waist before billowing out in a sweep of skirt. A wisp of lace trimming teased the eye, revealing tantalising glimpses of the low décolletage and of the slender arms above her long gloves. She halted and looked up at him, her chin slightly raised, as if in challenge.

He ought to greet her and perform the introductions, but at that moment, he couldn't utter a syllable. As her gaze met his, she drew in a sharp breath. Her expression went from wary to wondering as she inspected him from chin to boot tops, her obvious admiration sending a ripple of gratification through him. When her eyes came back to focus on his face with the same intensity that he was gazing at her, some wordless flash of sheer energy pulsed between them.

Before he could unfreeze his tongue, Stephen turned to him, his expression indignant. 'Hugh Glendenning, you rascal! You told me Miss Overton was a lady, but you neglected to mention she was dazzling!'

His friend hastened over and bowed, then clasped the governess's hand and brought it to his lips. 'In such a small gathering, we need not stand on ceremony. I'm Saulter, a former army comrade of Colonel Glendenning, and I count myself his best friend. Delighted to make your acquaintance, Miss Overton!'

He wasn't sure whether to be relieved or annoyed that Stephen's approach to Miss Overton ended the fraught moment between them. Looking startled at first when Saulter seized her hand, she recovered quickly and dipped his friend a curtsy.

'Very pleased to meet you, too, Mr Saulter. And good evening, Colonel. How fine you look in your uniform.'

Dropping her hand, Saulter laughed. 'Trying to show us all up in your gilded magnificence, were you, Glendenning? Sorry, but you can't hold a candle to the lady!'

Olivia blushed and shook her head. 'You exaggerate shamefully, Mr Saulter.'

'In this instance, he tells only the honest truth,' Hugh said, finally finding his voice. 'I'd no intention of trying to rival anyone, Saulter. Merely getting some more use out of these old rags.'

Before he could say more, Mansfield reappeared to announce that dinner was ready. Noting drily that Stephen immediately tucked Miss Overton's hand on his arm to lead her in, Hugh motioned them onward. 'Please proceed. As Saulter said, we'll not stand on ceremony, Miss Overton.'

Once they entered the dining room, he continued, 'Won't you both be seated? I saw no reason for us to shout at each other from opposite ends of the table, so I had Mansfield group us all together.'

'Allow me,' Stephen said, pulling out a chair for her.

Hugh winced, Saulter's action underscoring Somers Abbey's lack of the footman who would normally have performed that service for a lady. 'Not that we could stand on ceremony, even had I wished to. As you see, Saulter, we're lightly staffed enough to be almost dining *en famille.*'

'Dinner will be much more pleasant without having hordes of servants hovering about,' Stephen replied graciously, making him feel a little better. 'Goodness, Glendenning, remember all those grand dinners at durbars and cantonment dining outs? So many servers bobbing about, offering you this and that and refilling your glass, that you hardly had time to eat!'

'Dinners in India did tend to be sumptuous—and long. Though as dining in company was our major entertainment, it needed to last a long time.'

'Yes, and even then it was often not long enough. After the meal, and a short round of tea with the ladies, came the drinking—the real business of the evening for too many.'

'Though the courses will be far fewer, I don't propose that we drink each other under the table afterwards, so dinner will be the main entertainment I can offer you.'

'In such charming company—and I don't mean yours,

Glendenning—' Stephen looked at Miss Overton '—I expect to be delightfully entertained. As for the meal, I'm sure whatever courses are sent up will be delicious. Glendenning often expressed how much he missed Mrs Potter's cooking while we were in India, Miss Overton,' Stephen told her. 'I'm looking forward to sampling her expertise.'

'In my limited experience, she serves a fine meal,' Miss Overton replied, smiling at Saulter.

Watching closely, Hugh judged that smile neither shy nor excessively forward, as it might have been were she unsure of her place or of how to behave. No, it was the serene smile of a lady who felt entirely at home in the dining room of a gentleman's manor house.

Though Hugh had suspected that would be the case, none the less he released a small sigh of relief. He would have felt terrible, after having practically coerced Miss Overton to attend, if she had turned out to be ill at ease in company—or uncomfortable with his friend's gallant remarks.

She seemed to be taking both in her stride.

'You've not been here long then, Miss Overton?' Stephen was asking.

'Just a few weeks. Though I've not yet had time to explore very far, I've found the area lovely. Are you familiar with Somerset, Mr Saulter?'

'No, this is my first visit.'

'Somers Abbey is such an interesting building. You must get the Colonel to tell you its history.'

'Murdered monks in the basements, perhaps? Or priest's holes hidden in the walls?'

Hugh laughed, gratified at how deftly Miss Overton had skirted around a discussion of his wards. He couldn't be sure, but he guessed she was trying to avoid having the conversation turn in a direction that might be upsetting for him. He was both grateful and beginning to believe that inviting her to dine had been a splendid idea after all.

'If you truly are interested, Saulter, I'll give you the ghost's tour later.'

His friend shuddered. 'That should help me sleep better at night!'

After Mansfield brought the first course in, Miss Overton turned to Saulter. 'You are back from India on home leave, I understand? Will you be in England long?'

'For several months, at least. A chance to enjoy cool weather and green meadows before going back.'

'You and the Colonel were both in the army together, were you not? The Queen's Second Foot?'

'Yes. As the military mission was winding down, I transferred to the civil side. I'm a younger son, with no property to return to, so making a career in the India service seemed the best way to secure my future.'

'You might have heard, then, of a soldier who married the sister of a good friend. Lieutenant Johnnie Trethwell? I believe he served in the Second. He was invalided out of the service over a year ago.'

'Why, yes! You know Johnnie?'

'I only met him briefly, at his wedding to my friend's sister. But she related to me some of the wonderful tales he told of his time there.'

'That sounds like Johnnie!' Saulter said, smiling. 'He earned quite a reputation in the service. Perhaps the best India hand we had for reconnoitring the countryside or going out in mufti to discover what was going on in the marketplaces and bazaars. Although Englishmen who only wanted to recreate "Little England" in the cantonments scorned him, those of us who had more appreciation for the land and culture found him compelling—and learned a great deal from him. A shame about his injuries. Though I understand he married an heiress, I've heard he intends to return to India, this time on a trading venture. If anyone can sniff out the best swords, sabres and jewels to delight English collectors, it's Johnnie.'

Catching Hugh's eye, Stephen raised an eyebrow. Hugh knew exactly what that gesture meant. If Miss Overton were good friends with the sister of Trethwell's heiress bride, she must once have been well placed socially.

Certainly that sumptuous gown argued that she'd formerly occupied a much more elevated position in society. How in the world had she ended up as a governess in the Somerset countryside?

'If you, too, found the land fascinating, I can understand why you transferred to the civil service. Did you receive any additional training at Haileybury or the College of Fort William?'

Stephen's widened eyes reflected Hugh's own surprise at how knowledgeable she appeared. 'I returned for some language training at Haileybury. Do you have relatives or friends in India service, Miss Overton? You seem to know all about the process of becoming an officer there.'

'No one in my own family has served there, no. But my good friend has long been fascinated by India and hopes some day to travel there herself, if her husband's duties in Parliament permit. She's collected all the travel accounts she could find written by officers, officials and civilians who've lived there and been kind enough to lend some to me. The country sounds so interesting.'

'Which accounts have you read?'

'Mr Forbes's *Oriental Memoirs* and some of the journals of the Marquess of Hastings, from when he was Governor-General and Commander-in-Chief of the army. Although my favourites are Captain Skinner's *Excursions in India* and Captain Mundy's *Pen and Pencil Sketches* of his tours through the countryside. Such wonderful drawings!'

'Ah, you are well read! Perhaps you need to travel to India and experience the land for yourself, eh, Glendenning?'

She smiled. 'I'm not sure I'm brave enough for that!'

'Nonsense. You sound entirely intrepid! Travelling there is half the fun, isn't it, Glendenning! Remember those regimental voyages up the river? Imagine, if you can, Miss Overton, a flotilla of almost three hundred vessels of all shapes and sizes, from a sixteen-oared budgerow to a tiny skiff! Cook boats, baggage boats, hospital boats, soldiers' boats, officers' houseboats, boats loaded with carriages and gigs, provision boats filled with bellowing goats, protesting horses, nervous cows, squawking ducks, and all of this tended by a horde of servants in all varieties and colours of dress!'

She laughed. 'It sounds mesmerising!'

'Certainly loud, wasn't it, Glendenning? Then, as the sun began to lower, the navigator of the lead vessel would choose some auspicious place for the entourage to moor for the night. Out would come the planks linking boat to shore and on to land would scurry the servants, some setting up fires to cook the dinners, some wading into the river to begin the day's washing, others bringing the livestock on shore to graze, the headman going off to the nearest bazaar to barter for necessary supplies… Ah, and what wonderful meals they concocted in the open, with nearly as many courses as if we'd been at home in the cantonment! Quite extraordinary, wasn't it, Glendenning?'

Hugh found himself nodding. 'So it was. What I remember best are those evenings ashore, relaxing as night fell and the cooks prepared dinner for the various messes. Listening to the babble of voices in several different languages, savouring the scent of garlic and ghee, watching the fireflies rise like sparks into the darkening sky, sometimes catching sight of a flock of wild peacocks returning to their night roost, iridescent blue in the moonlight.'

'It sounds beautiful and how beautifully you describe it, Colonel,' she murmured, her compliment sending a wave of delight through him. 'I can understand why you wanted to continue serving there, Mr Saulter.'

As Hugh listened to Miss Overton's questions and Stephen's answers, he found himself beginning to relax and realised he'd been more on edge than he knew. But both his friend and the governess focused on exchanging information about the flora and fauna, the magnificent buildings and ruins, the colourful, ever-changing landscape, and the fascinating diversity of peoples and cultures. Not once did they stray into anything more personal.

He now had something else for which to thank Miss Overton, Hugh realised. Just as their chat in the attic had resurrected the fond memories of Charles that had been buried under the anger and resentment of returning to find his childhood home suffering from his brother's neglect, tonight's discussion had unearthed happier recollections of the time he'd spent abroad, before the tragedies that had devastated him.

It was as if, after wandering for long, barren years in

the hulk of a burned-out dwelling, one suddenly discovered a gold coin or a sparkling gem gleaming out of the blackened wreckage.

Not that any quantity of fond memories could sweeten the bitter aftermath of those tragedies. But the happy moments were as real and valid as the painful times. Recovering them warmed and soothed him.

As much as Miss Overton brightened and graced his dinner table. How easily, unconsciously, she'd assumed a hostess's role.

A vague feeling of guilt soured that pleasant observation. Though he'd certainly not intended to, by employing her as a governess, he was taking advantage of whatever tragedy had overwhelmed her. For as much as her previous behaviour had given him strong hints, tonight's dinner revealed with unmistakable clarity that Miss Overton had been bred to be an aristocrat's wife. She should be presiding over her own dinner table and tending her own children.

Ever since her arrival, she'd shown herself to be a confident and accomplished woman—not at all a shy, biddable female who waited for others to tell her what to do. The circumstances that had stolen away the life she'd previously known must have been dire and irreversible, else she would have been clever enough to overcome them.

Sighing, he shook his head. He really didn't want to wonder about her past. Certainly, he wouldn't abuse her privacy by asking vulgar, intrusive questions about it. But, nonsensical as it was, he had this strong urge to discover what those circumstances were and try to make them right, if he could.

And then he laughed soundlessly at himself.

The answer to the riddle was almost certainly a sudden loss of funds. With him barely able to make his own estate profitable, he had no assets left over to assist her in buying back her life.

The only other reason for a lady's sudden loss of family and position would be—scandal.

Has she been disgraced? Looking at her now in that figure-hugging gown, he could understand how some unprincipled man, inflamed with lust, might have been fired by the desire to possess her. Had she been seduced and abandoned, first by her lover, then by her family?

Or was it only his own increasing desire for her that led him to imagine such a scenario?

He needed to reel in those desires and put a stop to this line of speculation. As forthright, intelligent and perceptive as Miss Overton was, he couldn't really see her being lured down the path to seduction by some slick-tongued scoundrel.

Preoccupied by his thoughts, he was startled when Miss Overton suddenly stood up. Stephen must have finished relating his latest story, Hugh realised—an account to which he had been paying no attention whatsoever.

'I should leave you gentlemen to your brandy and cigars.'

'If you must,' said Saulter, who had risen when she did, Hugh belatedly springing up after them. 'But we won't linger for long. Promise you will await us in the salon for tea.'

Smiling, she shook her head. 'I appreciate the invitation, but the tasks for this Cinderella begin very early. I must thank you both for a delicious and enjoyable dinner, and take my leave. Colonel, Mr Saulter.'

With that, she curtsied to their bows and walked from the room.

Stephen waited until the echo of her footsteps faded before turning to Hugh. 'You blighter! Where did you steal her from? It's quite obvious Miss Overton is a well-born lady from a genteel household. How did she end up a governess?'

Hugh shook his head. 'I have no idea. I hired her through an agency. One would expect a governess to be of gentle birth, but not until this evening has she revealed her pedigree so...strikingly. Up until now, she has gone about quietly, keeping to herself, garbed from head to toe in forgettable black. I did note how competently she took charge and there were definite indications of a managing nature, but until tonight, I never thought to question how she came to be in service.'

Stephen made a grimace of disgust. 'Honestly, Hugh, for an intelligent man, sometimes you can be as dull as dirt. You never wondered about her background until tonight?'

'To be fair, until tonight, I've not seen her dress or behave other than as a governess,' he defended himself.

Which was not precisely true. Had she not challenged him about the girls from the first, with none of the deference he would have expected from an employee? Hadn't she confessed herself from the very beginning to be 'managing', informing him she had run her mother's household? Hadn't she told him she'd used her 'mistress-of-the-household voice' to commandeer a vehicle to travel to Bristol?

If he were brutally honest, he'd not wanted to acknowledge what these clues revealed about her. Because as long as he could tell himself she was merely another female member of his staff...as long as he refused to see her as a well-bred lady of his own class...he could avoid dealing with the fascination and physical attraction she stirred in him.

Stephen raised a sceptical eyebrow, clearly not buying his line of defence. 'You had no inkling at all?'

'Well, of course I had *some*. But it wouldn't have been polite to go prying into her background. We all of us have secrets—and pain—we don't wish to share with the world.'

That oblique remark was reminder enough to douse Stephen's irritation. 'Very true,' he admitted with a sigh. 'It is a conundrum, isn't it? But if I'm remembering, the heiress Trethwell married was the daughter of Lord Vraux—a very wealthy baron. If your Miss Overton was a good friend to the sister of one of Vraux's daughters, she's not just the gently bred offspring of some obscure country parson, she must have moved in the first circles of society. How does someone like *that* end up a governess?'

'The usual way, probably. Somehow her family lost all their money and left her with no dowry.'

He wouldn't insult Miss Overton's honour by mentioning his other speculation.

'With connections as elevated as those, I should have thought her family could have found her a husband rich enough not to have to worry about dowry.'

Hugh shrugged. 'As you know, I went straight from university to the army. I never took part in London society and have no idea how things are done there.'

'You also display a deplorable lack of curiosity! Not a sin I possess. I already planned to spend some time in London before I return to India. While I'm there, I'll see what I can find out about our puzzling Miss Overton. Shall I write you about what I discover?'

'Would it make any difference in her circumstances?'

'Probably not,' Stephen admitted.

'Then I prefer to continue thinking of her simply as my wards' excellent governess.'

'She's shown herself to be excellent at several things, conversation being one. You must have her dine with us every evening I'm here.'

See her every night, gowned in that siren's call of silk? Alarm and insidious desire warred in his belly. 'Probably not good to set that sort of precedent. Whatever her birth, she is now simply a governess.'

'Pish-tosh!' Stephen said dismissively. 'I doubt she'll start taking on airs merely because you deigned to invite her to dinner! Besides, after I leave, you can go back to dining on a tray in your library, if you like. But for now, your duty as a host is to entertain me and dining with that intelligent, lovely creature promises the best entertainment Somers Abbey currently has to offer. At least, until I beat you at cards tonight.'

'You can try,' Hugh said, trying to slip by without giving an answer.

'First, agree that you will invite Miss Overton to dine with us for the length of my visit.'

He should have known he couldn't elude his persistent friend. Telling himself his host's duty obligated him to entertain Saulter as best he could, he gave a reluctant nod. 'Very well—only because I need to make your visit as pleasant as possible.'

'Aren't you glad I'm giving you an excuse to do what you really want to do anyway?' Stephen shot back.

He had to admit—to himself, if not to Stephen—that tonight had been the most enjoyable dinner he'd experienced since his return from India. So enjoyable he could almost forget...

But, no, he would *never* be able to forget.

'I'll send her an invitation tomorrow.'

'Good. But let me write the note. I don't trust you not to dash off something so imperious she will deny us her company. I'll make it charming enough to entice her.'

'When did you say you were leaving?'

Clapping him on the shoulder, Stephen laughed. 'Let's get that brandy and then we'll see how much social isolation has deteriorated your skill at whist.'

Though he might claim to Stephen that inviting Miss Overton was just a favour for his friend, Hugh knew he, too, would look forward to seeing her again in a social role.

He'd forgotten how delightful it could be to have a lovely, intelligent hostess sitting at his table. He would never have one again, permanently...but Stephen's visit gave him the excuse to savour that pleasure—and the charm of Miss Overton's company at dinner—for a few more days before they must both revert to the restrictions of their respective roles.

Chapter Ten

Two evenings later, Olivia found herself once again standing in her bedchamber as Mary helped her dress for dinner with the Colonel and Mr Saulter. Watching in the mirror as Mary eased the skirt of the evening gown over her head—this time, a deep green satin with moiré ribbon trimming at the bodice and hem—she thought ruefully that the last two evenings had been like living in a dream.

Somehow, she'd been transported from a lowly employee reduced to taking a tray alone in her room back into dining as the lady of birth she'd once been. The abrupt contrast made her a little giddy—but oh, how she loved it!

Mr Saulter's visit would end soon. It might be a mistake to allow herself to take part in these evenings, but she'd found she lacked the will to deny herself the treat. She'd have weeks and months to toil in her spartan governess role before she could hope to return to London for the consultation she'd promised Sara. She had only a few more days to make the most of this stolen interlude.

Of course, there was one glaring difference between

dining at Somers Abbey and the same social ritual in London. An unmarried lady of quality could never have attended a London dinner with gentlemen present unless she had a suitable hostess to act as her chaperon. But a gently born woman who went into service forfeited her chance of making a respectable marriage and therefore no longer had a reputation to protect. As an independent woman who had often chafed at the silly restrictions society placed on unmarried females, Olivia could only approve that particular result of her change in status.

Once again, after Mary tightened the laces of the bodice and shook out the belled skirt and sleeves, she felt her spirits rise as she looked at her image in the glass. Savouring the warm kiss of satin against her skin, for another night she had become Cinderella, rescued from the ashes of the hearth and transported to accompany a prince.

And what a prince he was!

She recalled the magical moment that first night when she'd looked over to discover the Colonel dressed in his regimentals. He carried himself with an air of authority even in civilian clothes, but in uniform—oh, how handsome and commanding he appeared!

The scarlet coat with the gold epaulettes and braiding made his broad shoulders look even more imposing, while the sash at his waist emphasised his lean waist and hips, and the buff pantaloons hugged his saddle-muscled thighs. The sweep from scarlet coat, to gold sash, to buff pantaloons, to the ebony of his shiny black boots made him look even taller.

This was a man born to lead, a commander in whom every one of his soldiers must have had confidence—a man who could be relied upon to defend what was his and to shelter and protect anyone given into his care.

Her guilty attraction intensified, just gazing at him.

She'd conversed both nights mainly with Mr Saulter, who was quite handsome and charming in his own right. But he did not stir within her the same giddy awareness she felt when the Colonel's gaze rested on her, or evoke the tingle that shivered over her skin when he took her hand to lead her into dinner.

Though she tried to remind herself that these feelings were one-sided, silently repeating to herself Travers's contention that the Colonel had never got over losing his beloved wife, every instinct told her there *was* a connection between them.

Perhaps it was merely something physical, improbable as it seemed that a man who'd loved a delicate, fragile Beauty could be attracted to a tall, plain, brown-haired girl.

But what did she know of the ways between men and women? Lord Theo, the handsomest man she'd ever met, had become enamoured of her plain friend Emma. And married her.

She mustn't allow her thoughts to stray in that direction. Even if her far-too-inexperienced instincts were correct and the Colonel somehow found her attractive, with his heart still held by his late wife, the most he might feel for her was lust. A hunger she didn't dare encourage, no matter how strong her desire for him.

Not that he was likely to respond to any encouragement she might offer. Regardless of his own urges, a man of principle like the Colonel would never allow himself to trifle with an innocent, particularly one who was a dependent in his household.

Soon, they would go back to being merely governess and employer. Though probably not soon enough for her to extinguish the ever-growing attraction she felt for him.

How was she to deal with him, once they were again just governess and employer?

Having no good answer to that question, she pushed the problem to the back of her mind. For now, she would simply enjoy the moment.

'There, miss, you're all ready,' Mary said, interrupting her thoughts. After stepping back to inspect her, the maid drew in an awed breath. 'Oh, Miss Overton, that other gown was beautiful, but you look even prettier in this one! Just like a princess!'

'Thank you, Mary! Although the credit must go to the skill of London's dressmakers.'

'Oh, no, miss. I knew you was Quality by how gracious you treated me that first night you come here. A body can always tell who was born to it—and who weren't.' The maid giggled. 'I hope Mrs Wallace sees you tonight! Always trying to lord it over all of us, when I bet she's as common as the rest of us. She'd be that put out, to see you dressed so fine! I think that's why she's refused to wait at table while the Colonel's guest is here, like Mr Mansfield asked her. After all, it's not like she hasn't done it before. She used to wait on Mr Charles all by herself when he was master.'

Recalling the gossip Travers had related, Olivia pressed her lips together. Just what other services had the woman offered during those tête-à-tête dinners?

Recalling also the former lady's maid's warning, Olivia told herself to be watchful. If the housekeeper had been rebuffed when she tried to wheedle her way into intimacy with the Colonel, she might be incensed that the governess had been accorded the signal honour of dining with him and his guest. And look for some way to exact retribution.

Though that wasn't the most dangerous thing she needed to watch for. She must not lure herself into imagining her Cinderella role would last longer than Mr Saulter's visit. There was no prince in *her* story and only ashes awaited her at the end of this fairy tale.

Pushing away that unpleasant fact, Olivia said, 'I'd just as soon not encounter Mrs Wallace dressed like this. It would only aggravate her, and she's difficult enough to deal with already.'

Mary sighed. 'You've the right of it there. Go on, now, and enjoy your dinner! Mrs Potter's been fussing over it all afternoon. I have to tell you, it's the nicest spread any of us have seen since the Colonel come back to England! She's so hopeful that this visit from the Colonel's friend will cheer him. Now, you fetch me to help you out of that dress whenever you come back up, no matter how late. I wouldn't want you to tear none of that beautiful ribbon, struggling to get yourself out of the gown.'

'Thank you, Mary. Like wearing armour, I feel ready to launch into the fray.'

Anticipation—and a guilty excitement—swirling in her belly, Olivia gave her braided coiffure one last check and walked from the room.

Perhaps it wasn't just the gown's connection to her old life that had made her feel on these last few nights more attractive and confident than she'd been since the awful morning she'd gone up the family solicitor's stairs a lady and walked back down an indigent female.

Perhaps she truly did look transformed. Mansfield smiled with delight each time he saw her in her London garb and always whispered a compliment before he announced her.

Mr Saulter paid her even more extravagant compliments, although that was surely officer gallantry. But the Colonel, too, added his more measured praise. Reviewing in her mind his expression when he'd gazed at her in her fashionable gown, she couldn't help but believe the admiration in his eyes *was* real.

Would he forget himself enough to act on it? Did she really want him to?

'That meal was excellent!' Stephen declared as he tossed his napkin back on the table. 'Please, Mansfield, would you convey my compliments to Mrs Potter?'

'Mine as well, Mansfield,' Hugh said. 'She has outdone herself tonight.'

Especially knowing that she works with such limited staff and supplies, he thought.

'My mother herself would have been proud to serve her guests such a meal.'

'I shall certainly tell her, gentlemen,' the butler said. 'She'll be that pleased to know you were so satisfied.'

'I believe, Glendenning, that I would like to follow last night's pattern and dispense with brandy and cigars,' Stephen said. 'That is, if we can persuade you to play for us again, Miss Overton.'

'You do play wonderfully,' Hugh said. 'It was a true delight to have music in the house again.' He supposed he shouldn't have been surprised to discover she played as expertly as she did everything else, but hearing her perform so beautifully had been an unexpected delight.

Music was another of the pleasures he'd denied himself since India. Both by isolating himself from social contact with his neighbours and by working such long hours, he had neither time nor energy to play himself.

Like having a hostess at his table, as she'd begun the first piece last night, he'd been struck by how much he enjoyed it. How much he'd missed having someone create it for him.

Though these evening social interludes must cease once his guest departed, perhaps he could allow himself the pleasure of lingering within earshot when Miss Overton played the pianoforte for his wards, since part of her duties would entail giving them instruction on the instrument.

'Very well, gentlemen, if you insist,' she was saying. 'The meal was so excellent I couldn't keep myself from sampling every course. I'm so blissfully replete, I couldn't possibly sleep for a while.'

'Then you must play, by all means,' Stephen said, taking her arm to escort her towards the salon that housed the pianoforte. 'In fact, after you've regaled us for a while, we shall prevail upon Glendenning to play some dance music for us. Taking a few turns about the floor will provide just the exercise we need to settle in that meal and relax us for the night.'

Hugh held up a hand. 'Don't volunteer me, Saulter! I've scarcely laid a finger on a keyboard for years.'

'Oh, nonsense, it's like riding a horse. Once you've mastered the technique, you never forget and, as I recall, you performed for the mess quite competently on several occasions. If you don't remember any tunes, there's some sheet music in the bench. I looked through it just this afternoon.'

With a grimace, Hugh frowned at his friend, who returned a cherubic smile. 'Remember your duty as host, Hugh,' he murmured.

'I'm beginning to regret not having associated more with my neighbours,' he grumbled back. 'I could then have sent you elsewhere to dine. Surely there is some country family with unmarried daughters who could try to entrap you.'

Stephen merely laughed. 'You really should socialise more—or else the gentry hereabouts may start to believe you consider yourself above them. Perhaps we should ride by the squire's house tomorrow when we head out to the fields. Country gossip being what it is, he's bound to know you are entertaining a visitor. Chances are, we have only to pay a call and he'll invite us to dine.'

'I can still send you alone,' Hugh shot back.

'Not a chance. We should probably inveigle an invitation for Miss Overton as well.'

'You certainly must not!' she protested, her eyes widening in alarm. 'In fact, if you should be invited to dine with the squire, I would very much appreciate it if neither of you mentioned that I have joined you for dinner here. It…might not be thought appropriate.'

A single lady dining alone with gentlemen.

Standards being somewhat different in India, it hadn't even occurred to Hugh when he issued his invitation to Miss Overton that there were some who might think it immodest of the governess to dine with them without a chaperon.

'Are you concerned about your reputation?' he asked. 'I must apologise! I never gave the matter—'

'Oh, no, not that,' she interrupted, her smile, to him, seeming a bit strained. 'Some might consider a governess was acting above her station if she dined at her employer's table on anything other than a major holiday. I should not like to be thought…grasping.'

'You are certainly not that,' Stephen said indignantly.

'Thank you, kind sir,' she replied. 'Owing to that country gossip you mention, the neighbours may eventually learn that I joined the gentlemen for dinner during Mr Saulter's visit, but I should not like to advertise the fact. And you needn't worry, Colonel. A female in service has no reputation to protect.'

'Even if she is a gently born lady of good family?' Stephen asked.

'Even then. Once she hires herself out as a governess or companion, she is no longer considered eligible, so her reputation—or lack of it—is of no consequence.'

'That hardly seems fair,' Stephen said, releasing her arm as they entered the salon and she took her seat on the piano bench.

Miss Overton merely shrugged. 'It is the way of the world. So, gentlemen, what would you have me play?'

Hugh had not previously considered that in taking up her position, Miss Overton had forfeited the deference that she'd been accorded since birth. It did indeed seem unfair, he thought, frowning. And in her obvious haste to change the subject, he detected that she was not so indifferent to her devalued status as she wished to appear.

How could she be? It had changed her entire world.

And now he was once again fretting about matters he could neither change nor wished to dwell on.

'You played that complicated Beethoven piece so wonderfully, I should like to hear it again,' Stephen was saying.

'Beethoven it shall be, then,' she said, pulling out the sheets of music.

While Stephen remained by the piano to turn the pages for her, Hugh took a seat. Having always found music soothing as well as delightful, he forced himself to set aside all his questions, concerns and problems and let the power of the music wash over him. How magnificent it was!

He was as hearty in his applause when the last note faded as Stephen.

'Wonderful!' Stephen exclaimed. 'Now we gentlemen owe you a treat. And if you try to tell me a lady as graceful as you does not love dancing, I shall accuse you of uttering falsehoods.'

Laughing, she gave him her hand as she stood up. 'I will not even attempt to utter such a falsehood. On the contrary, I adore dancing.'

'You heard the lady, Glendenning,' Stephen said. 'Dancing we must have. Here,' he said after a moment of rummaging through the sheet music atop the piano, 'I found these pieces and set them out earlier. Nothing as complicated as Beethoven, so you should have no problem.'

Though he made a token protest, in truth, Hugh was happy to sit down at the instrument. He was by no means as accomplished a musician as Miss Overton, but he'd always enjoyed playing. As Stephen had mentioned, he'd often been called upon to perform for his fellow officers, sometimes even at evening entertainments when the ladies were present. But, like everything else he associated with light and joy and peace, he'd given it up after Drew's death.

He'd been a fool, he thought, delight at the melodious notes beginning to ripple through him as he played a few scales to limber up his fingers. His stark self-denial wouldn't bring back Drew or Lydia.

As he played one reel and then another, the healing balm of the music seeped into the still-ragged places in his soul, until he felt almost…tranquil. However deep his guilt, in future he promised himself that he would definitely allow himself this pleasure.

Was that promise another gift for which he owed thanks to Miss Overton—and Stephen, of course?

As the dance concluded, Stephen halted with his partner beside the piano. 'The reels were fine, but now I'd like a waltz. Here—I found the music for one,' he said, placing it on the music stand.

A waltz? Hugh's expansive sense of well-being abruptly ended. It was one thing for Stephen to perform the complicated figures of a country dance opposite Miss Overton, take her hand to turn her, or skip her across the room in a reel. But to wrap his arm around her waist and hold her close, their two bodies moving as one to the music?

Stephen Saulter was an attractive gentleman—and he obviously liked Miss Overton. Hugh could only be selfishly glad that his friend's life and career were established far away in India. He wouldn't want her exposed to the dangers there—and he felt a strong protest rising within him at the idea of her going off with any man, even Stephen.

Which was ridiculous. He had no claim on her. If he admired her and regretted the unknown circumstances that had robbed her of the chance to become mistress of her own household—and he did—he should welcome the idea that a man of upstanding character like his friend might value her enough to overlook her lack of dowry and consider courting her.

Just because he had promised himself never to take on the responsibility of a wife again didn't mean his friend should deny himself the pleasure.

And from the way Stephen was gazing at Miss Overton admiringly, Hugh suspected his friend's thoughts might already be turning in her direction.

Why did he find the idea so distasteful?

True, it would be difficult to find another governess as competent and protective of his wards as Miss Overton, or one to whom the girls had taken so quickly. But surely what would be best for the governess ought to sway him—

'The *waltz*, Hugh.' Stephen's voice interrupted his musing. 'Some time this century would be good.'

Suppressing all his contradictory and turbulent thoughts, Hugh set his lips in a thin line and played, trying to keep his eyes on the music and not on what a handsome couple the two made as Stephen twirled her around the room. Then played the song again when, after the first rendition, Stephen called for a reprise.

Finally, his friend guided Miss Overton to a halt. 'As delightful as it is to waltz with you, I'm in need of a break. Shall we pause for some refreshment, Miss Overton?'

'I would certainly enjoy some,' she replied.

Tearing his eyes from the enchanting picture she made, with her face flushed and her dark eyes sparkling, Hugh walked over to ring for the tea tray.

After they'd shared a refreshing cup, waving off Miss Overton's protest that she really ought to retire, Stephen said, 'Not quite yet, Miss Overton. I've prevailed upon my good friend to do yeoman duty, playing for us. Now it's only fair that I play and allow *him* the pleasure of dancing with you.'

Her eyes widening, Miss Overton looked over at Hugh. Once again, their gazes caught and held. 'I... I doubt he has any interest in dancing with me,' she faltered.

She was wrong—oh, how wrong she was! With the music having lightened the weight of all his burdens, he felt more alive than he had for months. And every fibre of that more responsive body craved the feel of her in his arms.

Painfully conscious of how sharp that desire was, Hugh probably would have refused her hand had Stephen not practically shoved Miss Overton at him. 'Come now, Glendenning! Surely you don't mean to insult the lady by refusing to dance with her.'

'It's probably not appropriate—' she started to protest.

'Perhaps not in the squire's parlour,' Stephen cut her off. 'But we're at Somers Abbey, among just old—and new—friends. And I promise you, Glendenning is eager to dance with you. As you should be with him. He was accounted one of the finest dancers in the regiment—after me, of course.'

'I'm sure he doesn't—'

'Oh, but he does,' Hugh found himself saying. Hell and damnation, he knew touching her wasn't wise, but the presence of a guest that made this opportunity possible wouldn't last much longer. Easily shrugging off the feeble protest of his conscience, he held out his hand. 'Miss Overton, would you do me the honour of this dance?'

Gazing up at him, she swallowed hard and for a moment he feared she would refuse. But apparently she was no more able to resist the madness than he was. 'I would be delighted, Colonel,' she said at last.

A moment later, Stephen played the opening measures and Hugh pulled her close. Close enough to smell the delicate rose scent she wore, to feel the warmth of her waist under his hand, a warmth that seemed to burn through his gloves and set his fingers—and his desire—ablaze.

As he moved her into the rhythm of the dance, he sensed the softness of her skin under the gown's satin veiling. The brush of her breasts against his chest as he twirled her around the room hardened him instantly, making him ache with need.

Intoxicated by her nearness, he whirled her through the movements, each spiral further loosening the years-long stranglehold he'd maintained over his senses. Leaning his chin into the silk of her hair, he tightened his grip on her waist, his fingers memorising the curve of hip and the swell of belly. He pulled her closer still, until he could feel the whole length of her torso against his, his deprived senses devouring the feel of her and ravenous for more.

When the last note sounded, he glided to a halt with her still in his arms. Standing there, the rapid tattoo of her heartbeat vibrating against his chest, he couldn't seem to let her go.

When he did not release her, she looked up at him, her gaze questioning—but made no move to pull away. In her eyes he saw the same reckless need that was pulsing through him.

Exultant, conscious of nothing but the woman in his arms, he bent down to kiss her.

In the last instant before his lips would have touched

hers, he heard it—just a breathless little gasp. Of surprise, of need—or of protest?

Whatever it meant, that small sound gave his appalled brain just enough time to wrench control back from his rampaging body.

Trembling, he straightened and pushed himself away from her. Had he really meant to commit the incredible folly of ravaging her mouth, right here in the salon, with his best friend looking on?

Calling upon every ounce of discipline instilled in him through fifteen years' service as a soldier, he made himself drop his hands to his sides and back away.

But before he could summon words to frame an apology, with a stuttered 'Ex-excuse me', she picked up her skirts and ran from the room.

'Confound it, you idiot, go after her!'

Stephen's strident voice completed Hugh's return to full recognition of where he was—and what he'd almost done.

'Now?' he objected, looking over at his friend. 'Granted, I owe Miss Overton an apology for...'

Luring her in? Frightening her with his inappropriate passion?

Leaving the sentence unfinished, he went on, 'Given the haste of her departure, I imagine at this moment I'm the last person she wants to see. I... I should allow her time to compose herself.'

Certainly *he* needed time to gather his scrambled wits and make sure his randy body was back under control before he faced *her* again.

'Well, you're not the only one who owes her an apology,' Stephen said grimly. 'And mine had better not wait.'

Chapter Eleven

Halting in the corridor several rooms away, Olivia raised a hand to lips that tingled in the wake of the Colonel's nearness.

He had been about to kiss her—she was absolutely sure of it. Though everything within her had yearned to respond, some primitive sense of impending danger had sent her fleeing from the room.

Alarm coursed through her anew as she thought again about what she had nearly done. Or rather, what she had nearly let the Colonel do.

No man she'd ever waltzed with had affected her like the Colonel. Despite the mindless yearning that drew her to him, her limited experience hadn't prepared her to know how to manage such powerful feelings.

Feelings that she, as merely an employee, absolutely could not allow herself to develop for her employer.

It was past time for her to return to her duties and forget she'd ever been granted the indulgence of dining with him, dancing with him…

'Are you all right, Miss Overton?'

Startled, Olivia looked back to find Mr Saulter hurrying after her, concern in his gaze. 'Won't you come into the dining room? Let me pour you some wine.'

Still too stunned to feel embarrassed, she let him take her arm and lead her into the silent room, where he swiftly relit several branches of candles on the table and sideboard before pouring them each a glass.

Motioning her to a chair, he said, 'Please, sit and drink this. You've had…something of a shock, for which I fear I am mostly responsible.'

'What just happened?' she murmured as she seated herself—and was aghast to realise she'd uttered the question aloud.

Taking a chair beside her, Mr Saulter gave a short laugh. 'Something I should have managed better. You see, these last few days, Hugh has seemed so much more alive, so much more like the man I first knew in India, that I got ahead of myself. I was so excited to observe how he responded to you, I pushed him too hard. And was most unfair to you in the process. I assure you, he meant no disrespect!'

Feeling her face colour, Olivia shook her head. 'It wasn't his fault. The dance—the music—I'm afraid I was carried away, too.'

'Please, you aren't the one who needs to apologise!' Sighing, he continued, 'I've observed what a great help you've been to him, taking care of his wards and easing him into shouldering a burden that can't be anything but painful. I don't think I'm in error in thinking you admire the Colonel and are concerned for his well-being.'

'No, of course not. I wish to assist him in any way possible.'

Saulter nodded. 'That's what I thought. So believing that, I hoped you wouldn't mind my encouraging his attraction to you. You can't imagine how much it gladdened my heart to see him show signs of admiring, and coming to trust, another lady, after what he's endured! I had begun to despair that he would ever get over Lydia's betrayal and the manner of her death. After all, to suffer the pain and humiliation of having your wife run off with another man hard on the heels of losing your only son—I can't even imagine the agony!'

About to take a sip of her wine, Olivia's hand froze on the glass. 'What?' she gasped, certain she could not have heard Saulter correctly. 'I—I thought his wife died shortly after the death of their son.'

'Oh, she did—' Saulter broke off abruptly. 'D-Didn't you assure me, when I enquired earlier tonight, that you were fully aware of the sad circumstances surrounding the tragedies that occurred to Glendenning in India?'

'I… I know that his son died suddenly of a fever, and that his wife perished a short while later—that is all.'

Closing his eyes briefly, Saulter swore under his breath. 'Then I'm afraid I've just been horridly indiscreet.'

Olivia shook her head, unable to make sense of it. She simply couldn't imagine how any woman lucky enough to have won Hugh Glendenning's love could have ended up betraying and abandoning him. 'You can't be telling me that the Colonel's wife…*left* him?'

Catching herself, she added hastily, 'I shouldn't enquire further, particularly if you have pledged to keep silent about the matter. I'm just…shocked. And heartbroken for him. As if losing his son and wife alone weren't enough of a blow.'

Grimacing, Saulter nodded his agreement. 'Horrible, all of it. Having dropped such a lighted cannon ball to explode in your face, I suppose I can't leave it at that. I'm not pledged to silence and, sadly, all the tawdry details were soon known to every Englishman and woman in the cantonment, and probably passed along to every English settlement from Delhi to Calcutta.'

'How perfectly awful for him. I... I wouldn't enquire, but knowing the circumstances surrounding the deaths of his wife and son would allow me to guard against inadvertently saying or doing something that would touch on that grief. By the way, as far as I can tell, no one in Somerset knows more about his wife's death than that she passed away soon after their child died.'

'That's a mercy anyway. I'd halfway feared Hugh had imprisoned himself here, refusing to see any of the neighbours, to avoid the scandal.'

'I'm not acquainted with any of the gentry in the neighbourhood, so I can't say for sure about them, but none of the long-time retainers at Somers Abbey are aware of it, I'm certain.'

Travers couldn't have assured her of the Colonel's undying love and loyalty to his wife had she known of it, Olivia thought.

'Very well, with the goal of having you avoid any missteps, I'll give you the bare details.' After taking a long pull on his wine glass, Saulter said, 'Not that Glendenning ever discussed it with me, but it had become obvious for some time before his son's death that all was not well between him and his wife. Lydia...never adjusted to living in India. The smells, the insects, the wild animals, the unintelligible languages and strange customs of its people—all the *foreignness* that made the land so fascinating to her husband and me made her anxious and fretful. In those last months, she often complained

publicly that Glendenning neglected her. Not that she
lacked for companionship, not when even the plainest
European females are besieged with invitations to dance
or play cards or stroll about the cantonment. I think...
I think the death of their son was simply the last straw
for her and Hugh was too submerged in his own grief to
be able to help her.'

'How sad for them both.'

Saulter nodded. 'In any event, she persuaded one of
her most fervent admirers to run away with her, intent
on returning to England. But the rivers, always treacherous, were swollen from the monsoon rains. Somewhere
on the trip downriver, the boat capsized. There were no
survivors.'

'Awful,' she murmured. 'Simply awful. I can't imagine how he managed to keep going.'

'I have to admit, I worried for a while that he might
put a pistol to his head. Instead, he pushed everyone
away, refused to attend any social functions, even with
the officers of the regiment, and buried himself in his
work. Until he was notified of his brother's death and
was obliged to come back to England to claim his inheritance.'

'Where he once again buried himself in his work.'

'Yes. He...he does admire you, Miss Overton. And
I can see that he has begun to trust you, at least in the
matter of his wards. I can only beg you to proceed...
kindly with him. As for the debacle of that waltz, I'd be
willing to bet he hasn't touched a woman since the last
time he embraced his wife, and—well, a man is a man.
But Glendenning is a man of iron will. He wouldn't have
lost control of himself if he hadn't...let down his guard

around you. Please remember that and don't judge him too harshly.'

'I can only repeat, he wasn't the only one…letting down his guard,' she said ruefully. 'This does…somewhat complicate things moving forward.'

Saulter sighed. 'I'm afraid my little trick with the waltz may have made things awkward for both of you.'

'Well, we shall simply have to get beyond it,' she said briskly. 'Much as I've enjoyed your company, I think it best if I resume my place as the governess of the household and no longer dine in your company.'

'Although I am most unhappy with that proposal on my own account, I have to admit, that would probably make it easier for Glendenning. For both of you.'

She nodded, despite the protest rising within her. But she squelched it. She needed time to think through the implications of the horrifying truths she'd just discovered before she could chart out how best to go forward while causing herself and her employer the least amount of embarrassment.

'Then I shall finish my wine and bid you goodnight, and goodbye, Mr Saulter. I truly have enjoyed our evenings together.' She smiled ruefully. 'Save for the last little bit tonight.'

'Not nearly as much as I have enjoyed them, I assure you, Miss Overton! These evenings and also the chance to meet Hugh's charming wards yesterday. What sweet girls they are! Finally, you must let me apologise again, as I shall do to Glendenning, for thrusting you into so uncomfortable a position.'

'Apology accepted.' Taking the last sip of her wine, she set down the glass. 'Let me thank you again for trusting me with a full account of the Colonel's losses. Good-night, Mr Saulter.'

'Goodnight, Miss Overton,' he said, rising as she did. Just before she reached the threshold, he said, 'I do hope my…unfortunate revelations tonight haven't altered your opinion of—or will alter your behaviour around—the Colonel.'

She shook her head. 'I can only admire him more for enduring what he has suffered. And I assure you, he will never receive the merest hint from me that I am aware of the true circumstances of his wife's death.'

'Thank you, Miss Overton. You are a princess among women.'

The princess whose time at the ball was over, she thought as she made her way upstairs to her chamber. Back to her rags and ashes…and thinking through how she was to meet the Colonel again without her cheeks flaming at the wanton encouragement she'd given him for that kiss that never happened.

She wasn't sure what pained her more—returning to the loneliness and isolation of her governess's life, or being cheated out of the kiss she'd wanted so badly.

Fortunately, Mary was sleepy enough that she was content to help Olivia out of her gown and go straight back to bed without peppering her with questions about her evening. Once the maid had gone, she carefully folded the gown in tissue paper and slid it to the back of the wardrobe.

She wouldn't be needing it again at Somers Abbey.

Cinderella's day was done and it was for the best. Worse than having her employer nearly kiss her tonight was admitting how much she'd wanted him to. Though her treacherous emotions had initially rejoiced at realising that Saulter's revelations about the death of the Colonel's wife meant, contrary to Travers's belief, he had not set his late wife up on a pedestal, a paragon to whom no other female could measure up, a parallel realisation soon dissipated that excitement.

Being betrayed in your most desperate hour by the person who had pledged to remain beside you, for better or worse, for the rest of your life, would have to scar the soul with the deepest of wounds. A wound so grievous, a person would naturally retreat into himself.

How could he allow himself to love or trust any woman again? Why would he even want to?

Even though, as Saulter had put it, 'a man is only a man', and natural physical desires couldn't be repressed for ever, she suspected that only the exceptional intimacy of the waltz had induced the Colonel to relax the iron control he maintained over himself. No matter how much lust he might feel, under normal circumstances, so rigidly honourable a man would let no sign of it show.

What had happened tonight did not change the truth she'd been repeating to herself ever since the dining adventure had begun. There was no prince waiting for her. She was an indigent female who would live out her life earning her bread. The Colonel was simply her employer.

She thought he liked her and hoped that he approved of her handling of his wards, but that was as far as any relationship between them could go. As attractive and admirable as she found him, she'd be a fool to let her emotions become any more entangled. Especially not for a man whose tragic past meant it would likely be impossible for him to ever truly love or trust a woman again.

As for the physical attraction between them, she was

more at risk from the promptings of her own desires than she was from the Colonel's. She must guard against the dangerous temptation of indulging herself, just a little touch or brush against him there, lest she tempt the Colonel against his will into compromising her. Or worse, lured him in so completely, she became his fancy woman, forfeiting whatever respect she'd earned and being sent off in disgrace once his lust was sated.

She must shut her heart and mind to all the tantalising possibilities her attraction to him whispered about and focus on her sole reason for being at Somers Abbey— caring for the Colonel's wards—no matter how much it saddened her to let those dreams go.

As for maintaining her sangfroid when next she met him, she would simply pretend that her time as his dinner guest had never happened and resume her original brisk, matter-of-fact demeanour. She would see him in future only when she needed to consult him on a matter concerning the children and do that as seldom as possible.

Except…except when she needed to try to bring them together.

Exasperated, she hopped into her bed. It would be impossible to avoid the man completely if she meant to engineer that rapprochement between guardian and wards she felt both needed so badly.

In fact, knowing now the whole of what had befallen the Colonel in India, she felt he needed the pure, uncomplicated love and devotion only a child could offer even more than she'd initially imagined.

Well, she would manage it somehow. By being brisk, efficient and impersonal. And never, ever, putting herself close to him, or dancing with him, again.

Punching her pillow and lying back, she had to laugh. There weren't likely to be many opportunities in future for a governess to dance with the master.

Chapter Twelve

The next morning after breakfast, Hugh dawdled in the library. He would need to leave momentarily to meet Stephen and ride out, stopping along the way, as they'd discussed at breakfast, to call on the Squire.

His friend was probably right in predicting that an invitation to dinner would be forthcoming. In the English countryside as much as in India, visitors from other parts of world excited the interest of the neighbours. Besides, since he'd hidden himself away and turned aside potential invitations with the excuse of being too preoccupied with work, he knew the Squire was curious about him and eager to become better acquainted.

At breakfast, Stephen had also made him an oblique apology for pushing him into dancing last night, to which he'd returned simply a nod of acknowledgement.

He owed Miss Overton a much more articulate apology and it should be delivered immediately. However, his uncertainty over how to do it, and what to say when he did, had kept him lingering in the library.

He was too honest with himself to blame what had happened just on the wine, the magic of the music and the intimacy of the dance. Miss Overton had attracted him from the first. If last evening proved anything, it showed that his control over his desires was not as firm as he'd imagined it.

He would have to reinforce it. He didn't intend to spoil the burgeoning trust between them, or let some further glimpse of lust scare away the immensely capable woman who was making the duty of overseeing his wards so much easier.

Even more important, he didn't want her to perceive any inkling of his interest in and growing regard for her. Anything that might have her develop…expectations.

He sighed. It would be so easy to develop expectations himself. After dealing with an unexpectedly demanding spouse around whom he'd sometimes felt he must walk on eggshells, Miss Overton was refreshingly straightforward and resilient. He didn't have to watch every word to avoid distressing her—indeed, she was more likely to take *him* aback with her tart remarks. She was also reassuringly independent, able to make decisions on her own, only consulting him when she ran into some obstacle—like the housekeeper—she needed his assistance to overcome. Sometimes she even challenged his direction and was never shy about putting forward her own opinions.

But excellent as she was, the colossal failure of his marriage had left him with no desire ever to repeat the experience. He mustn't allow himself to consider—or let his behaviour hint to *her* that he might consider—chancing wedlock again.

Exasperated with himself for his indecision, he jumped up from his chair.

Choose simple words, man, and just do it. And in

*future, rein in both desire and fascination by keeping
your distance.*

He would look for her first in the schoolroom, which
he must pass by to reach the bedchamber wing where
Stephen was billeted, then proceed to collect his friend.
If he could catch her attention as he walked past and
beckon her into the hallway, he could deliver the apology
quickly, privately and in a straightforward manner that
befitted an exchange between employer and employee.

Perhaps more important, with his wards nearby, awaiting her return, he could deliver it in a setting that did not
tempt either of them to linger.

Quickly navigating the warren of halls and stairs,
he approached the schoolroom. Steeling himself to the
murmur of young voices—he needed to do better by
his wards, but not today—he glanced through the partly
opened door to discover Miss Overton seated at the nursery table, reading with her charges.

The nursery table so recently brought down from the
attic. His mind flew back to that moment under the eaves
when he'd first inhaled the subtle scent of her rose per-
fume. When an intense consciousness of her as a woman
had first stolen over him...the same attraction that had
got him into so much trouble last night.

An attraction that therefore needed to be ruthlessly
squelched.

He was shaking his head over how he was to manage
that when she looked up and spied him. To his quick wave
of a hand indicating he didn't wish her to invite him in,
she raised an enquiring eyebrow, then nodded when his
gesture towards the hallway silently conveyed his desire
for her to join him there.

'I must speak with your guardian, girls,' she said as she rose. 'I'll only be a minute.'

Quelling with irritation the skitter of nerves that seemed to afflict her whenever her employer was near, Olivia wondered what the Colonel wished to see her about.

Surely not to reprimand her for her undignified flight from the music room last night. He couldn't help but agree that the less said about that unfortunate incident, the better.

It must be some minor detail, otherwise he would have bid her to come to his library—wouldn't he? She sincerely hoped that episode hadn't ruined the growing rapport they'd developed—an ease she would need if she were to continue working effectively with him on his wards' behalf.

If she met him with composure, without seeming flustered or embarrassed, surely he would act in kind, she told herself as she crossed the schoolroom, leaving the door ajar behind her.

Yet much as she tried to armour herself against him, even from several feet away, she sensed the vital force of him that had so intoxicated her last night as she danced in his arms.

Be brisk, efficient and impersonal, she reminded herself, trying to resist his appeal.

Halting as far from him as possible while still appearing respectful, she said, 'You wished to speak with me, Colonel?'

'I did. First, I owe you an apology for my...overly familiar behaviour during the waltz last night. It was not the conduct I expect of myself as a gentleman and I am sincerely sorry. It won't happen again.'

Even if I wish it might?

Squashing that inappropriate response, she said, 'No need for apologies, Colonel. Waltzing can lead to madness, sometimes—on the part of the lady no less than the gentleman.' Which was as far as she could go towards admitting he hadn't been the only one carried away by music and desire.

'I hope the last few evenings, when you've been kind enough to grace my dinner table, haven't given you the... wrong impression. I never intended to cross the line of the respect and protection an employer owes his employee, or to take advantage of my position to...lure you into a situation that made you feel uncomfortable. Clearly, I did so last night. I want to assure you that you need not fear being subjected to such inappropriate behaviour again.'

She ought to be relieved that he was confirming what she'd already suspected about his sense of honour and his commitment to doing the proper thing for—and with— an employee.

Instead, she felt...sadness and a sense of loss for something longed-for that was never to be. Along with a hurt that went deeper than it should that he seemed able to dismiss so easily an incident which had shaken her so profoundly.

But then, what had she expected? Of course it would affect her, an inexperienced maiden, more profoundly than a man who had loved, and made love to, the beautiful woman he'd made his wife. Why should he feel anything more than a twinge of conscience at becoming momentarily swept away by the long-denied feel of a woman in his arms—even a tall, plain, opinionated spinster like her?

Suppressing the hurt, she nodded briskly. 'Let us speak no more of it. It would probably be best if we return to our customary places, the master dining with his guest and the governess in the nursery with the children.'

Not that she'd really expected him to protest, but she felt another frisson of sadness when he nodded. 'I agree. In fact, I was about to inform you that Mr Saulter is probably correct in predicting that when we call on the Squire this afternoon, he will invite us to dinner tonight, which will be Mr Saulter's last evening at Somers Abbey. He leaves tomorrow to visit family in Yorkshire.'

So Cinderella's run of magical evenings was definitely at an end. Tonight, she would return to her solitary governess existence. Olivia tried to tell herself she was glad, that it was better to avoid temptation than try to resist it.

Resist the employer who was to her temptation incarnate, but who intended to treat her only as an employee.

'One other matter,' he continued, his voice and manner now completely matter of fact. 'Mansfield came to me yesterday about another instance of Mrs Wallace creating a disturbance with Cook and the tweeny. I hadn't planned to do anything about her position until later, but with the staff already reduced, I can't have her harassing my remaining employees. I shall have to deal with her now.'

Apparently, he was able to dismiss the matter of their inappropriate behaviour and move on much more easily than she was. Somehow, the impersonal manner she'd initially hoped he'd adopt when they met after that disturbing waltz was turning out to be more distressing than reassuring.

Trying, despite the sinking feeling in the pit of her stomach, to respond equally with calm, she said, 'You intend to discharge her?'

'I should like to do so immediately, but I have to have someone to run the house. You certainly have the experience, but you're fully occupied with the children. It's not as easy to find staff here.'

Firmly suppressing her turbulent emotions, she said, 'What about Travers, your mother's former lady's maid? I was told that she filled that position when the last housekeeper retired upon your mother's death, before your brother hired Mrs Wallace. I know she is in retirement, but she's still quite spry and capable. Perhaps she would agree to temporarily fill the role again, until you can find a replacement.'

His eyes brightening, he nodded. 'An excellent suggestion. It would be good to have her at Somers Abbey again. I will be preoccupied with my guest until Saulter leaves, but after that, as soon as my work allows, I shall call on her and ask.'

Which gave her the perfect opening to try to advance the true purpose for her continuing presence at Somers Abbey—bringing guardian and wards together.

'Might the girls and I go with you?' she asked. 'When I visited Travers, she expressed a great interest in meeting them. I know they would love to hear any tales she could tell them about their papa when he was a boy.'

Raising his eyebrows, he said, 'When did you visit Travers?'

'The other day, after I took the girls for their first long walk. They managed to muddy their gowns thoroughly, particularly the fine embroidery work around the hems. I don't imagine a gentleman would realise it, but cleaning such delicate stitching without damaging it is quite difficult. Knowing I was responsible for creating a good deal of extra work for her, I felt I should deliver the gowns personally, with my apologies. Mrs Travers was kind enough to ask me to stay for tea and was curious about the girls. I promised one day I'd bring them to meet her.'

He nodded. 'I imagine she would be curious. With their father visiting here so often, she knew him well. I'm sure the girls would like to hear more about their papa as a boy.' He laughed ruefully. 'I only hope Travers won't relate too many of my own escapades while she's at it.'

'Escapades by their stern, unsmiling guardian? I imagine they would enjoy those stories even more!'

He shook his head. 'If it will help little Sophie to look on me less like an ogre ready to devour her if she opens her mouth, a few embarrassing stories might be worth it.'

Emboldened by his positive response to that initiative, she pressed further. 'If you will allow us to accompany you when you visit her, along the way, might you point out some of the places you enjoyed playing as a boy? So I may take the children back later. They have been cooped up so much of late, I would like to get them out every day for a good long walk.'

She held her breath, hoping that she hadn't pushed him too far. But knowing, with her employer's dedication to his work, there wouldn't be many opportunities to get guardian and wards together outside the formal setting of his library, she needed to make the most of the few that came along.

To her relief, after a long moment during which she feared he might change his mind about allowing them to come along on his visit to Travers, he exhaled a long sigh. 'I suppose on the way back from the village, I could show you several places you might take them to play. And several that, though I romped there myself as a boy, you should avoid, as they are much too dangerous for young children.'

'Information I should very much like to have! I want to take them all around the estate, so they can become more familiar with and appreciate their father's homeland, but I certainly don't want to put them into any danger.'

'No, you want only to nurture and protect them.' The slight edge of sadness in his voice had her looking up at him with concern. He gave her a half-smile—of reassurance, perhaps?

'As do you—despite the cost,' she replied softly, wanting him to know she appreciated the pain he endured to associate with them.

'With your help, I shall do so. My very commanding Miss Overton.' As their gazes caught and held, his smile faded.

Olivia felt that sense of connection surge between them, even stronger than before. And she was almost certain she saw in his eyes the same bittersweet longing she was trying so hard to quell.

'Are we going to visit someone?'

Startled by Elizabeth's voice, Olivia jerked her gaze free. What was it about the potent force the Colonel exerted that made her forget there was anyone else nearby? She looked over at the little girl, who stood by the open doorway, wondering just how much she had overheard.

Meanwhile, kneeling down to the child's level, the Colonel said, 'We were talking about taking you to visit a lady who knew your father well when he was a boy.'

'There is a lady here who knew Papa?' Elizabeth

echoed, with a wistful longing on her face that touched Olivia's heart.

Poor mite. She would instinctively latch on to anything that offered her a glimpse back at the happiness and security she'd had when her father was alive, she thought.

'Yes, Elizabeth,' the Colonel replied. 'Mrs Travers knew your papa almost as well as I did.'

'Can we go tomorrow?'

Olivia watched the rather aloof and formal expression the Colonel usually wore around the children soften—as if he, too, was touched by the little girl's obvious need.

'Not tomorrow, I'm afraid. But soon after.'

'I should like that so much,' she whispered, tears glistening in her eyes.

A look of pain flitted the Colonel's face, so briefly she wouldn't have caught it had she not been staring at him in a most unladylike manner. Replacing it with a determined smile, he said, 'We shall have to make it happen, then, won't we?'

'We mustn't keep the Colonel, Elizabeth,' she said, motioning the child back towards the school table. 'I'll join you in a minute.' For the rapprochement she wanted to happen, she mustn't let the girls cause the Colonel more pain than he could bear.

The child dutifully retreated into the schoolroom, then paused by the table to make her guardian a curtsy. 'Thank you, Colonel. I'll be waiting and waiting to meet the lady.'

'We *will* go soon, I promise, Elizabeth,' he replied, that softened look on his face again. 'Goodbye to you and to you, Miss Overton.'

'Good day, Colonel. Please convey my farewells and good wishes to Mr Saulter.'

'I will do so.' Giving her a nod, he turned and continued down the corridor.

As she walked back into the schoolroom, Olivia felt a swell of hope that, before she left Somers Abbey, she might have the satisfaction of seeing the grieving guardian and bereft children grow close enough to comfort each other.

As for her unsuitable attraction to the Colonel... That unexpected surge of connection between them towards the last might have made her foolish heart rejoice, but she needed to focus instead on the bittersweet look he'd given her immediately after. An expression of sadness and longing which said without words that however attracted to her he might be, he was fully committed to re-imposing on them the normal constraints of a relationship between employer and governess.

She'd already promised herself she would not try to entice him into forgetting them again.

Tonight, she would turn away again from the tantalising glimmer of life as it used to be and return to the servant's role she now filled. Over the next few days and weeks, she would work to snuff out her hopeless attraction to her employer.

But if, over her time at Somers Abbey, she could reconcile the Colonel and the children, that would be enough.

It would have to be.

Chapter Thirteen

Despite the promise she'd herself made not to seek out
the Colonel for any private consultations, late that evening Olivia found herself lingering in the corridor beyond the library door, waiting for Mr Saulter and his host
to finish the convivial brandies they'd gone up to share
after returning from dinner at the Squire's.

Of course, they might have settled into the time-
honoured regimental tradition of drinking until dawn.
But the information she needed to convey was important
enough that she was willing to wait a while longer. She
feared if she put off her mission until the morning, occupied by the children as she would be then, she might miss
catching the Colonel before he headed out to the fields.

Besides, if she did wait until morning, he would likely
be in the breakfast room or parlour, probably accompanied by his guest. She needed to speak with him alone
and at a place and time where there was little chance Mrs
Wallace might be about to eavesdrop.

To her relief, after a few more rounds of pacing the
corridor, she heard the squeak of the door opening, followed by Saulter's voice calling goodnight. She slipped

into the shadows of the hallway, waiting until the guest had turned the corner, heading away from her towards the wing of bedchambers, before she hurried to the library door.

After quickly rapping, she stepped inside. 'Colonel, might I have a word with you?'

Engaged in returning the brandy decanter to the sideboard, at the sound of her voice, he turned sharply towards her, alarm on his face. 'What is it? Nothing wrong with the girls—'

'No, no, they are fine. Sleeping like angels.'

As he exiled a sigh of relief, Olivia felt a pang of guilt. *He slipped away between dusk and midnight.*

Her sudden interruption must have recalled to the Colonel the night he'd returned to learn the son he'd left happily playing in the afternoon was dead.

'Sorry, I didn't mean to worry you.'

'What do you need to tell me, then? It must be important, or you'd not have lost sleep, waiting up for me.'

'It is something I thought you needed to know immediately—since it may cause you to alter your plans about visiting Travers,' she replied. She wouldn't add that finding sleep would have proved elusive in any event, the stark contrast between her solitary evening tonight and the three wonderfully convivial ones that preceded it making her too restless for peaceful slumber.

To say nothing of recalling that almost-kiss.

Dragging her mind back to the matter at hand, she walked over to stand in front of his desk, shaking her head when he motioned for her to take a seat. 'This won't take long. After the girls were in bed—' *being too agitated to read through the long, lonely evening that stretched ahead* '—I went down to ask Mrs Wallace if the household had any extra cloth. Though my trip to Bristol equipped the girls with warm nightwear and spencers to go over their light dresses, they still need several gowns made from heavier material for daytime wear, which I could sew for them if I had dress lengths. Mrs Wallace told me she had no extra material, but there were several trunks of old gowns in the attic. That if you gave your permission, I could pick them apart and re-make them for the children.'

'You certainly have my permission. The trunks must be Mama's. She would approve of having her old gowns refashioned for such a good cause.' He angled his head at her, that half-smile she found so attractive lighting his face. 'Informing me about your upcoming sewing project was important enough for you to lose sleep over?'

Despite her intent to remain brisk and impersonal, she couldn't seem to help smiling back. 'My sewing skill is not worth that! It's what happened afterwards. I went up to the attic—'

'The one I showed you?' he interrupted again, frowning. 'I certainly hope not! Those stairs are much too steep for you to be climbing up in skirts, holding a lantern. I'll—' He halted abruptly, then continued, 'I'll have one of the grooms show you up tomorrow.'

'I didn't make it all the way up. As you say, the stairs are too dangerous for me to negotiate with lantern in hand, so I didn't take one. I'd hoped there would be enough light from the gable windows to illumine the space, but by the time I was nearly at the top, I realised that, with night coming on, the attic was too dark for me to even locate the trunks.'

'You would need help to carry them down anyway.'

'Yes, but I thought to inspect the contents first, to discover whether or not it was worth having them hauled down. But that's beside the point.'

'So there is a point?'

Despite her resolve to distance herself, the warmth and delight she felt at his teasing tone was in such stark contrast to the desolate loneliness of her evening, she was sorely tempted to respond in kind.

Which should be warning enough for her to conclude her business as quickly as possible and leave, before all her other wise and noble resolves crumbled.

'I'm about to get to it,' she said tartly. 'By the time I picked my way back down the stairs, Mrs Wallace had retired to her rooms for the evening. In case the material in the trunks turns out not to be suitable, I intended to go ask her to remind me how much I'd spent on the spencers—the trip to Bristol was done in such a rush, I remembered the total but not how much the individual garments cost—so I could advise you of the sum. Mary stopped me, explaining that the housekeeper had long ago instructed the staff that once she retires to her rooms, she is not to be disturbed, except for an emergency. Mansfield, who was still in the butler's pantry, seconded Mary's appeal that I not excite Mrs Wallace's wrath. He suggested instead that I consult the household account book she keeps in her desk in the servants' hall. While he suspected she would be livid if she learned I'd looked through it, he felt it would be safe enough for me to take a quick peek, as long as I replaced it in precisely the same position in the drawer that I'd found it.'

'Worrying over the price of spencers is enough to keep you awake?'

What she'd discovered being too alarming to joke about, she continued soberly, 'I found the entry quickly enough, but the amount she listed as having been dispensed for my Bristol trip was almost twice what I actually spent. Did you authorise her to take extra money from the household funds, beyond what you repaid me, perhaps to set aside towards purchasing more clothing for the girls?'

The Colonel's smile faded, too. 'No. She asked me what the total was and I told her. Exactly the amount I gave you.'

'I thought as much,' Olivia replied, nodding. 'I was going to dismiss it—it really was too trifling a matter to disturb you about, but something about it seemed so strange. On impulse, I tracked down Mansfield and asked him how much last week's order of wine and spirits had cost. You see, he'd told me he used to enter the totals for the goods he receives into the book himself, but Mrs Wallace began complaining that he didn't write clearly enough. So for some time, she alone has made all the ledger entries. The cost he quoted was a little more than half the amount entered in the ledger. So I rousted Cook and asked her if she knew how much had been paid for the last order of flour from the mill.'

'Also significantly less than was recorded in the ledger?'

'Yes. If you run your household as I used to run mine, money is taken from the storeroom and given into the housekeeper's hand to be dispensed to pay bills as the household incurs them. In this case, it appears Mrs Wallace has been drawing from those funds a good bit more than what the actual bills totalled.'

'You mean to say that she's been embezzling money from the household funds?'

'I don't really have enough evidence to make that

accusation. There may be another explanation. But the appearance of impropriety is strong enough, I felt you needed to know about it at once. So you have time to decide how you want to proceed.'

The Colonel shook his head.

'One expects the servants to keep the proceeds when candle nubs are sold off, or older garments discarded, each servant selling his own traditional share of cast-offs. But to have someone actually *stealing* funds? The bald-faced arrogance staggers me! When I think of all the hours I've slaved away, trying to restore this estate and drag it back from the edge of bankruptcy, all the while trusting Mrs Wallace for its proper management... Damnation!' he cried, slamming his fist on the desk. Almost immediately he collected himself and looked back up at her. 'Forgive me, Miss Overton.'

'No need for forgiveness, sir. It's a serious charge and will require some careful investigation—especially if you intend to discharge her. Should she get wind of that, she might flee, or try to destroy any evidence that might serve to incriminate her.'

'Like that ledger. Keeping her from suspecting anything may be difficult, though, if the other staff starts whispering about discrepancies in the bookkeeping.'

'I didn't mention the discrepancies to anyone else. When I was asking about expenditures, I just told Mansfield and Cook I found it interesting to compare the expenses from month to month and season to season, and was pondering ways I might use the varying costs as a lesson in sums for the girls.' She laughed wryly. 'Though they offered the information, they both looked at me like I was rather odd.'

The Colonel shook his head, his expression still furious, but his anger now tightly controlled. 'You're not odd—you're exceptional,' he retorted. 'If you hadn't had the wit to question this, none of it would have been discovered. And if further enquiry does prove what you suspect to be true, I might have sent Mrs Wallace on her way with impunity—even providing her a good character!—after she'd bilked the household funds of who knows how much.'

'If it is true, she may have secreted the funds here somewhere. After all, she only has a half-day off and seldom goes beyond the village. There would have been talk if she'd been spending large amounts with the merchants there.'

'I must discover the truth of this immediately, before she suspects I mean to turn her off, else she might run off with her ill-gotten gains,' the Colonel concluded. 'You are right—as always—Miss Overton. This *was* important enough for you to wait up and tell me about tonight. How can I thank you?'

He turned on her not just the half-smile she'd glimpsed several times, but a full smile that lit his blue eyes, softened the harsh planes of his cheekbones and glowed with warmth. Dazzled, the description of his younger self that Mansfield and Travers had given her came to mind—confident, commanding, eager to go out to India, ready to conquer the world.

If the world-weary Colonel was attractive, this version of him was breath-stealing.

'Knowing you will discover the truth of it, one way or the other, is thanks enough,' she said at last, making herself look away from the tantalising sight of him—before her delight at his praise made her forget the boundaries she must maintain.

Then, to her shock, he reached up and took her hand, cradling it in his large one. She felt the warmth of it zing to her toes, lighting off nerves all over her body as it went.

While she stood there, barely breathing, he brought her fingers to his lips. 'I owe you much more than this simple salute, Miss Overton,' he murmured, his gaze capturing hers. 'Once more, you intervene to lighten my load. I hope one day to repay you for it. How I wish I might…'

For long moments after his words trailed off, they remained frozen in place, gazing at each other. Completely lost in him, as his grip on her hand tightened, she found herself leaning closer—hoping he would give her the kiss she'd truly prefer as her reward.

Instead, with a sharp shake of his head, he abruptly sat back in his chair and released her hand. 'You should get some sleep,' he said, his voice now gruff. 'I'll let you know what I find out and how I wish to proceed. Until then, please do your best to pretend that nothing is going on. Goodnight, Miss Overton.'

Unable to prolong their talk after so clear a dismissal, she balled her tingling hand into a fist and forced her trembling body to walk out the door.

The next afternoon, Hugh accepted the reins of the landau from the coachman and prepared to set off for the front entrance of Somers Abbey.

'Are you sure you don't want me to drive you, Colonel?' the coachman asked.

'Certain,' he replied. 'It's been a while since I've had the pleasure of handling a team and having me on the box will give my wards and their governess more room while they take in the sights of the countryside.'

'As you wish, sir.'

Nodding to the coachman, Hugh set the vehicle in motion. He was pretty sure his facile explanation was satisfactory enough—the ways of the Quality were mysterious, after all—that the man wouldn't speculate about the trip to any of the other staff.

Though he did enjoy driving, Hugh was more concerned that no one else at Somers Abbey discover his real reason for calling on Travers. Leaving the coachman behind would ensure there was no possibility of the man overhearing anything during their visit.

Driving himself did offer two more important benefits. He would have to concentrate on managing the horses, allowing him little time to notice Miss Overton, and he would not have to share a narrow coach seat beside the far-too-tempting governess.

He already had to contend with the dreams that tortured him, waking to remember the scent and feel of her in his arms as he'd waltzed with her, clasped against him more tightly than propriety allowed. Or the memories of the aching sweetness of her lips he'd sensed and craved and almost kissed before denying himself that pleasure.

Then there'd been last night in the library. Wrapped in candlelight and longing, he hadn't been able to resist teasing her. He'd indulged himself, too, using the natural gratitude one would expect him to feel after she'd warned him of such a serious offence as an excuse to touch her—kissing her hand so he might resist the urge to take her lips.

She made him feel young and vibrant, and alive again, things he'd forgotten he could feel after three years of shutting down every emotion, putting one foot in front of the other and merely going through the motions of life. She'd revived for him happy memories he'd forgotten and reawakened him to music, perhaps the one pleasure he could let himself enjoy. She'd even made it seem possible that he might be able to give Robert's children the care and affection his cousin would have wanted for them.

Grateful as he was for all those gifts, it didn't lessen his burden of guilt or his resolve to remain a widower—which was why he needed to walk a very careful line in keeping his desire for her under control.

By now, he'd rounded the drive from the stables and was pulling up at the front entrance where Miss Overton and her charges were to meet him. 'Your chariot awaits, ladies,' he called down to them as he set the brake.

'I'm so glad you are taking us today!' Elizabeth said as Miss Overton helped her and her little sister into the vehicle, then clambered up herself.

Though he remained fully aware of the governess seated just a few feet away, the distance between them was great enough that he was able to concentrate on his driving. In the passenger space behind him, she was asking the girls to tell her what they would see if the carriage were driving through the countryside of St Kitts. By the time Elizabeth had finished describing big houses with wide walkways all around them, shaded gardens, tall skinny trees with large nuts growing on them and bushes with prickly yellow fruit that tasted delicious—coconut palms and pineapple plants, he assumed—he was pulling up the team in front of Travers's little cottage.

The lady herself, who'd been outside cutting roses as they approached, ran up to the carriage as soon as it came to a halt. 'How wonderful of you to pay me a visit,

Master Hugh! I see you've brought Miss Overton and your wards, too. Please, do come in! I'll put the kettle on for tea.'

'So good to see you, too, Mrs Travers. These are indeed my wards, Robert's daughters, Elizabeth and Sophie,' Hugh said, pointing them out from his seat on the box. 'Girls, I'm pleased to have you meet one of Somers Abbey's most faithful employees, Mrs Travers, who was lady's maid to my mother. Hop down now and I'll leave the carriage at the livery and be back in a trice.'

'Welcome, welcome, all of you,' Travers said, her face wreathed in smiles. 'How fortunate that I decided to bring home some fresh tarts from the bakery this morning! Hurry, Master Hugh, or I expect these two lovely girls will finish every last crumb before you get back.'

He lingered for a moment after all his passengers had disembarked, watching Travers as she ushered her guests up the walk and into the cottage, before setting the coach in motion with a feeling of relief. He hadn't visited the older lady in many months, but as Miss Overton claimed, Travers appeared healthy and vigorous—quite capable of assuming a housekeeper's duties.

If she were also willing, that would solve one problem. Thanks again to Miss Overton for suggesting it.

By the time he returned to the cottage, Miss Overton was pouring tea while Travers dispensed berry tarts to her guests. As soon as all the adults were seated on a settle by the fire, the little girls on cushions on the floor, and their hostess perched on a footstool, Elizabeth said, 'Did you really know our papa?'

Her smile gentling, Travers said, 'Yes, I did, young lady. And how you two remind me of him, with your dark hair and those beautiful blue eyes! He was a serious lad, but always ready to kick up a lark—led on by Master Hugh.'

Miss Overton chuckled. 'A rascal, were you, Colonel?'

'He was a lively one,' Travers confirmed with a laugh. 'Remember, Master Hugh, the time your mama had a friend visiting with a little daughter? You must have been all of seven or eight, same as Master Robert, and that little girl wanted to tag along after you everywhere. Nothing would discourage her until you led her to the kitchen, promising some of Cook's sweet rolls. Then, while she ate them, you and Robert dipped her braids in honey!' The old lady chuckled. 'Took your mama and me near on an hour to wash it out.'

While the girls giggled at that, Travers continued, 'Then there was the time you two boys decided to climb Hunscombe Hill, looking for abandoned mine shafts that might contain pirate treasure. Came back covered in coal dust.'

Hugh laughed ruefully. 'I remember that all too vividly! When Papa discovered where we'd been, I got an unforgettable ear-blistering about the dangers mine shafts posed for reckless boys, plus the promise of a caning if we ever strayed there again.' His mirth fading, he turned to Miss Overton. 'I think all the shafts have been boarded up by now, but just in case, don't take the girls climbing on Hunscombe Hill.'

'Duly noted,' she replied, amusement in her voice—at his youthful indiscretions, no doubt.

'Although Mama's revelation that there were no pirates around Bristol—most of the free trading in the British Isles took place on the Cornish and Devon coasts—was nearly as daunting to us as Papa's scold. She cheered us up, though, by going on to tell us tales of Caribbean pirates. Which I believe, girls, is what first interested your papa in living there.'

'Please, can you tell us more stories?' Elizabeth begged.

Over another cup of tea, Travers obliged her. Hugh settled back to listen, chuckling at his boyhood escapades—and watching Miss Overton. While listening attentively, she assisted Travers, made sure the girls were comfortable and seemed content to sit back and enjoy the moment, without needing to participate or be the centre of attention.

Not that she was meek or retiring, like the governesses he remembered from India. She had instead an air of quiet competence, a self-confidence that announced she didn't need attention or reassurance from others to feel important or worthy.

What a serene, comforting presence she exuded! No wonder her two charges had gravitated to her so quickly.

She'd already smoothed his path in several major ways. What would it be like to have someone as competent—and attractive—as Olivia Overton beside him, smoothing the way permanently?

He squelched the thought as soon as it formed. Before he started having adolescent visions of happy homes and willing helpmates, he needed to remember how what he'd thought was a firm friendship, underscored by love and a strong physical bond, had disintegrated into anger, recrimination and betrayal. It made him sick to imagine the warm feelings he had for Miss Overton ending in such a bitter fashion.

No, he would admire Miss Overton's handling of the girls, appreciate her physical allure from afar and leave it at that.

* * *

When tea had been drunk and the tarts finished, Miss Overton stood. 'Time to be heading back to Somers Abbey, girls. You must thank Mrs Travers for your tea and treats, but most especially for those stories about your papa.'

The adults and the girls rose and exchanged bows and curtsies. 'Can we visit you again and hear more stories?' Elizabeth asked.

'Of course, my child,' Travers replied, patting the girl's hand. 'Come visit me any time Miss Overton can bring you.'

'Miss Overton, would you escort the girls back to the village? You might see if the baker has any more of those tarts they might take back to Somers Abbey. I'll have a word with Mrs Travers and meet you at the livery.'

'Of course,' Miss Overton responded. 'Thank you for a delightful tea, Mrs Travers. We now have a store of anecdotes about their papa—and the Colonel—that the girls may talk about over and over again for the fore-seeable future.'

'Alas, I've been left with only the shreds of my dignity,' Hugh said, slapping a hand to his chest in a dramatic fashion that made the girls giggle.

As the children said their goodbyes and Mrs Travers walked them out, Hugh put a hand on Miss Overton's shoulder, staying her when she went to follow. 'I'll discuss the housekeeper's position with Travers,' he said softly. 'If she's agreeable, I'll see how soon she might be able to take it up.'

'The sooner, the better,' she murmured. 'You'll want someone ready to start immediately, once you've determined exactly what Mrs Wallace has been up to. If

Cook or Mansfield should happen to mention I was curious about the cost of goods, she might get suspicious.'

For a moment longer, he savoured the feel of his hand on her shoulder, the delicate curve of bone and warmth of skin under his fingers, before he made himself let go.

'We'll talk more after I know something,' he continued, stepping away, acutely conscious of how his heartbeat—and other parts of his body—surged at her nearness. Could she sense it as well? Perhaps so, for she avoided his gaze.

The knowledge both pleased—and concerned him.

You must stop indulging yourself and keep your distance, the voice of reason growled in his ear.

Trying to shake off the distracting sensations, he said, 'Would you mind if I delay our drive around the estate? I'd like to drop you back at the Abbey and return to the village to make some enquiries among the merchants.'

'Of course, we can tour the estate another day. Though you will have to confront Mrs Wallace soon, if you talk prices and provisions with the shopkeepers,' she cautioned. 'Having the master himself enquire about such things will be so unusual, it's bound to cause speculation and she's sure to hear about it.'

'I plan to be ready, perhaps as early as this evening. Now you'd better catch up to your charges.'

With that, he sent her towards the door and waited for the lady's maid to return. And indulged himself by watching the graceful movement of her lithe body until she disappeared from sight.

Chapter Fourteen

After settling her charges in bed and reading them several stories—she was happy to indulge them and delay returning to her silent room as they were to hear the tales—Olivia walked with a sigh back to her chamber. For the second night, she'd dined with the children, which made the dinner hour much livelier. But after they were fed and put to bed, there was no escaping the lonely desolation of her empty chamber.

The Colonel was dining with the Squire again tonight. She tried to resist the strong urge to go to the library and linger there, her excuse the desire to do a more thorough survey of its contents, so she might still be present when he returned home. Perhaps to chat for a few moments, or offer to play Beethoven for him again.

She smiled as she wandered down the hallway, recalling the stories Travers had related about the Colonel's boyhood escapades. It warmed her heart to hear how adventuresome, optimistic and full of life he'd once been—and how relaxed he'd appeared, laughing with Travers at the memories. More relaxed and at ease than she'd yet seen him.

He seemed to be doing better with the girls, too, able to look them in the eye while he talked to them, his smile when he did so less forced and more natural. After catching tantalising glimpses now and then—those smiles in the cottage today, his hearty laughter at Travers's stories—she felt even more driven to try to bring back to him the warmth of the children's love—and perhaps let him recover more of the man he'd been before the tragedies in India.

She halted before her doorway, dithering, before deciding to head to the library after all. She would make a cursory inventory of its contents and choose a book to engage her. But she would not be so pathetically weak as to linger until her employer returned.

True to her resolve, a little over an hour later Olivia returned to her room, several books in hand. Knowing how early the Colonel must rise to ride out, she hadn't dared remain there any longer if she truly meant to avoid him.

It hadn't been the same as dining or conversing with him, but just being in the library had cheered her. There was so much essence of him in that room—the estate ledgers stacked on the desk, the brandy decanters and glasses on the sideboard, a vague lingering odour of tobacco, the battered but comfortable leather chairs before the hearth that she guessed he would not replace, even when the estate's finances improved, their cushions indented as if he'd just arisen from one and would return any minute.

She could almost imagine herself seated beside him, conversing about fields and drainage and the progress of the apple crop.

Warmth curling in her belly, she remembered the tingling of her hand when he'd kissed it in the library. The heat of his palm grasping her shoulder in Travers's cottage today.

Making a life in Somerset wouldn't hold the same thrill as fighting on the sidelines to forward the major legislation of the day, but what a contented life it could be! What sensual delights it might offer...

And she really needed to stop indulging in these idiotic daydreams once and for all, she told herself, angrily bringing that line of wistful imagining to a halt.

Yes, there was an attraction between them. Yes, she believed the Colonel had come to value her—perhaps even hold her in some affection. But he had also made it quite clear that, despite those facts, he was not prepared to offer anything beyond temporary employment. And perhaps a respectful friendship.

She couldn't give in to the temptation to use the physical attraction he was fighting to resist to lure him into anything more and keep her self-respect.

She must accept that the most she would ever be to him was a valued employee—who would be discharged as soon as one of his female relatives agreed to take over raising the girls.

On that deflating note, she entered her room—to find Mrs Wallace waiting for her, arms crossed, a furious expression on her face.

'Not dining with the Quality tonight?' the housekeeper said scornfully. 'Ah, that's right—you're only Quality enough to dine with gentlemen here, not good enough to be invited by the neighbours. But my, how you do keep trying to rise above your station!'

In no mood to put up with the housekeeper's insults,

Olivia said shortly, 'Did you wish to see me about something?'

'Indeed I did,' the woman said, walking around the chamber, running her hand over the polished mahogany of the dresser, the silken edge of the counterpane on the bed. 'I should have thought by now that you would understand it's me who takes care of all these fine things— a position I intend to keep. So you may as well abandon your attempts to try to replace me.'

'Replace you?' Olivia echoed, startled.

Tread carefully, she told herself, not sure how much the housekeeper knew.

'It has never been my intent to take up the housekeeper's position,' she replied at last.

Mrs Wallace gave a disdainful sniff. 'So *you* say. Why else would you be flitting about, trying to impress everyone with your talents? Offering to sew gowns for those orphan brats. Chatting with Cook and Mansfield over the price of goods, as if you actually knew anything about victualling a household! Most especially you should stop trying to entice the master with your satin gowns and your sly cream-puff ways. Do you really think he could want an ageing, dried-up spinster like you when he could have any of the young ladies in the country, if he so much as looked in their direction? When his first wife was an accomplished Beauty?'

Blast the woman. She knew just where to insert her poisonous knife. Olivia had no doubts about her competence to manage the girls or the house. But the attraction between her and the Colonel... Plain though she was, she was *almost* sure the feeling was mutual, that they were both struggling to resist it.

'Good and well you look troubled,' the woman continued, an expression of triumph on her face at having hit her mark. 'My, if you could only hear what the Colonel and Mr Saulter used to say about you in the breakfast room over their coffee and toast of a morning! Laughing at your airs and mocking your pathetic attempts to play the Great Lady!'

'I think you've said quite enough,' came a deadly quiet voice from the doorway. Both women whirled to face it, Olivia feeling sick as she recognised the Colonel. Just how much of the woman's vitriol had he overheard?

Surely he and Mr Saulter hadn't really...*mocked* her behind her back.

'Mrs Wallace, you will attend me in the library at once. Miss Overton, I would appreciate your coming along as well.'

Spots of colour burned in the housekeeper's cheeks at having been caught haranguing the governess, but despite the icy anger in her employer's voice, she walked out with her spine erect and her head held high. The woman's ugly words touching her deepest vulnerability, Olivia couldn't bear to look at him as she passed by.

They proceeded in silence to the library, the Colonel shutting the door behind them before walking over to his desk. 'I will postpone, for the moment, any comment on your effrontery in attacking Miss Overton. First, I should like you to explain this, if you can.'

From the drawer of his desk, he pulled out a large leather bag. Olivia heard the unmistakable clink of coins when he dropped it on the desktop.

Mrs Wallace's face went white, then flushed. 'I... I am in the habit of putting by as much of my salary as possible. I've done so for years.'

'So you don't attempt to deny this bag is yours. Interesting that I only turned it up after a thorough search of your quarters—and remembering the old housekeeper's desk had a secret drawer.'

'Of…of course I would want to keep it in a safe place. I'm counting on it to keep me comfortable in my declining years.'

'Amassing a sum like that would have required you to save more than your entire salary for all the years you've been employed here. Still, that explanation might have been somewhat credible, had I not been tipped off to check the entries in the housekeeping book.'

'I can't imagine what—' she blustered before stopping short and turning to Olivia. 'You!' she accused furiously. 'This is all your doing! It's *you* who's been meddling in things not your business, interrogating the other servants, trying to discredit me!'

'Given your attempts to discredit Miss Overton, you might have been able to argue that she planted evidence against you out of spite,' the Colonel answered back. 'But I've had a chat with our providers in the village. Claiming I wished to reconstruct entries in our account book that was damaged by an accidental spill of wine, I had them check their own ledgers and detail the prices paid for goods delivered to Somers Abbey over the last year. Which I then compared to the figures in your book. Given the amount in this bag, I suspect I could have gone back further than a year and found the same results.'

For a few long moments, the housekeeper remained silent, as if trying to find some explanation that might exonerate her. Finally, she burst out, 'It should have been mine—yes, that and even more! I gave Charles everything—my honour, my loyalty! *I* should have been mistress of Somers Abbey, and so I might have become, had he not died so suddenly! Then *you* came and there was nothing I could do to get back my position. What was I to do? Charles owed me more than to have me thrust back into being a lowly housekeeper!'

'How soon after I inherited did you begin collecting what you thought was due you?' the Colonel retorted. Then, waving his hand, he continued, 'Never mind, it doesn't matter. I could have you transported for this, you know. The only reason I might refrain from seeing you prosecuted to the full extent of the law is to avoid scandal and the possibility of bringing dishonour on my brother's name. But I warn you, if you deviate in the slightest from my instructions, I *will* have you bound over for trial.'

'Of course, we must spare the Glendennings and Somers Abbey from scandal,' she said bitterly.

The Colonel fixed her with a level stare. 'I understand life in the penal colonies isn't very…pleasant.'

'What do you want, then?'

'You will be paid your last quarter's salary—only the last quarter. You will leave here by daybreak tomorrow, most certainly without my writing you a character. Where you go after that is your own business, but if I ever see or hear of you in Somerset again, I will prosecute. Do you understand?'

'You don't give me much choice, do you?' she muttered, defiant to the last.

'Indeed.'

After a moment, she nodded.

'Very well. By daybreak, I expect to find no trace of you at Somers Abbey. You may go now.' He waved his hand towards the door.

'Take care *you* do not end up lying in the same bed,' she growled at Olivia as she passed.

As soon as the door closed, the Colonel went to the sideboard, poured two glasses of wine and waved her to a chair. He handed her a glass, from which she took a grateful sip.

'Are you all right?' he asked, studying her face anxiously. 'I hope you didn't let her spiteful venom upset you.'

'Reeling from the attack, but recovering,' she managed to say, trying to tell herself the housekeeper's hurtful claims were only jealous invective.

'When I went to the kitchen to find her, Mary warned me she'd been ranting about going to your room and "putting you in your place". Wretched woman!'

'She did seem to be working up to a veritable harangue,' Olivia said, trying for a bit of humour. 'So, the shopkeepers provided evidence to confirm that she had been stealing money from the household funds?'

'Yes. Only a small amount at first, but as the scheme continued undetected, she grew bolder. She must have guessed, after she became sole keeper of the ledger, it was unlikely I would discover her thievery. Even when I review the books annually, checking current expenditures in order to estimate what will be required in the following year, I wouldn't have thought to go round to the various merchants and double-check that the figures listed in the ledger were correct.' He shook his head. 'Heaven protect us from a woman scorned.'

She wanted to ask him to refute the housekeeper's most wounding assertions, but couldn't bring herself to do it. What difference did it make anyway? Their time for being master and guest was over. 'I suppose life works best if we all keep to our proper place.'

He sighed. 'I hope you didn't believe any of her lies—

that disgusting bit about us "mocking you"! Surely you know both Saulter and I were sincere in our admiration of your musical talent and your conversational abilities, and truly enjoyed the evenings you dined with us.'

She hadn't dared ask, but a warm glow lit within her to hear that her instincts had been correct. 'Thank you for affirming that.'

Even reassured, her feelings were still too unsettled to want to think any more about the relationship between them. 'How did you manage to search her rooms undetected?' she said instead, veering back to the safer matter of the housekeeper.

'I enlisted Mansfield's aid. After returning from talking with the village merchants, I had him lure her down to the cellar with the excuse that he didn't think the amount of wine and sherry that had been delivered matched the entries he'd checked in her ledgers. Of course, she had to accompany him to make a count of the bottles and try to persuade him that the figures were correct.'

'Devious,' she said with a smile.

'I hope so. It took only a few minutes of glancing through her ledger to confirm all her entries exceeded the amounts the merchants had given me. I went directly to her room and began ransacking it. Fortunately, just before they emerged from the cellar, I remembered the old desk had a secret drawer and found the stash of coins. I should have dismissed her in any event, but without that proof, I wouldn't be able to hold the threat of prosecution over her. I intended to confront her tonight, after I returned from dinner. I'm just glad I arrived back soon enough to spare you some of her invective.'

Olivia took a deep breath. 'Imagine, a household without Mrs Wallace's malevolent presence. Mary is going to be ecstatic!'

'I think we will all be relieved. Again, I owe you thanks. You're becoming quite the Somers Abbey's saviour.'

Ah, that she might be his! But if she did not mean to take to heart anything else from the housekeeper's spiteful words, she should be mindful of the last taunt thrown her way.

The Colonel wasn't the only one who must keep desire in check. She didn't need to end up like Mrs Wallace, just one more female servant who found herself in the master's bed—before being discarded.

Finishing her wine, she set down the glass. 'I think I'm revived now. Perhaps the girls and I could drive over and pick up Mrs Travers tomorrow.'

He shook his head. 'I'll send over a wagon. She'll probably have more than a bandbox she wants to move into the housekeeper's room.'

'The children will enjoy having her near. They can pester her every day for more stories!'

'I shall like having her about the house, too.' Tossing down the last of his own wine, he stood as she rose. 'Thank you again, Miss Overton. May you sleep well, knowing the dragon of Somers Abbey will be gone in the morning.'

She was chuckling at his image, glad to have restored the friendly rapport between them, as she walked to the door. Just before she went out, he said, 'Mrs Wallace was wrong on every count, you know. You're not "an ageing spinster", but a young, dynamic, desirable woman. An employee of integrity whom I very much respect

and one I would never insult by making a dishonourable proposal.'

Even if I wanted one?

But once again, in a few succinct phrases, he'd voiced
the conclusion his actions had already been signalling to
her. Yes, the attraction was there. But he didn't wish to
pursue any relationship beyond the formal link between
them, nor would he ever act out of lust.

She would have to resign herself to that fact.

Chapter Fifteen

In the early morning, a few days later, Olivia lingered in her chamber before returning to her charges, rereading the note Mr Saulter had sent her. After thanking her again for her delightful company at dinner and for the excellent piano performances with which she'd entertained him afterwards, he'd ended by penning, 'I don't think Glendenning knows how lucky he is to have found you.'

Was he implying that he still believed the Colonel was attracted to her and ought to pursue that attraction? she wondered. Or might he be hinting of his own interest in her?

Not at all sure how to interpret his statement, she shook her head. Despite having had five Seasons, she had little experience with men. Even before she'd lost all her money, with her modest looks and minimum dowry, she'd not encountered any potential suitor who intrigued her enough to converse with him at length, to say nothing of flirting. She'd found working for the political causes that inspired her far more exciting than pretending interest in the few, boringly conventional society gentlemen who tried to engage her, gentlemen who didn't attract her in the least.

She sighed. That was certainly not the case with the Colonel.

After placing the letter back in the drawer of the bedside table, she was walking back to the schoolroom when a squeal from Sophie startled her. Picking up her pace, she rushed into the room to find the two sisters tussling over possession of a chalkboard.

'I had it first,' Elizabeth said hotly, pulling the slate from her sister's grip, then slapping her hand as she pushed her away, making Sophie whimper.

'Elizabeth!' Olivia chided. 'You and Sophie need to share. And you should never, ever strike your sister.'

Looking suddenly aghast, Elizabeth froze. Alarm and trepidation replacing the anger in her eyes, she said 'I'm sorry, I'm so sorry, Miss Overton. You—you won't send me away, will you, because I was naughty?'

'Of course I won't send you away!' Olivia said, struck by the girl's anxiety. No wonder the sisters had been virtual pattern cards of perfection, if they feared any infraction of the rules would mean they'd be abandoned again. 'I'm here to take care of you and I will do so for as long as you need me.'

Pulling both girls into a hug, she said to the elder, 'You got angry and made a mistake. We all do sometimes. You just need to recognise you were wrong and try very hard not to make the same mistake again. Now,' she continued, releasing them, 'you must apologise to your sister.'

Elizabeth turned to her sibling. 'I'm sorry, Sophie. I promise to share. And I'll try not to hit you again—ever.'

Just then a shaft of morning light slid through the schoolroom window. Jumping up, Elizabeth ran over to look out. Turning to Olivia, she said, 'Please, Miss Overton, may we go for a walk? It's been raining and raining and raining! But it's stopped now.'

The girls had seemed impatient and fretful—as Olivia had felt herself—after being cooped up for several days by foul weather. 'I imagine it's still too wet to walk around the grounds, but we could go to the walled garden. As long as you stay on the brick paths, you won't get your shoes too wet or your petticoats muddy.'

'Thank you, Miss Overton,' Elizabeth cried, bounding over to the wardrobe to pull out her spencer. 'I'm sorry I was naughty.'

'I am, too—but I'm also a little bit pleased,' Olivia told her with a smile as she helped Sophie into her outer garment. 'If you forgot yourself enough to be naughty, it means that, deep down, you trust me to continue to care for you, even when your behaviour isn't perfect. Now, let's get a basket from the kitchen and collect some flowers while we're out. We can arrange a bouquet for the table in the salon.'

In the meantime, Hugh lingered in the breakfast room, drinking another cup of coffee and trying to fight off a sense of melancholy. Having lived in self-imposed isolation for so long, he'd forgotten how enjoyable it was to have a friend around, someone to chat with on his way back and forth from the fields, to talk to about the work of restoring the Abbey, to dine with and share brandy and cigars with afterwards. He already missed his friend.

He also missed the distraction, and the buffer, Stephen had provided from Miss Overton. Having had his taste for companionship resurrected and knowing what a fine dinner companion and conversationalist she could be, he found it even harder to resist the temptation to ask her to join him occasionally. To seek her out for an afternoon chat when the girls were napping, or invite her to accompany him on a stroll through the gardens.

But it was imperative that he resist it. He'd already received several clear indications that his control over the desire she inspired in him was not as rock-solid as it should be. Loneliness, attraction and long-frustrated lust were a combustible combination he must be careful not to bring too close to her bright flame.

Unless...he *could* enjoy her company, as long as their meetings included his wards. He owed them a tour around the estate in any event. Perhaps, once the work on the north meadow was complete, he could take a day off and take them for a picnic on the heights across from Hunscombe Hill, with its beautiful views over the valley. At the very least, he could encourage their governess to bring the girls to the library for a longer visit every evening before dinner, so he'd be sure of seeing her at least once a day.

That approach might work, for it was slowly getting easier for him to tolerate being around his wards. The slash of pain that ripped through him at the sound of the children's voices wasn't as devastating and he was starting to see them—animated Elizabeth and still-silent Sophie—more as reflections of Robert rather than needle-sharp reminders of grief, guilt and loss.

He was wondering what he might say to coax Sophie into speaking to him when, coming from the direction of the walled garden, a distant scream shattered the silence.

A child's scream.

Terror exploded in his chest. Tossing down his coffee cup, Hugh ran for the door to the garden.

* * *

Several more screams tormented him before he skidded to a halt on the brick walkway, peering down allées separated by fruit trees, once neatly espaliered on wooden railings, now riotously overgrown. The sounds seemed to come from the walk furthest from the kitchen, where his mother had trained her prized roses up the brick wall. Breaking back into a run, he headed there at full speed.

As he careened around the corner, he spied the group huddled together at the far back edge of the garden, surrounded by a cascade of roses, their rain-heavy heads drooping. As he approached, he scanned the girls, looking for blood, for limbs dangling at an awkward angle.

It wasn't until he was nearly upon them that he concluded there were no visible injures. In fact, as he slowed his steps to approach the garden bench on which Miss Overton sat, he realised both girls were now…giggling?

Relief that they were unharmed was so strong, he felt light-headed.

'You are all right, all of you?' he demanded. 'No one is injured?'

The smile with which Miss Overton had greeted him turned to a puzzled look, then one of contrition. 'Oh, my, I'm so sorry! I thought we were far enough from the house not to be overheard.'

He shook his head. 'I heard screams. I thought—'

Feeling dizzy, he sucked in a ragged breath.

Miss Overton slid over and patted the bench. 'Please, sit. You ran all the way from the house, didn't you? Elizabeth, take the scissors and go cut some of those pink flowers and white flowers, down there on the pathway. Sophie, you hold the flowers so your sister can snip them, but watch out for the thorns, just as I showed you. Then you can put them in the basket.'

As the girls walked away, Hugh sank gratefully on to the bench, heart still hammering in his chest. He pulled in several deep breaths, closing his eyes as he pushed from his mind the horrific image that had sped him from the breakfast room—a small body, broken and bleeding, gasping for air.

He opened them to find Miss Overton gazing at him, looking concerned—and guilty. 'I'm so very sorry to have worried you,' she repeated. 'I didn't think anyone would be able to hear us in this far back corner of the garden. Obviously, I was mistaken. I shall wait for better weather, so we may walk further away the next time we want to indulge.'

'What happened?' he demanded once he'd caught his breath.

Blushing a little, looking as guilty as a schoolgirl caught with treats in her hand, she said, 'You see, the girls—and I—were restless after being confined to the house because of the rain storms. So I told them what my brother and I used to do when we were finally able to go outside again after being trapped indoors by snow or bad weather.'

Hugh angled his head at her. 'You...screamed?'

Her giggle was as engaging as her charges'. 'Yes. We used to have contests, to see who could scream the loudest or the longest. Of course, we only indulged in this when we were quite far from the house.'

Their flowers cut and scissors set inside the basket, the girls skipped back to the bench. 'I like the screaming game, Miss Overton,' Elizabeth said as they halted. 'Can we play it again?'

'Yes, but we must go further away. The Colonel heard us and was worried because he thought you were hurt.'

'I'm not hurt, sir,' she said, grinning at him. 'The game is very amusing. You must play it, too.'

'We'll play again later,' Miss Overton said. 'Now, you girls may go pick some of the wildflowers at the corner before we return to the house.'

His heartbeat, which had finally settled into normal rhythm, kicked up again as the girls scampered off—leaving him close enough to their governess to inhale her faint scent of roses.

Thank goodness the girls were still within sight.

'The screaming game?' he repeated, shaking his head, distracting himself by trying to picture the quiet, competent, serene Miss Overton running through a meadow, yelling at the top of her voice. 'Miss Overton, you never fail to amaze.'

'It's an effective technique for relieving frustration,' Miss Overton told him with a grin. 'But only if you can get far away from everyone. Not suitable for London, so I haven't played for years—much as I've needed it at times!'

Her smile faded. 'I am very annoyed with myself for letting our silly game alarm you. I hope you know I would never wish to cause you anxiety.'

No, you have only tried to ease my burdens.

'I know. I suppose when it comes to a child's welfare I have a tendency to…overreact.'

Now that it is too late.

'Most understandable. It's such a delicate balance, isn't it? You must care for children and do all you can to keep them from harm, but you can never entirely protect them. I do have some idea of the grief and guilt that occurs when you cannot. My older brother died from a sudden illness when I was a girl. I don't think my family ever truly recovered from the experience.'

He'd never talked to anyone about the devastation of losing Drew. But somehow, in the aftermath of his recent terror and with the warmth of her sympathetic understanding wrapped around him, he found himself saying, 'With all the poisonous creatures in India—snakes, lizards, spiders, scorpions—Drew was never allowed anywhere without someone to keep watch. But illness can strike so swiftly. He seemed perfectly fine when I left him that afternoon for the regimental dinner. My wife...sent me a note, saying he'd fallen ill, asking me to return home. She often sent me messages asking that I come home for some urgent matter that turned out to be a squabble among the servants, or a lizard that had got caught in the pantry. So I...ignored it. Though I did leave early, long before the group broke up, by then, it was too late.'

He gritted his teeth, nausea spiralling in his gut, the accusations Lydia had flung at him as she pummelled her fists against his chest echoing in his ears.

'How could you be so neglectful?'

'All you think about is your precious career!'

'You should have been more concerned with Drew's well-being!'

'Had she sent for a doctor?' Miss Overton's soft tones startled him, recalling him from the morass of memory.

'No. No, she was waiting for me to do that.'

Miss Overton frowned. 'Could the doctor only be summoned by the military member?'

He looked at her, puzzled. 'It generally was done that

way, though it wasn't absolutely required. But Lydia was…used to having me handle everything.'

Miss Overton shook her head. 'I don't wish to sound critical, but if someone I loved was gravely ill, I would have run for the doctor myself and dragged him back by the collar, if necessary. Although, if the fever were as deadly as it appears, perhaps there wouldn't have been anything he could have done anyway.'

His stomach still churning, Hugh nodded. 'I sent for him the minute I got home. He told me the same thing after he arrived. It didn't help. And I don't think my wife believed him.'

'She blamed you.'

Suddenly weary, he simply nodded.

For a long time they were both silent, Hugh fighting back the memories. Finally, Miss Overton said softly, 'Though it's the height of presumption for me to venture an opinion, I can't help thinking your wife insisted on blaming you because the guilt she felt herself was too terrible to bear. My mother felt the same, when my brother died. That she was his mother. That she should have been able to do *something* to save him. Even though the doctor and everyone else assured her that there was nothing more she could have done.'

'Nothing more you could have done.'

The regimental doctor had repeated it over and over as Hugh stood by his son's bed, locked in a grief so terrible, so painful, he couldn't move, could barely breathe.

To his shame, he felt tears well up. Dashing them away with one hand, he muttered, 'Sorry.'

While he sat there, buffeted again by grief, he felt her take his hand and twine her fingers in his. 'No, *I'm* sorry, so sorry,' she whispered. 'For bringing it all back. I promise in future to be more careful.'

He looked down at her, seeing in her face no condemnation for his failure and his weakness, only sympathy and a deep understanding.

Suddenly, he thought he knew why.

'Your brother was the only son?'

Eyes widening in surprise at his abrupt question, she nodded. 'Yes.'

'So your father's estate was inherited by someone else.'

'A distant cousin. Who, after my mother's death, also became owner of the house in which we were living.'

'And you preferred hiring yourself out to living on his charity.'

Looking away from his penetrating gaze, she whispered, 'Yes.'

He'd lost his family, but he still had his ancestral home and the land on which he'd been born. She'd lost her family—and everything.

For several more long moments he sat with her in silence, fingers entwined, sharply conscious of the heavy losses they both had endured. Though Hugh still felt the siren call of her nearness, the aching desire was tempered by a…tenderness, a sense of closeness and kinship he wasn't sure he wanted to feel even as it sifted into him, cooling the raging fires of grief like a gentle snowfall.

Finally, as the girls came skipping back, their arms full of the wildflowers they'd plucked, she pulled her hand free and stood. 'What lovely flowers! Come add them to the basket and let's go in. We must put them all in water before they wilt.'

Turning back, so that he only now saw the tears glittering at the corners of her eyes, she made him a curtsy. 'Good day, Colonel.'

He watched her walk away, the anguish of which he'd just caught a glimpse once again submerged beneath her façade of quiet calm.

Chapter Sixteen

Two afternoons later, after settling the girls in for a nap, Olivia walked down to a small salon across the corridor from the breakfast room, where two large trunks awaited her.

With the assistance of the groom the Colonel had detailed to accompany her, she'd discovered them in the attic yesterday, just in the spot Mrs Wallace had described. While the groom held a lantern, she'd lifted out the dresses and carefully removed them from their tissue-paper wrappings. The material was so lovely and in such good condition that, reluctant as she was to use anything recommended by the housekeeper, it seemed a shame to let them go to waste, mouldering in the attic. So, with the Colonel having already given her permission to pick them apart if she wished, she'd asked the groom to bring the trunks down for her.

Mrs Travers, once again installed in the Abbey in her housekeeper role, had recommended that they be brought to this small salon, rather than to the schoolroom, as it would allow her to work while the girls napped. The room also contained a large, west-facing window, which would offer the brightest afternoon light for doing fine work. It was her late mistress's favourite room for sewing and needlework, Mrs Travers told her, and had been closed up since the woman's death. But she'd been delighted to open it back up and air it out, assuring Olivia that she'd send the tweeny up to keep watch over the sleeping girls while Olivia worked.

After extracting several gowns from the first trunk and spreading them out on the sofa—she hoped to be able to take apart at least two of them at this first session—she moved a chair and a side table close to the window. Setting her sewing box and scissors on the table, she sat down and began to carefully snip apart the seams of the first gown, a light woollen in a lovely sky-blue that would highlight the colour of the girls' eyes.

She smiled, picturing the girls walking out in the new gowns, matching blue ribbons in their hair and buttoned up in their dark navy spencers. They would be toasty warm and look charming.

She was snipping the last seam on the bodice when, to her surprise, there came a knock from the doorway. She turned to see the Colonel standing on the threshold. 'I'm not disturbing you, am I? Mrs Travers said you were working in here.'

An eager warmth rose in her as a smile sprang to her lips. 'Not at all. Please, come in. What did you want to see me about?'

His smile was warm, too, as if he were as happy to catch her for a private chat as she was to see him. 'That tour of the estate we had to postpone. The weather is supposed to...'

Halfway into the room, he halted abruptly and went silent, his smile fading. Olivia watched him, puzzled—

until she realised that his gaze was fixed on the gowns arrayed like brightly coloured butterflies on the sofa. Dismay and anger swept through her as his expression went from surprise to pained recognition.

Stifling a most unladylike curse, she jumped up, snatched the gowns, stuffed them back in the trunk and slammed the lid. Turning to face him, once again as vexed at herself as she was angry, she said, 'Those weren't your mother's gowns, were they?'

Still standing stiffly, his lips pressed together in a thin line, the Colonel shook his head.

'Damn Mrs Wallace!' she exclaimed furiously. 'Still mischief-making! I'm sure she knew exactly to whom those gowns had belonged. How foolish of me to believe she would actually give me helpful information.'

Taking a deep breath, the Colonel gave his head a shake, as if trying to slough off an injury. 'Gone, but not yet forgotten,' he said drily. 'The best way not to give her that victory is to close the lid—figuratively as well as literally—and forget about her nasty trick. Shall we?'

'I will if you can,' she said. 'I hope it goes without saying that I would never have—'

He held up a hand, cutting her off. 'No need for apology. I know *you* would never deliberately try to injure. But my dear Miss Overton,' he continued, his tone turning determinedly light, 'I was shocked—shocked!—to hear you use such unladylike language! I certainly hope you don't talk that way within my wards' hearing.'

He was making such a game effort to put the unpleasantness behind him, she could only play along. Abandoning the rest of the apology she had intended to make, she said instead, 'No, indeed, sir. Why do you think I introduced them to the "screaming game" as a means of venting frustration?'

'Not an alternative that would be any more acceptable in polite company. But a tolerable alternative as long as one plays it outdoors and far from anyone's hearing.'

'Which I make sure I do.' Dropping her scissors back in the sewing box, she said with a sigh, 'Perhaps I ought to find an isolated meadow now, before the girls wake up. I was so hopeful of having their new clothes ready for them within the week! At least I discovered the... unsuitability of the trunk material before I had spent hours constructing gowns from it! But now I shall have to wait until after I can get to Bristol and purchase material to even get started.' She smiled ruefully. 'And pick your pocket into the bargain, for the funds to procure the yardage. Once the weather clears and the roads dry out, may I take the girls there —with your permission, this time?'

Frowning, he shook his head. 'You know I don't like you travelling that far without an escort.'

'On a fine summer day, with it remaining light so late into evening, I'm sure we would be fine.'

The idea came to her suddenly, and though she hesitated to ask, knowing he'd just been upset again by walking in to discover his late wife's gowns draped all over the salon, it was too precious an opportunity not to take the chance.

'Unless...if we were to wait until the north meadow project was complete, would you consider driving us there? I know the girls would love having you along.'

And it would give him a whole day with them, on a light-hearted outing with many new sights and interesting objects to engage the children and show them in their best, most curious, most innocent light.

He stood for a moment, turmoil obvious in his eyes. She held her breath, hoping he wouldn't consider an entire day with his wards too much to endure.

'Though the north meadow work won't be completed for some time,' he said at last, 'I came here intending to propose taking all of you, not just on the promised tour of the estate, but also on a picnic afterward, high up in the hills, where one can see the whole of the valley. I wanted to show them where the boundaries of the estate run, with the Abbey set like a jewel in the centre. But if you prefer, I suppose I could escort you to Bristol instead.'

The breath she hadn't realised she'd been holding whooshed out. What a victory that would be for the girls! She would do everything she could to make the excursion a happy one for both guardian and wards. As the afternoon at Mrs Travers's cottage had been.

She ignored the guilty knowledge that having the Colonel escort them to Bristol would be as much a treat for her as it would for the children.

'A tour and picnic would be wonderful, sir, but right now, they really do need more gowns as soon as I can get them sewn.'

He nodded. 'Bristol it is, then. Perhaps you can find them a few ready-made gowns while we're in the city, to serve until you have time to complete new ones.'

'That would certainly be helpful—but are you sure? The extra expense?'

He gave her a severe look. 'I am not Mrs Wallace, haggling over the price of gowns and spencers so I may line my pockets. I do not propose to have my wards going about their walks shivering, or wearing their few frocks into rags.'

'Thank you so much, sir! I know it is a sacrifice for

you to take a whole day off from your work on the estate. I'll make sure you don't regret it.'

He looked down at her, smiling faintly. 'Spending a whole day in your company, Miss Overton? I assure you, I will not regret it.'

Then, giving her a short bow, he walked out. While she forbade herself to speculate on exactly what that statement could have meant.

A guilty indulgence is what this trip really is, Hugh thought as, a little more than a week later, he drove the farm wagon back from Bristol.

Two happy children, their bellies full of lunch and treats, had just fallen asleep on the benches behind him, while the open area between the benches was stacked with paper-wrapped lengths of cloth, bags of the requisite trimmings, net and straw for constructing bonnets—and the large, covered cage of a colourful parrot.

The instigator of that last purchase sat companionably beside him on the driver's bench, humming, a little smile on her face as she gazed at the road ahead.

Amusement, tenderness and a stronger, deeper feeling he didn't wish to put a name to stirred in his chest as he glanced at her. Ah, what a wonder was the Managing Miss Overton!

Initially, aside from the lure of her company, he'd been dreading this trip. But over the last week, she had slowly, quietly prepared him for spending an extended time with his wards, bringing them to the library each evening with a picture they had drawn to show him, or some rock or bird or flower they'd seen in the gardens to ask him about, or having Elizabeth repeat for him some story or fable about their island home that Robert had taught her.

Like a painting taking shape, going from pencil sketch to the basic outline in oil, to the full application of shading and hue, his wards had slowly metamorphosed from sharp reminders of Drew's loss, to hazy reflections of Robert, to engaging small beings in their own right. Even as the grieving father in him tried to hold himself aloof, unwilling to risk incurring the agony of loss again, his heart whispered it had room for more and love was always worth the risk.

He'd also allowed himself to ease slightly the prohibition he'd placed on encountering Miss Overton without the children in tow. When he'd asked if she would be agreeable to playing piano for her charges each evening before she took them up to bed, she'd requested in return permission to resume playing after they were asleep, as long as it wouldn't disturb him.

He'd immediately agreed—knowing guiltily as he did so that he would arrange to linger nearby and listen. Knowing that lingering there, watching her, entranced by the music her clever fingers created, would 'disturb' him profoundly, though not in the way she'd meant.

He did retain enough self-control to refrain from taking a seat in the salon as she played. It would be only a few steps more to join her on the bench. Only a few inches more to lean down and touch his lips to the smooth curve of her bared neck as she bent over the instrument. Only a small lift of his hand to grasp her chin, angle her head up and take the lips whose tempting sweetness still haunted his dreams.

'Daydreaming, sir? I should recommend you keep your attention on the road.'

Her amused voice broke into his erotic imaginings, jolting him back to the present—but doing nothing to quell the sharp desire still filling him. In the silent, drowsy sunlight, he was suddenly all too aware of the physical essence of her he'd been ignoring all day, assisted in that effort by the presence of one chattering and two giggling little girls.

Her subtle scent of roses. The warmth radiating from her body. The plump fullness of the lips in the smiling face she raised towards his, golden highlights sparkling in the depths of her brown eyes.

At this moment, the sleeping girls behind him were of no help whatsoever.

Uncomfortably aware of his arousal, fighting the sensual need pulsing in his blood, he needed to find some other way to distract himself.

Conversation, he thought disjointedly. If he kept her talking, maybe he could withstand the urge to kiss her.

So he said, 'After I've magnanimously devoted a whole day to fulfilling your wishes—including, God help me, the purchase of a parrot—it's most unkind of you to question my driving skill. Inaccurate as well, for I have these two sturdy plodders well in hand.'

She chuckled. 'Not a high-stepping matched pair, are they? I expect your fellow soldiers in the regiment would gasp in horror at seeing you driving a farm dray.'

'They'd approve of nothing less than a flashy curricle, for sure.'

'Don't mistake me—I am very grateful you have devoted a whole day to us. The girls will be talking about this excursion for weeks—that is, Elizabeth will. I suppose Sophie will finally talk to us when she's ready. But though she might not have offered any words, the expression on her face could be read plainly enough. I'm not sure which delighted her more: drinking chocolate at Fry's, or gobbling those sweets at the inn where we had our bread and cheese.'

'She certainly packed away a quantity of them,' Hugh observed.

'Probably the molasses and sugar reminded her of the islands. Whereas Elizabeth was most delighted to be able to choose a new gown and have a hand in selecting the material and trims for others. But nothing, sir, absolutely nothing, will top in their minds the delight of the parrot. Having a living, breathing reminder of their homeland will be such a comfort to them!'

'So you assured me when you talked me into purchasing it. A living, breathing, *talking* reminder.' He chuckled. 'I shudder to imagine what John Coachman will say when I inform him the creature is going to be kept in the stables.'

'Only temporarily, sir, until we can set up a proper space, perhaps in a corner of the schoolroom. The merchant said such birds are very intelligent. We want him to help coax Sophie into talking by repeating what Elizabeth says, not to learn to speak horse.'

'Very well, but if he's too much disturbance in the schoolroom, he'll have to remain in the stables.'

'He might be just as much disturbance there. I'm not sure how English horses will deal with a tropical parrot. If necessary, I'll bring him into my room.'

'And what will you tutor him in? Parliamentary speeches?' At her puzzled look, he said, 'I've noticed that my London newspapers are sometimes left turned to the pages describing the current happenings in Parliament.'

Her cheeks flushed. 'I'm so sorry! Sometimes I get

called away by the girls and forget... But I should have asked permission—'

'No, no, you don't need my permission to read the London papers!' Reading about the goings-on in Parliament—action she had once worked to shape—was little enough from her former life to cling to.

Curious to know more about that life, but concerned to avoid triggering the distress he'd witnessed the other time they'd spoken of politics, he said carefully, 'Are the bills in which you were interested moving forward? As I confessed to you before, having spent my adulthood in India and then coming back to find Somers Abbey in such disarray, I've not taken the time to find out much about what's been happening in England. Significant changes, I think you mentioned? As a responsible landowner, I should know more about them.'

Though her eyes lit, she said guardedly, 'Well, if you are truly interested...'

'I am. Would you be kind enough to give me a short summary of the major events?'

'Just a short one, then. And please do tell me to stop once you've heard enough. I'm afraid I have a tendency to prose on at length.'

And so she launched into a discussion of the major legislation the reform politicians had pushed through over the last few years. The bill ending slavery he'd known about, but almost nothing about the overhaul of election rules to eliminate rotten boroughs, or the regulation of working hours and conditions for children employed in factories.

She talked about her work with the Ladies' Committee run by Lady Lyndlington, a friend whose husband was apparently a leading member of the reform group in Parliament. When he teased about her family perhaps preferring her to spend more time finding a husband than writing exhorting letters, she laughed and replied that, in fact, she and two good friends had managed to obtain their respective families' agreement to let them abandon conventional society, lease a house together and devote themselves to their Committee work.

As he listened attentively, watching how her face glowed and the very tenor of her voice became imbued with passionate purpose, it was impossible not to realise how much playing her part in the reform movement had meant to her.

She had indeed lost so much—not just family, home and friends, but the work that had been the driving force in her life.

He marvelled that she had borne it with such fortitude. Other than the few rare glimpses of distress he'd caught, she'd hidden her heartache under a serene exterior and a cheerful smile.

How unfair it was that this woman, who would have made a splendid helpmate for a man in government, or at the very least the superbly capable wife of a landed aristocrat, had ended up a servant. Whereas he'd seen too many bored and indolent officers' and gentlemen's wives in India, gossiping and complaining as they lived lives of leisure and did little of importance for anyone.

'Well, the Judd Street house was not to be,' she concluded, the enthusiasm fading from her face, a pensive look taking its place.

'Did you never encounter a dashing young politician who could persuade you to accept his hand?' he asked, voicing a curiosity that, he was ashamed to admit, carried more than a trace of jealousy.

'Alas, no.' She smiled faintly. 'None of the society gentlemen I met over five Seasons interested me in the slightest. Though to be fair, their only interest in *me* was the possibility of obtaining a modestly dowered, well-bred female to manage their household and eventual children. The Members of Parliament were either already married, or had attachments elsewhere.'

Because you were meant to come here—to me.

Quickly stifling that inappropriate thought, he made himself focus back on her losses.

'I'm sorry you had to leave London and your work,' he said, knowing his regret could make little difference, but compelled to express it anyway.

'I suppose all of us stagger under the weight of real tragedy. But facing the small slings and arrows of everyday life, one can be as happy as one chooses—paying attention to the things that please, or letting ourselves focus on those that annoy. For myself, I choose as much as possible to be happy.'

'I hope that you find helping my wards adjust to life in England a worthy cause too, if not as important as the work of your reform Committee.'

Smiling more broadly, she nodded. 'In some ways, it is more important. When I left London, there were others to take up the pen and continue that fight. Arriving with no nurse or maid from home, the children had no advocate. And they are darling girls. Although I've been with them less than a month, I'm terribly fond of them already.' After a moment's hesitation, she added, 'I hope that, with time, you are finding it...easier to be with them?'

'I am. Thanks to you. I suspect I'm even growing...

somewhat attached,' he added, surprising himself with the truth of that statement.

Her face had grown melancholy, but at that admission, she brightened again. 'That's wonderful! At the risk of being presumptuous—again—I can't help thinking that sharing a fond affection would be a blessing for all of you.'

As you have been a blessing to me.

He stifled the thought before he could utter the words aloud. A sweet tightness constricted his chest again, along with a strong desire to pull her into his arms. Not just from the carnal desire he had to battle constantly. But also for the simple pleasure of offering her the comfort of his embrace and a poignant yearning to help her carry her burdens, as she had helped him lift his.

Before he could succumb to it, Elizabeth stirred sleepily. 'Are we almost back?' she asked, sitting up and rubbing at her eyes. 'When can we uncover Pierre's cage?'

Hugh welcomed an interruption that brought him up short before his thoughts veered off in a direction they had no business taking. Even had he the funds, with no excuse of kinship between them, there was no way he could help Miss Overton recover the life she'd lost. And despite his daily growing regard for her, he dared not offer anything else.

'Another mile or so down the road and we'll pass through the gates into the drive leading to the Abbey,' he told Elizabeth. Turning to Miss Overton, he had to chuckle. 'I can't wait to see the expression on John Coachman's face when the grooms unload Pierre.'

Chapter Seventeen

That night, after the children were in bed, Miss Overton again returned to the music room to play the piano. Abandoning his usual listening post by the library door, Hugh slipped into the hallway and drifted to the threshold of the music room, captivated by the melancholy beauty of the music and irresistibly drawn to be closer to her.

As she caught him in the gentle web of her music, he found himself thinking again about the proposition that had occurred to him after she'd told him more about her life on the way home from Bristol this afternoon. A proposition he'd almost blurted out, before Elizabeth awoke and interrupted him.

If some relative volunteered to take over the girls—though the more days that passed without a reply to his letters requesting assistance, the less and less likely that seemed—he would have to discharge Miss Overton and send her back to London.

Back to search for another position, where she would have to start over again with a new employer who might—or might not—appreciate what a talented, committed, sterling woman of character she was.

Someone who might treat her merely as a convenient servant. Or even worse, mistreat her.

Unless… If they were to enter a *marriage* of convenience, it might be a happy solution for all of them.

He'd instinctively recoiled from the idea. He'd been a star student, a natural commander who could direct a company of soldiers, analyse the threat facing them and send them out with a plan to meet it with perfect confidence. Though the hours of work required were long and the progress frustratingly slow, he had no doubt that eventually he would restore Somers Abbey to the prosperous estate it had been in his father's day.

But when it came to figuring out matters of the heart, he felt as inadequate and uncertain as a green lieutenant leading his first patrol into hostile territory.

After having longer to ponder the idea—and he'd thought of little else since returning this afternoon—he'd once again rejected the possibility, even more grateful that Elizabeth's return to wakefulness had stayed his tongue. Despite all the advantages such a marriage might offer them both, with his dreadful record as a husband, he couldn't bear risking the possibility that the warmth and respect they now shared might disintegrate into the bitterness and anger his union with Lydia had become.

But just now, as he listened to the music, a more encouraging realisation had struck him. If, in some distant future, they should fall into discord, Olivia could live apart from him—in England.

Where she would be safe. Safe to return to her political world in London. With the increase in income he expected the estate would produce by then he'd able to rent her that house in the capital, where she might devote herself to the political causes she loved. Still linked to the girls, still shielded from penury and proposals from unworthy suitors. Still *his*, even at a distance.

The thought of having her near, protecting her—and at last, at last, being able to make love to her—made his senses and spirits soar.

She might well react to a proposal with indignation and summarily reject him. Despite that probability, he'd summon up his courage and speak to her—this very night.

He had his eyes closed, savouring the last chord, when her soft voice startled him. 'It won't…disturb me if you wish to sit in the room,' she said, turning on the piano bench to face him. 'Heaven knows I make enough mistakes not to be vain about my performance. If you have the time to listen, you don't need to stand outside the door.'

'Thank you. I truly didn't wish to disturb you.' It was her disturbing effect on *him* he always struggled to resist, he thought as he walked into the room.

Though perhaps, if she were willing to take on a conflicted widower, a not-yet-restored estate and the care of two little girls not her own, he might no longer have to resist her.

But how to begin?

While he pondered that, she said, 'Now that you are here, I wanted to thank you again for driving us to Bristol today. The girls are still so excited! I had to promise Elizabeth I would take her to visit Pierre first thing tomorrow before I could get her to lie quietly enough to fall asleep.'

She chuckled. 'Then I had to return to the stables and tell John Coachman again how grateful I am that he allowed us to keep Pierre in the stables tonight, how much

I appreciate his forbearance in giving temporary shelter to a creature that brings the girls so much comfort, being such a beautiful reminder of their homeland. I promised him I'd have another home for the parrot by tomorrow.'

'Laid it on thick, did you?' he asked with an answering chuckle, coming over to stand beside the piano bench—his heart skipping a beat at her nearness and the audacity of the proposition he was about to make.

'Inches deep. You saw the look he gave when we brought in the parrot! I might have also promised him I'd have Cook prepare a basket of his favourite foods tomorrow. Else I feared we might find the poor bird had mysteriously expired in its cage some time in the night, which would devastate the children. I… I'm also glad that you are feeling easier around the girls. I still feel guilty for berating you about them when I first arrived. I've lost brother, father and mother and I know how much that hurts.'

'Your mother's loss was quite recent, wasn't it?' he asked quietly, giving in to the temptation of sitting beside her.

She nodded. 'It was losing her that sent me into service. As you guessed, I didn't want to become a charge upon the cousin who'd inherited the estate and then my mother's house.'

'I find it strange that neither your father nor your mother left you a legacy.'

She laughed shortly. 'My father left me quite a handsome one. Unfortunately, my trustees saw fit to invest virtually all of it and my mother's in an investment that went bankrupt.'

Yet one more loss to add to all she had suffered. 'I'm so sorry. It must have been a terrible shock. To believe you would be living in comfortable circumstances, and then discover…you would not.'

She shrugged. 'What was there to do? One takes stock of the choices one is left and m-moves on.'

It was the little catch in her voice as she spoke those brave words, the soft sheen of the tears in her eyes he saw gleaming in the candlelight, that gave him the courage—and the opportunity—to broach his proposition.

'It occurred to me on the road home today that there might be an alternative to you continuing a life in service. What if you were to enter into a marriage of convenience…with me? Don't respond at once,' he added quickly, as her eyes widened. 'I know the suggestion comes as a surprise. Please, let me explain.'

Too shocked—or horrified—to speak, she sat silently as he continued, 'I know you've grown fond of the girls and they certainly adore you. Were we to marry, you would have a legal and permanent claim to them, while they would finally have that lady of wisdom and breeding so necessary to guide them into becoming capable, refined young women. It would be no less a blessing for me, gaining me a skilled hostess, a clever and amiable companion, and a partner in raising the children and restoring Somers Abbey to its former splendour. While it would offer *you* a return to your rightful status and position, eliminate the necessity for you to earn your bread among strangers and permanently free you from the threat of penury.'

Hardly stopping for breath, he forged on to the most difficult part. 'On a more personal level, I—I couldn't, in all honesty, pledge you my heart. I'm not sure, after the events of India, I have one left to offer. But I could promise you respect, kindness, compassion and fidelity. And this,' he concluded, easing her into his arms.

He'd planned to immediately release her after one brief hug. But as he held her, she snuggled closer and rested her head on his chest. As if she, too, had longed to be there for ever, in his arms.

'Will you consider my proposition, my lovely, Managing Miss Overton?' he whispered into her hair.

'I can't... I... Oh, I don't know how to answer!'

'Don't answer—not yet. Take time to think about it, as much time as you need. Whatever you decide, you may be assured of my continued respect and protection.'

Saying that, he released her, his heart beating rapidly with both hope and trepidation. He couldn't say which frightened him more—the possibility that she would refuse—or that she might accept.

Had he really had the audacity to propose to her, when he couldn't pledge the soul-deep love so beautiful a soul deserved?

But now it was no longer his decision. He would abide by hers—whatever it turned out to be.

Feeling calmer and more at peace than he had in months, Hugh rose, dropped a kiss on the top of her head and walked from the room.

All through the following day, Olivia went about her work absently, tired after a sleepless night spent tossing and turning as she examined the alternatives over and over, without being able to reach a decision.

In the afternoon, she took the girls for a long walk across the meadows and through the nearest orchard, hoping the crisp, warm air fragrant with the aroma of growing apples would clear her mind and bring her endless circular arguments to a halt. But she arrived back at the house without reaching any conclusion—other than that she must make up her mind soon, before she drove herself mad with indecision.

After tucking the girls into bed that evening, she wandered back to her room and hopped on to the bed, her mind once again filled with conflicting thoughts and desires.

The advantages of such a match were so overwhelming, she ought to accept without another thought. To know she would have her darling girls with her for ever, a home in the countryside she was growing to love, the security of a permanent place—and the affection and protection of a man as honourable, stalwart, and attractive as Hugh Glendenning should be more then incentive enough.

Were she to know Olivia had been offered so attractive a proposal, Lady Patterson would call her an idiot for hesitating a second before seizing it.

Still, if she'd been content to settle for a convenient marriage with a man who wanted her to run his house and mind his children, she could have accepted one of the several offers she'd received over the years in London. Hadn't she vowed never to give up her independence for anything less than marrying a man who *loved* her—without reservations?

The Colonel *was* honourable, stalwart and almost irresistibly attractive. Despite the huge incentive of knowing she would have him at her beck and call in her bed, she knew she was more than half in love with him already. If she were to have the girls to love and the Colonel in her bed, knowing all she could hope for from him was respect and affection, spiced with a fiery passion, would it be enough?

Or would she condemn herself to a lifetime of heartache, losing her heart to a man who'd already confessed he no longer had one to give?

Over time, once he grew to trust in completely in your fidelity and affection, he would learn to love again, a little voice whispered.

Perhaps, she answered it back.

But what if he could not? The heart and soul, like the body, were capable of recovering from grave injuries. But not from all.

Was she willing to gamble on the possibility that the Colonel would eventually recover from his?

Would you throw away the potential for a lifetime of happiness, because you are too cowardly to accept that risk?

When she phrased it in those terms, she swayed towards accepting him. She had never backed down from a challenge, or refused to take a risk that had a good chance for success—as she had when she'd abandoned the security of remaining her cousin's dependent to brave the uncertainty of striking out on her own.

Then another, more troubling, thought occurred. Now that he knew the truth of her circumstances, knew also how attached his wards had become to her—and she to them—had the Colonel felt almost *obligated* to offer for her? Had he done so out of a sense of duty and chivalry—nobly rescuing an indigent gentlewoman whom he admired—while secretly hoping she would refuse?

Still torn, she shook her head. The Colonel had said

she could have as long as she liked to make her decision. She simply *couldn't* make it right now.

Giving herself permission to postpone her final answer eased the turmoil churning within her. To be able to put it from her mind completely, at least for an evening, she needed the soothing effect of music.

Hopping down from her bed, she shook out her skirts and headed for the music room.

While working on the estate books in his library a half-hour later, the supper tray Mansfield had brought him set aside, mostly untouched, Hugh heard the muted chords of the first few measures of a Mozart concerto.

A mingling of disappointment and relief filtered through him. Miss Overton must not have yet decided whether or not to accept his proposition, else she would have come to see him directly after putting the children to bed.

His own emotions continued to seesaw wildly from a muted excitement about the possibility of having her permanently in his life, to a deep foreboding that trapping her into marriage with a man who'd never fully recovered from the disaster of his first union was a prescription for misery.

He knew what she wanted to hear—vows to love and cherish. Much as he told himself the proposal he'd made her had been offered purely out of a desire to find an honourable solution to problems posed by the clash of his passions and responsibilities, he knew it was more than that. He'd been strongly drawn to Olivia Overton from the first. But his ever-strengthening affection was all tangled up with lust and loneliness and longing…and fear.

Fear that something that started out so precious might

somehow, inexplicably, fall apart, like waves at the Indian Ocean seashore washing away one's handful of sand, no matter how tightly one tried to cling to it.

Fear that he couldn't risk having his heart shattered again and survive.

Though he might not be able to make Miss Overton the sort of proposal she wanted, he very much wanted her to remain at Somers Abbey.

For his wards' sake. And his own.

Much as he yearned to know his fate, until she made her decision, he would not have to deal with the consequences of either choice.

Closing the ledger, he leaned back in his chair and let the distant chords wash over him, the music seeping under his skin to loosen the knots of tension in his neck and shoulders.

Though it would do a much more effective job of soothing if he could hear it better. Besides, hadn't Miss Overton invited him to sit in the salon while she played?

He decided he'd take her up on that offer. And be able to fully enjoy one of the beauties she'd brought back to his life.

Not wishing to distract her, he walked in silently and slipped into a chair. But with a sixth sense—probably the same one that always alerted him when she was near—she seemed to sense his presence. As soon as the movement concluded, she turned towards him.

'If you are going to listen, do you have any requests?'

To his relief, the question was framed in a smile, with no trace of the awkwardness he feared she might feel upon seeing him again after his unexpected proposal. Smiling back, he said, 'Beethoven again, if you please.'

'Beethoven it shall be.' Turning back to the keyboard,

she said, 'If I continue to practise it, I might even learn to play it competently, instead of dodging the most difficult parts.'

'Your performance sounds wonderfully competent to me.'

She chuckled. 'Which makes you a pianist's ideal audience—uncritical and appreciative.'

Still smiling, he settled in to listen, content to lose himself in the music that filled his ears and trickled a sense of calm and content into his soul.

If she accepted him, he might look forward to evenings like this for ever.

When the final chords sounded, he gave her a round of applause. 'That was beautiful! Dare I request an encore?'

Shaking her head, she rose from the bench and walked towards him. 'With the girls waking so early, it's time for me to retire. Before I do, though,' she added, halting by his chair, 'I wanted to let you know that, though I'm not yet completely sure, I am leaning towards accepting your kind proposal. If you are still offering it, of course.'

A wave of excitement swept through him as he stood up beside her. 'I am. And I would be happy and honoured, should you decide to accept.'

He reached over to take her hand and bring it to his lips. 'Thank you again for the concert. I shall bid you goodnight and live in hope.'

Though the little exhale of breath he heard as he kissed her fingertips fired his always-smouldering desire, he knew he must release her. To his surprise, though, tightening her grip, she retained his hand. Then gazed up at him.

'You do know how to tempt me,' she murmured, rubbing her fingers against his.

The sultry look in her eyes sent a shock through him and ratcheted desire up several notches. Was she asking for what he thought she was?

Eager enough to take a gamble, he said, 'Do I? Then let me tempt you further.'

Tipping her chin up, he leaned down and finally, finally gave her the kiss he'd dreamt of since practically the moment he'd first seen her. And exulted that he must have read her wishes correctly, for she leaned into him.

He'd meant it to be chaste, an expression of how much he cared for her and wanted to ease her burdens. But that first, simple brush of his mouth against hers wasn't enough.

Apparently, she didn't think so either, for when he lifted his to move away, she wrapped her arms around his neck and pulled him down again, her mouth seeking his.

Despite an arousal now so hard it was almost pain, he truly intended to take just one more kiss. But then he simply had to trace her lips with his tongue, then slip it into her mouth and taste her.

She gasped, then opened to him and pressed closer still.

And then he was lost in her, drowning in the honeyed sweetness of her mouth, the delectable shell of her ear, the smooth soft expanse of neck she arched for him. He kissed his way down to the froth of lace of her collar and back to her mouth, where she met him tongue for tongue, her lack of expertise more than made up by her passion.

Conscious thought submerged by desire, he slid a hand down to her breast and felt the nipple tighten beneath its imprisoning layers of gown, stays and chemise. Still caressing her, he wrapped his other arm around her shoulder and bound her close, worshipping her mouth with deep, thought-numbing kisses.

A mindless imperative roared at him to bury himself in her and find bliss. Trying to resist it, he forced himself to move his hand back to her shoulder.

Where, to his surprise, she caught it and slid it back down.

Delighted to comply with her unspoken demand, he caressed her again, damning the multiple layers that barred him from touching the soft, sweet skin of her breast and the pebbled texture of her nipple. The mere thought of her, bared to the waist and open to his hands and mouth, fired him with longing.

But while he fought to limit himself just to kisses, when she pressed herself against his aching erection and moved her hand down his side, as if intending to touch him, he knew he must break off the kiss and step away.

After he did, she looked up at him, her expression befuddled, her eyes dark with passion, and her mouth so seductively reddened from his kisses it was all he could do not to pull her back into his arms.

Instead, biting back a curse, he took another step back.

She reached out to grab his wrist. 'Don't stop now, please! I want *more*.'

He uttered a ragged sound somewhere between a laugh and a groan. 'Sweet tormenter, if I don't stop now, I won't be able to stop. I'm thrilled that you want more. But I respect you too much to take you unless my wedding ring is on your finger. The consequences of doing so without that are too dangerous.'

For another long moment, she simply stared at him, as if the words he'd uttered made no sense. At length, she shook her head, seeming finally to break free of the sensual spell. 'Yes, you are right, of course.'

She uttered a ragged sigh that echoed his own frustrated need. 'Then I'd better make up my mind quickly, mustn't I? For now, I will bid you goodnight.' Dropping him a deep, formal curtsy, she walked towards the door.

At the threshold, she paused to glance back. 'I'll say goodnight and go to bed. My lonely, *lonely* bed.' Giving him a saucy, come-hither look, she slipped out.

Hugh tightened his hands into fists and concentrated on taking long, even breaths as he resisted the desire to follow her.

Chapter Eighteen

Her body still throbbing with frustrated desire, her mind swerving from euphoric visions of a happy future to the possibility of heartbreak, Olivia drifted up to her room and wandered over to her bed.

The Colonel had been wise to pull away from her when he had, she thought as she hopped on to it and collapsed against the pillows. She'd been one slender scruple away from urging him to pull her on to the sofa, strip down her drawers and take her.

Not until tonight had she fully realised just how primitive and powerful the pull of passion could be. Even now, every needy, aching feminine part of her was protesting being denied that ultimate, intimate closeness.

A closeness she wanted to experience only with him. Because, she realised with sudden clarity, she wasn't just 'more than half' in love with Hugh Glendenning. She'd fallen for him completely.

Had it truly been little over a month since she'd determined to leave London? In the brief handful of weeks she'd been at Somers Abbey, her life had changed dramatically. She'd become attached to two little girls desperately in need of affection and security. And foolishly thinking she could indulge her attraction to the Colonel and remain heart-whole, she'd let herself stumble into love with him.

Even after learning of the tragedies that would make it difficult, if not impossible, for him to love again.

For a moment, agonised as she tried to decide between accepting and rejecting his proposal, a third, if craven, alternative occurred to her—packing her few things and leaving Somers Abbey.

Returning to Sara in London—and doing what? Wallowing in the misery she'd brought on herself, while she searched for a new position?

But…she'd promised Elizabeth she would remain at Somers Abbey as long as the children needed her. The little girl had only just begun to feel safe enough to laugh and play and even misbehave on occasion. Olivia couldn't strip her of that budding sense of security just because staying on threatened her with heartache.

So she wasn't going anywhere.

Which left her one stark choice. She could marry the fascinating, honourable, driven man she desired so much. Or simply remain governess to his wards, suppressing her love and passion for him, until time, or some female relative, relieved her of that role.

An almost impossible task.

If she meant to stay on, she might as well cast aside her doubts and accept the risk. Accept the Colonel's proposal and throw all her heart and soul into loving him, hoping he might one day love her in return.

She held her breath, waiting for the protective little voice in her head to protest that decision. When, instead, the choice settled in with a sense of calm and rightness, she felt the first stirrings of peace descend over her troubled spirit.

Relieved to be headed towards a return of her usual calm, she began preparing for bed. Preparing for what might well be one of the last few nights she would sleep alone, she realised, excitement at the prospect of sensual fulfilment overriding her lingering anxiety.

For a moment, she considered going to find the Colonel to announce her acceptance at once. But he had doubtless already retired. She didn't relish the prospect of creeping around this dark warren of a house, searching for his bedchamber.

Instead, she'd wait until tomorrow and inform the Colonel of her decision at her first opportunity.

As it happened, the next morning, Olivia was setting out reading books and slates in the schoolroom, preparing to give the girls their first lesson, when Mary halted on the room's threshold. 'The master asked if you would come to the library, miss.'

Delight, dread and anticipation washed over her. She'd let him detail whatever task had led him to summon her, then reveal her news. The knowledge that she was about to announce a decision that would have enormous consequences for the entire future course of her life stirred up nervousness and a touch of nausea in her belly.

Best to get it over with quickly, and move forward—into the rest of their lives together.

'Tell him I'll be down directly.'

Trying to quell her nervous excitement, Olivia halted on the library threshold. Before she could speak, or even curtsy, the Colonel said, 'Please come in and take a seat, Miss Overton.'

Surprised by his cool, formal tone, so markedly different from the warm friendliness of the past few days, she walked over to the place he indicated.

'What was it you wished to see me about, sir?'

As she gazed up at him after taking her seat, the look of anguish on his face sucked the breath from her. He appeared more miserable and weary than she'd ever seen him. Instinctively she knew that whatever he had to convey was far more dire than some question of supplies for the schoolroom, or finding a more appropriate room to house the new parrot.

'What's happened?' she cried. 'And what can I do to help?'

'I'm afraid there isn't anything you can do,' he replied, forcing a smile. 'Except to be careful what you wish for, I suppose. You'll recall when you first arrived, I indicated that your period of employment might be shorter than six months, as I'd written to several female relations, looking for one who might want to take on the raising of the girls. After having received not a single offer, I'd concluded I would have to keep them here.'

Olivia's chest tightened, already anticipating the blow. 'But now you have an offer.'

He nodded. 'I received a letter today from my great-aunt, Lady Laversby. Apparently she was on the Continent when my note arrived at Laversby Hall and just recently returned to find it. She writes that she would be thrilled to have the children. It would, she said, remind her of the happy time when her own long-married daughters were growing up. To sum it up, she's already given orders for the old nursery rooms to be freshened, hired two nursery maids, recalled her daughters' former governess and is on her way to Somers Abbey to collect the girls.'

Absently, Olivia noted the ticking of the mantel clock in the silence as she tried to wrap her mind around the shocking news. Finally, the most pertinent question surfaced. 'You...you're not really going to send them away with a stranger, are you? When they are just now, finally, beginning to feel at home? At home...with us?'

Sighing, he wiped a hand across his brow. 'As I'm sure you're aware, one of the driving reasons for my offering you a marriage of convenience was to ensure that a proper female would oversee the upbringing of my wards. Much as I dislike having to displace them again, my great-aunt could provide that. She's a warm, outgoing, sympathetic woman who genuinely loves children. I'm sure, in time, the girls will flourish with her.'

Her concern for the girls distracting her, for the moment, from considering the implications his decision would mean for her, Olivia stared at him. 'But...you told me yourself you'd become...fond of them and I know they care about you! Are you really going to just...let them go?'

'What else can I do?' he cried out. 'Lady Laversby has the means, and the staff, to create a perfect environment for them. Wardrobes full of pretty dresses, toys, dolls, trips to London, nursery maids to wait on their every need. I can't give them that. Not now. Perhaps not for years to come.'

'But those things are only of surface importance! As one who has sustained enough losses to know, pretty dresses and dolls and servants can't compare to being somewhere you feel secure, with someone you can depend upon to love and care for you! Please, please, if you care about them at all, don't uproot them again!'

He closed his eyes, as if bracing himself against a pain too difficult to bear, before continuing, 'You haven't yet asked what I planned to do about my other, major reason for suggesting a marriage of convenience—securing *your* future. But despite my concern for that, and the girls, I should never have allowed myself to propose, when all I have to offer is debts…and brokenness.'

The implications of what he'd just said hit her with the force of a hammer blow. 'So you are…withdrawing that offer.'

Giving her no answer, he jumped up from behind the desk, pacing the room in anguished silence before finally stopping beside her.

'You can't imagine how spectacularly wrong my marriage went. I wouldn't wish that kind of misery on anyone again—myself, or anyone else.'

It struck her then that he didn't know she was aware of the real circumstances surrounding his wife's death. Now, with him already upset, didn't seem the right time to enlighten him.

Besides, he'd just confirmed her worst fears—that he had offered for her, not for the chance to build a future and recover from the tragedies of the past, but to provide for his wards—and save her from a lifetime in service.

She ought to nod and say she understood, and retire with as much dignity as she could muster, grateful she hadn't humiliated herself by blurting out on arrival her acceptance of the proposal he had just withdrawn.

But despite all the reasons she should remain silent, she couldn't help seizing one last chance to argue for their future.

'Why do you feel you must be responsible for the happiness and well-being of everyone? The girls, perhaps—they are just children. But I'm an adult. As I told you before, it is *my* job to make the best of where I am—and who I'm with. To face, and communicate about, any difficulties that might arise. The tragedies life throws at one can make any of us splinter and crack. It's not weakness, but strength, to reach out to someone else, someone who truly cares for one's well-being, to help weather them.'

Seeing the turmoil so clearly written on his face, she wanted to push him harder. But she'd already gone further than she should. Her mother would have expired of mortification on the spot had she been present to hear her.

'You don't understand—how could you?' he said softly at last. Looking at her with longing—and resignation—he said, 'I can't take the chance of ruining any more lives. Lady Laversby should arrive tomorrow. She indicated in her note that she wished to make only a short stay, perhaps just overnight. She's anxious to meet the girls and escort them to their new home.'

Willing herself not to complete her humiliation by bursting into tears, Olivia swallowed hard. Hugh Glendenning obviously desired her and she was almost certain he cared for her, too. Perhaps enough to glimpse, glimmering on the horizon, the same hazy vision of a happy future together that beckoned her.

A future they could never reach unless he was willing to move beyond the past. But sadly, he wouldn't, or couldn't, take that leap.

'So that's that. You will, I hope, at least tell them in advance what is going to happen?' she asked, trying to keep the bitterness and distress from her voice.

'Of course. I'll come up to the schoolroom and tell them later today.'

The schoolroom—where she'd been about to have Pierre transferred. Inane as it was in the face of her whole world collapsing, she found herself asking, 'What will happen to the parrot?'

He gave a grimace of a smile. 'If Lady Laversby won't have it, I think I'll put Pierre in the library.'

'So when do you wish me to leave? Today? Or am I permitted to say goodbye to the children before they go?'

He closed his eyes briefly again at the sharpness of her tone. 'You may leave whenever you like. Though I would appreciate your remaining until after Lady Laversby collects the children.'

'So they may have another day or so with someone they know, before they are shipped off with strangers again?'

She was being unfair, but she couldn't seem to help herself. In a mere handful of hours, she would be losing both the girls—and him. She felt as though her bones were splintering inside her, whole seas of organs dissolving and washing away.

He didn't bother responding to that jibe. 'You will receive your full six months' salary, of course. Let John know when and how you'd like to travel back to London and he'll make the arrangements. There's just one thing more. As I'd already mentioned, the other driving reason for my offering marriage was to secure your future and see you restored to your proper position in life. I still intend to do that, but in a manner that will not threaten your happiness by entangling your life with mine.'

Returning to his desk, he pulled a small leather pouch from a drawer. As he dropped it on to the desk, she heard the musical clank of coins. 'Before you leave, I want you to have this. By rights, it belongs to you.'

Confused, she examined the bag with a frown. 'I don't own a pouch like that and I certainly don't have extra funds to place in one.'

'It contains the money Mrs Wallace embezzled over the years. Since you discovered her villainy, it really should be yours. What would you say if I told you this bag held enough to pay for two years of rent for the house on Judd Street? So that upon your return to London you might secure the home you told me about and share it with Miss Standish. Resume your place in society, take up your work again with the Committee and the orphan school. Do all the things that mean so much to you.'

The generosity of his gesture dropped into the vast sea of her anguish and disappeared without a trace. After he'd shattered her heart and ground the pieces into his library floor, he had the gall to offer her *money*?

A pain that cut so deep she couldn't breathe was followed by an all-consuming fury. Leaping up from her chair, she marched to the door and turned to look at him.

'Many thanks for your *kind* consideration, but I think not.'

With that, she stalked out of the library, slamming the door with every bit of strength she could muster.

At least she wouldn't have to break the awful news to the girls, Olivia thought as she walked numbly back up to her room. Since the children, who after their experiences were particularly sensitive to changes in emotion, would be able to sense in an instant that something was amiss, she couldn't go back to the schoolroom just yet.

Not until she'd composed herself enough to show them a serene face.

She supposed it was some sort of victory that the Colonel had almost—almost—managed to pry himself from the ghosts of his past. She already knew he desired her and he'd just come very close to admitting he loved her.

Just not close enough.

Not that she blamed him for that failure—after all he had endured, how could she? There wasn't a cowardly bone in his body—indeed, if he had a fault, it was in trying to take responsibility for everyone and everything, rather than shrinking away from the challenge.

He was already trying to open his heart again to children whom experience told him could die. How could she fault him for not wishing to open it further for a woman who could betray?

Was it just yesterday that they'd returned from that trip to Bristol? When, for that blissful day, they'd seemed almost like…a family? Not truly a family yet, of course. There hadn't been enough time to solidify those tentative bonds. But oh, how sure she was that they might have become one!

But instinctively she knew, too, that everyone has a limit beyond which a loss cuts too deep to heal. No one could decide what that limit was for another and it wasn't kind or fair to try to push the Colonel past his.

If only she'd met him before India—when his heart was still open and undamaged.

And hadn't her life these last few months been filled with might-have-beens?

Idiot, her practical mind responded. If she had met him before India, he would have been in love with a golden Beauty and wouldn't have looked twice at a tall, plain, managing, brown-haired spinster.

What would happen to her and the girls had already been decided and she had no power to change that decision. Rather than indulge in pointless imaginings, she would do better to pack her few things, decide how and when she meant to travel back to London…and figure out how she was going to say goodbye to the girls.

She already knew she couldn't bear saying goodbye to the Colonel.

In the afternoon two days later, Olivia put the last item in her trunk, latched it and gave it to the waiting groom to take to the stables. She would go to the schoolroom, say goodbye to the girls before their new nursery maid summoned them to join Lady Laversby, who was waiting downstairs with the Colonel to escort them to her travelling carriage, and then leave Somers Abbey.

She'd decided that she would not share her last few minutes with the girls with a roomful of strangers—and the Colonel—looking on. It had been bad enough last night, escorting them down for their first meeting with his great-aunt and then sitting in the corner, stiff and silent and invisible, like a proper governess, while their new protector embraced them and chatted about all the delights that awaited them at Laversby Hall.

She was trying to steel herself to be as cheerful and positive as possible before she went to the schoolroom, knowing her distress would only make her apprehensive charges—former charges, she amended—more uncertain and uneasy than they already were.

Deciding she was as ready as she was likely to get, she squared her shoulders and left her room.

She barely made it inside the schoolroom before Sophie flung herself at her, arms around her knees and clinging to her skirts. Elizabeth remained seated on her bed, ankles crossed decorously, misery and trepidation on her face.

'Do we have to go, Miss Overton?' she asked.

Putting an arm around Sophie, she walked her to the bed, lifted her up beside her sister and then sat beside them.

'I'm afraid you do, my dear. But you are going to like your new home very much. Lady Laversby is such a kind lady, isn't she? And she is so excited about having you come to live with her! Remember how she described the rooms you will have, with large bright windows, and curtains and coverlets of whatever colour you choose? She has a dressmaker waiting there to make up new gowns for you. And a whole family of dolls! I expect there may be ponies, too.'

'Why can't we stay with you?' Elizabeth asked.

'Well, you see, the Colonel is your papa's cousin and Lady Laversby is his great-aunt, so you are all family. I'm not related to you in any way, so I don't have the right to keep you.'

'Couldn't you come with us?'

'I'm just the governess. I'm…hired, a servant, like Cook or Mary. The Colonel engaged me to work here at Somers Abbey, but Lady Laversby decides who will work at her home. She already has two maids to help you and she wants the very, very nice lady who was governess to her own girls, who loved them and took such very good care of them, to take care of you, too. So…she doesn't need me to work for her.'

'We do.'

Her heart stuttering, Olivia took a deep breath. 'It will be strange at first, but I'll write to you, so you must work hard and learn your letters so you can read my notes all by yourself. And there will be so many wonderful things to see and do that, soon, you'll be so happy there you will hardly remember being here at Somers Abbey.'

Elizabeth shook her head. 'I won't forget. The warm soft nightgowns you got for us and picking flowers in the garden and the screaming game. We won't be able to play the screaming game at the new house, will we?'

Olivia could only imagine the reaction of the Colonel's very proper great-aunt. 'Probably not.'

'New gowns will be nice, but I want the ones from the material we picked out. The ones you were going to make for us.'

'I can still make them for you, sweetheart.'

'You promise?'

'I promise.'

'Will you come and bring them to us when you're finished? Please?'

She really ought not to promise anything. Even with her fare back to London paid and the six months' salary she'd found on the table in her room last night, she would have to be very careful with funds. She didn't know how long it would take her to find another position and she really didn't want to depend on Sara's charity.

Just as she'd refused to depend on the Colonel's, she thought bitterly, pain slicing through her again at the memory of his misplaced generosity.

Lady Laversby probably wouldn't be thrilled at having the girls' former governess showing up uninvited, either, creating a rather awkward social situation. She was no longer a lady to be entertained as a guest, but not exactly a servant to share a room with the maids, either.

To say nothing of the fact that the best thing for Olivia personally would be to return to London and try to relegate every heartbreaking detail of her life at Somers Abbey to the deepest, darkest part of her memory as quickly as possible.

But looking at the woebegone expression on Elizabeth's face, and with Sophie silently weeping on her sleeve, she couldn't bring herself to refuse.

'Yes, sweeting, once I finish the gowns, I will bring them to you.'

'How soon will you finish them?'

Despite her own tears that threatened, she had to smile at the little girl's persistence. 'It will be several weeks. You must not worry if it seems like a long time. I promised to come and I will.'

There was a tap at the door, Lady Laversby's nursery maid entering after the knock. Giving Olivia a curtsy, she said, 'My mistress is waiting downstairs for the young ladies. If you would follow me, girls?'

Sophie clutched her shoulder, but brave little Elizabeth swallowed hard and, with quiet determination, slipped off the bed.

'Now, if you please, miss,' the maid said to her, making a 'shooing' motion at Sophie.

'Give us a moment, won't you?' Olivia said sharply, glaring at the girl, who rolled her eyes, but retreated into the hallway.

Anguish building within her, she helped Sophie off the bed. 'Best go down now, girls. We don't want to give Lady Laversby a bad impression, being late from the start.'

Nodding, Elizabeth took her sister's hand. 'We have to go, Sophie.'

'Goodbye, sweet girls,' Olivia whispered.

'Goodbye, Miss Overton. I l-love you,' Elizabeth whispered back.

And then they were both clinging to her, Olivia kneeling to wrap them tightly in her arms. She could feel Sophie's shoulders shaking, the wetness of Elizabeth's tears at her shoulder where the little girl had buried her face. Her own breathing was ragged as she struggled to hold herself together.

At last, she released them, placed a kiss on each girl's forehead and gently ushered them out into the hall, where the maid waited.

'Come along, young misses,' the girl said and shepherded them towards the stairs.

Not sure she could stand it if either of them looked back, Olivia hastily retreated into the schoolroom. Once the echo of their footsteps faded, she placed both hands over her mouth to hold in the wail she mustn't utter. Light-headed, agony slashing her chest, she leaned against the doorframe, gasping for breath as she choked down sobs.

It took her a few minutes to master herself. Once she was reasonably calm again, she walked back to her room, scanned it one last time for any items she might have overlooked, then donned her pelisse and gathered up her reticule and a small bandbox. She headed for the door, hesitated and, unable to prevent herself, walked over to the window, which overlooked the front drive.

She stood there, numb and aching, until she saw Lady Laversby's carriage bowl down the carriageway.

Suddenly feeling driven to quit Somers Abbey as

quickly as possible, she hurried out the door and over to the servants' stairs, swiftly descended to the kitchen, slipped out the back door and hustled towards the stables.

Her silent, solitary exit was fitting. No one had welcomed her to Somers Abbey. She couldn't bear to have any of the staff she'd come to like and appreciate bid her farewell.

She walked into the stable yard to see the landau hitched up, her trunks strapped to the back, one of the grooms at the horses' heads.

Leaning out the stable door, John said, 'I'll be ready to drive you to the posting inn in a minute, miss. Just as soon as I help the grooms carry that great hulking bird up to the library.'

Chapter Nineteen

Three weeks later, Hugh set his horse towards the Abbey at a trot. One of the grooms, returning from the village past the north meadow where he was supervising the drainage work, had mentioned a letter had been delivered for him.

Though he told himself that it was most unlikely the missive came from Olivia Overton, he knew he wouldn't be able to wait until nightfall to find out.

She'd left without a word—not that her silent exit had surprised him. What other words were there to say, after all? And though he did hope she might pen him a note, just to inform him she'd arrived safely back at her friend's house in London, that was probably asking too much as well. After he'd tendered her a proposal and then revoked it—even though he'd done so for her own good—then offered her the funds to return to her former life—an offer she'd taken as an insult, rather than the testament to his affection and regard he'd intended—she probably wanted nothing further to do with him. Undoubtedly, she was still furious with him for sending the girls away.

In time, she would recover. At least he'd let her go

before he'd roped her into a union where any misery he caused her could be permanent.

Which was why *he* had not sought *her* out to say goodbye. He hadn't been sure his resolve wouldn't have cracked, driving him to promise her whatever she wanted to keep her at Somers Abbey.

Arriving at the stable yard, he jumped down from the saddle and tossed the mare's reins to the groom who came running up. 'Rub her down and give her some water. I'll be riding out again shortly.'

Nodding to the groom's salute, he walked briskly to the entrance, calling for Mansfield as he crossed the threshold. When the old man appeared, he said, 'Thomas said there was a letter for me?'

'Yes, sir. I put it on your desk in the library.'

He didn't care that Mansfield stared as he took the steps up two at a time.

But, as he'd feared, the handwriting on the missive that sat on his desk was Lady Laversby's.

Foolish to feel desolation spiral in his gut over a letter from the wrong sender.

At least he knew his wards had safely arrived. Gritting his teeth to move past the pain, he broke the seal and began reading.

Though the girls missed him, his aunt wrote, they were settling in well and she was making sure they received lots of cuddling and coddling. Cook had been instructed to make all their favourite treats, she'd promised them a lovely English dog to replace the nasty parrot they'd left behind and she was certain they were all going to get on splendidly.

Smiling faintly, he remembered Elizabeth's gasp of awe when she'd first seen Pierre in the Bristol market, mimicking the voices of the passers-by. How Sophie had jumped up and down and clapped her hands when he finally agreed to purchase the parrot.

And how Olivia—now that she was safely far away, he would call her Olivia—had teased and cajoled, admiring the parrot's beauty, urging him to see how good it would be for the girls to have this feathered friend to remind them of home—until Somers Abbey *became* home.

But the girls would forget him, too. The sting of leaving Somers Abbey would fade into the delight of living with a lady who could provide the host of material benefits and motherly guidance he could not. Who would bring them up to be acquainted with other young ladies of their class, introduce them to other society leaders who would assist Lady Laversby in making sure their eventual debuts were successful and guide them to choose perfect husbands.

No, as much as he'd felt new holes being carved in his chest as he watched his great-aunt's carriage carry them away, he knew his duty as their guardian was to place them in a situation that was best for them.

Not where it was best for him.

And he would visit them, as he'd promised Elizabeth as he walked her to Lady Laversby's carriage. As soon as he thought he could do so without giving in to the urge to tell his great-aunt he'd changed his mind and was taking them back.

Putting her letter in the drawer, he swiped a hand over his face. He'd thought he'd experienced the worst a man could suffer when he lost Drew and Lydia. But this wasn't much easier.

His gaze flitted to the whisky bottle on the sideboard. Thus far, he'd resisted the urge to find oblivion at the bottom of a glass, making himself sip the fiery liquid slowly as he sat at night in the dimness of a library lit only by the fire in the grate, most of the dinner Cook had sent up to tempt him sitting untouched on the tray. Food didn't appeal and he tried his best not to return to the Abbey until the summer sky had fallen completely black, the winking stars guiding him home. Not returning until he was as exhausted as he could make himself after taking up a shovel to help with digging the drainage ditches, or pollarding row after row in the willow groves, heaving the heavy limbs into the wagons.

Even then, sleep eluded him. But lying awake was better than the dreams that delighted and tormented him.

The ones where Olivia lay under him, arms and legs wrapped around him as he entered her, making them one. Where he loved her long and slow until she shattered with ecstasy, calling his name. Where he watched her as she slept, her unbraided hair spread over his pillow, then dozed and awoke to a marvellous new day, with every new day marvellous, because he could lean over and gather her into his arms.

We might have been happy, his stubborn heart kept whispering.

But you were certain you and Lydia would be happy, he answered it back. *And how terribly awry that went.*

More importantly, he wanted Olivia to be happy. One only had to see the glow that came over her when she talked about London to know she belonged there.

Enough! Shaking his head, he pulled his mind free from those torturous, and ultimately fruitless, arguments.

He'd survived before. He would survive this. And he should content himself with the knowledge that having taken these painful steps would, in the end, make the future better for both his wards and Olivia.

That *should* make him feel better—but it didn't.

'Fool,' he muttered to himself—only to have Pierre, who'd been looking out the window his cage had been placed in front of, turn to him and echo, 'Fool! Fool!'

'I wonder if you would have persuaded Sophie to talk,' he said to the bird.

'Sophie talk! Sophie talk!'

That remark stuck another little needle of pain into his chest. 'Maybe I should cover your cage,' he retorted.

After which, wisely, Pierre went silent.

He was about to rise from his desk and return to the stables when Mansfield rapped at the door. 'Your friend, Mr Saulter, just arrived, Colonel,' he said as he walked in. 'He said he couldn't stay the night, as he is on his way to London, but didn't want to pass by without at least stopping in for a drink. Shall I show him up, or would you prefer to join him in the salon?'

'Bring him up, Mansfield. And see if Cook can put together a tray. I doubt he would refuse a bit of meat and cheese with his wine before he resumes his journey.'

His spirits brightened slightly at the thought of seeing his old friend. Although he dreaded the explanations he was going to have to make.

Hugh rose to shake the hand Stephen extended as Mansfield ushered him in, then set the tray of meat and cheese on the desk before bowing himself out.

'Good to see you again!' he said, motioning his friend to a chair. 'I trust you had a pleasant visit with your family.'

'Very pleasant. Although a shocking reminder of how swiftly time passes. My sister's boy, who was a plump toddler when we left for India, will be going up to Oxford next year! Seeing that, I was about to ask for a cane and an ear horn.'

'We may have a few good years left,' Hugh said with a chuckle. 'Wine? And please, help yourself.' He motioned to the provisions laid out on the tray.

'Thank you, I will. And who is this fine fellow?' Stephen asked, pointing to the parrot.

Preening, Pierre repeated, 'Fine fellow! Fine fellow!'

'A mistake,' Hugh said flatly, trying to ignore the hollow ache in his gut. 'An indulgence I was persuaded to buy in Bristol for my wards.'

Pierre cocked his head reproachfully. 'Not a mistake. Not a mistake.'

'That's enough from you, or the cover goes back on!' Hugh said, waving a warning finger at the parrot—who promptly turned his back and resumed looking out the window.

Laughing at that exchange, Stephen said, 'How are those charming girls?'

'Doing quite well, or so my great-aunt tells me.'

His smile turning puzzled, Stephen angled his head at Hugh. 'Your great-aunt tells you?' he repeated. 'What does that mean? Has Miss Overton left you?'

Hugh sighed. 'It's…complicated.'

'So explain.'

Trying to keep his expression and tone as neutral as possible, Hugh detailed his receipt of his great-aunt's offer to take the girls, her arriving at Somers Abbey to sweep them away and the subsequent departure of Miss Overton.

Taking a long sip of his wine, Stephen observed, 'You don't look very happy about it.'

'I admit, I miss them terribly. But I've known from the first that they should be raised by a well-placed female who can train them to run a genteel household and then see them properly presented and married. It's just that, not initially having had any suitable relations respond to my letters, I had rather grown used to the idea of raising them here.'

'And what about Miss Overton? Are you missing her?'

'She's returned to London. If you remember with what passion and enthusiasm she talked about her work there, you will know she is better placed now, too.' He wasn't about to reveal he'd suggested a marriage of convenience—and then rescinded the offer.

Stephen studied him. 'You just…let her go, without trying to do anything about it?'

'What would you have had me do?' Hugh spat back, anger and frustration and misery sharpening his tone. 'London is her proper milieu—not a struggling estate in the Somerset countryside! If I'm truly lucky, the proceeds from this year's apple crop may finally clear the rest of the debts my brother left, but the estate is still far from prosperous.'

'You think a lady who has lost her dowry and her position in life would care about that?'

'Perhaps not,' he admitted. 'But…you know how things ended with Lydia.'

Stephen was silent for a long time. 'Having no experience with wedlock, I won't presume to give advice on what makes for a happy union. If you feel you can't bring yourself to face the prospect of marriage again, I respect that decision.' He paused. 'You are *very* sure you do not want to make a push to win Miss Overton?'

He made himself nod. 'Yes, I'm sure.'

So sure he'd wrestled with the decision through every one of his many sleepless nights.

Stephen blew out a breath. 'Very well. Much as I enjoy your company, old man, I didn't make a detour on my way to London just to see you. I wanted to discover how matters stood between you and Miss Overton. Because if you have decided not to pursue her, I will.'

Hugh shook his head, not sure he'd heard correctly. 'You're going to what?'

'Pursue Miss Overton. Granted, pleasure is easily had in India. But I've come to the point in my life where I want more than just release for the body. I want a companion—someone to preside over my table as well as fill my bed. A lady of taste and refinement, who can play Beethoven and discuss politics and handle children. In short, a wife. Now that I know you've released any claim on her, when I get to London, I intend to look up Miss Overton—and court her.'

The implications registered in a blast of anger and disbelief. 'You can't mean you'd try to entice Miss Overton into marrying you—and carry her back to India!'

'A wife generally does accompany her husband,' Stephen said, smiling.

'That's not what I meant and you know it!' Hugh said furiously. 'You wouldn't be so irresponsible as to expose her to all those risks and dangers!'

Stephen's humorous expression vanished. 'After your dreadful experiences, I can understand your reluctance,' he said quietly. 'But even you must admit, not *every* English lady who goes out to India perishes. Indeed, every year the Fishing Fleet brings boatloads of single ladies from the homeland, all eager to find husbands on the subcontinent.'

What his friend said was true, but Hugh couldn't banish his dread or his furious resistance to the idea of Olivia marrying—Stephen or anyone else. 'Do you love her?'

'For reasons of which you should be very well aware, I've held my emotions in check,' he retorted. 'I don't intend to do so any longer. Granted, she isn't a Beauty in the conventional sense, but in my experience, Beauties require a tiresome amount of coddling. Better far to wed a woman of sense, competence and proven talents. Once I arrive in London, I will seek out Miss Overton and I will use every means at my disposal to persuade her to accept my suit.'

Hugh had been listening in growing agitation, but at this, he cried, 'You cannot mean that! Marry her, take her to India and I will no longer count you my friend!'

For a long moment, unsmiling, Stephen held his gaze. 'I would be very sorry to lose your friendship. But if you have truly relinquished any claim to the lady and my choice was between her hand and your good will, I think you know which one I would choose.'

All Hugh could think was what a catastrophe this whole conversation had become. He could tolerate living without Olivia, knowing she was safe in London, where she might find some way of continuing to live out her dream of involvement in politics. But married, in India? Exposed to the dangers of childbirth, fever, heat, ravaging tigers, poisonous reptiles and insects?

Clasped in some other man's arms, in some other man's bed?

Even considering it made him want to wrap his hands around that man's throat and strangle him.

If Stephen were truly planning to court Olivia, Hugh had better send him away before he said—or did—something violent. Whether or not he would be sorry for it later was debatable.

'It's getting late,' he said abruptly. 'You should be on your way to London.'

Rising from his chair, Stephen nodded. 'I won't ask you to shake my hand.'

'A wise decision,' Hugh spat out, closer to despising the man who'd once been his best friend than he would ever have dreamed possible.

'You're a fool, Hugh Glendenning,' Steven said as he walked out.

'You're a fool, you're a fool,' Pierre echoed.

For a timeless interval after Saulter departed, Hugh paced the library in circles, a maelstrom of emotion raging within him. He wasn't sure which notion disturbed and incensed him the most: Olivia exposed to all the dangers an Englishwoman faced in India—or Olivia married to someone else.

He already knew she wouldn't accept a marriage of convenience. But he also suspected, even though he hadn't intended it, his failure to follow through on his proposal had hurt her.

As he knew only too well, Stephen Saulter was a very charming fellow. A charming fellow who, he'd revealed to Hugh, now possessed a tidy fortune.

As she recovered from her disappointment in Somerset, she might well be vulnerable to the lures of a handsome, charming man. One who could tempt her with not just a return to her former status, but a position of respect as the wife of a rising official and a life of adventure far from England.

Much as it made him want to throttle Saulter to even consider such an outcome, Hugh had to admit his former comrade was a gentleman of excellent character. He had little doubt that, as Saulter got to know Olivia better, he would soon be able to pledge her a love untarnished by doubt, something Hugh had not been able to promise. Could Stephen persuade her to love him in return?

How could she when I suspect she loves me? an anguished voice within cried.

Why should she hesitate when you were unwilling to take a chance on a future with her—even if turning her away was for her own good? he answered it back.

Sick with agitation, anger, grief and outrage, he threw himself back in his chair and picked up his glass—only to put it down again. In his current state of turmoil, even the wine was unappealing.

If he really wanted to save her from Stephen, India—and any other man—there was only one way to do that.

During those many sleepless nights, he'd long since admitted he loved her—how else would he have been able to let her go, if he hadn't thought doing so was the best way to protect her?

But not until she'd left Somers Abbey had he realised how deeply he'd come to rely on her wry wit, serene presence and easy companionship. The idea of losing her completely and for good by marriage to another man was…intolerable.

Another memory occurred—one that eased his agitation slightly.

When he'd rescinded his offer, she'd argued with him,

contending that she herself was primarily responsible for her own happiness. So perhaps...perhaps he *could* chance wedding her, if the whole burden of her contentment didn't rest on his shoulders alone.

If he meant to claim her, he'd need to approach her before Stephen could succeed in charming her.

He would speak to the supervisors on the north field work this afternoon, pack two small bags tonight he could carry on his saddle and set out for London tomorrow on his fastest horse.

Although the idea of speaking about it aloud made his gut clench, if he truly meant to offer for her again, he would first have to confess the full truth about the end of his marriage to Lydia—tawdry facts that might have her send him packing before he ever got down on one knee.

But he would do it, for a chance to make her his. Though he still had doubts about his abilities as a husband, he had no doubt whatsoever that taking *her* as his wife would make *him* happy for a lifetime.

After the debacle of his first proposal, he only hoped he could convince her to give him a second chance.

Chapter Twenty

That same afternoon, Olivia sat in the small back parlour of her friend Sara Standish's home in Hanover Square, putting the last few stitches into the gown for Sophie she'd fashioned from the Bristol-bought fabric Elizabeth had liked the most—a light blue wool check that would bring out the lovely hue of their eyes. She smiled, envisioning the sisters wearing it with their dark blue spencers.

Since there was no reason she could not remain a friend to her former charges, she had tried to concentrate all her emotions on remembering the delight of their company and anticipating seeing them again. She'd already sent them several cards, one bearing the sketch of an English terrier, like the one Lady Laversby had promised she would get them that night in the salon at Somers Abbey, and several others with drawings of London scenes. She hoped their guardian's great-aunt had allowed the nursery maid, or new governess if she'd arrived, to read the notes she'd written on the back.

She'd tried to push to the very back of her mind the heartache of loving their guardian—a colossal mistake in judgement she would likely suffer from for the rest of her life. She'd vowed to simply not think of him—a pledge she'd not yet been very successful in fulfilling.

And yet, miserable as she felt when she recalled the way his eyes crinkled when he smiled, his rare laugh at some of the comments Pierre had made while she was trying to persuade him to purchase the parrot, the stimulation of his conversation, the thrill of his touch, she couldn't regret loving him.

And she would never, ever regret the glimpse he'd given her into the bliss and power of passion.

The only thing she regretted about *that* interlude was the frustrating necessity to heed the voice of wisdom and stop short of experiencing the final act of possession.

Would she always feel like she was *his*, even though she'd never fully belonged to him? Even though he'd not been able to fight through the ghosts of the past to choose a future with her?

And now here she was, silly fool, thinking of him again.

Determinedly replacing the image of his face with one of Elizabeth as she played the 'screaming game', Olivia held up Sophie's gown and inspected it. She might be terrible at embroidering and fine work, but she was an excellent seamstress, she thought with satisfaction. Now that both gowns were completed, she was ready to plan how and when she would travel to Laversby Hall to deliver them.

She suspected it would be better to simply arrive unannounced, rather than write for permission for a visit that might well be politely, but firmly, denied.

And she was going to see them, come what may.

She might not be able to hold on to Hugh Glendenning, but nothing was going to exclude her from the life of his wards.

Perhaps during her visit, she thought, a sudden swell of hope rising, she could figure out a way to be useful enough to her hostess that she might be persuaded to let Olivia stay on at Laversby. If not as the girls' governess, then perhaps as a music teacher, or an assistant and companion to Lady Laversby. Though the Colonel's great-aunt had seemed in robust health, she was getting on in years. She might well need some assistance to keep up with two active little girls.

The permanent ache within her eased at the possibility of being able to remain at Laversby, where she might indulge to the fullest her love for the children who had stolen into her heart.

Where she might catch a glimpse of their guardian when he came to visit, as he certainly must, sooner or later.

Could she keep herself from running to Hugh Glendenning, if she did see him?

A deep pain lanced through her, sparking tears she brushed away with an impatient hand. For a man to whom she'd already practically proposed, there was no predicting how foolish she might be.

Still, if she were lucky enough to secure a position in his great-aunt's household and wanted to keep it, she would have to be circumspect. Succumbing to her passion for him, as she had in the music room at Somers Abbey, would get her discharged without a character in short order. She'd lose the girls, too, and she couldn't bear that.

Better to avoid him, when he did visit.

On that sensible note, she folded Sophie's gown and placed it in the box with Elizabeth's already completed one.

She was putting up her sewing supplies when Sara walked into the salon.

'Finished, I see,' she said, coming over to give Olivia a hug. 'Are you going to use the green material now and sew another set?'

'Perhaps later, but not right now. I don't intend to hang about here, a charge on your household indefinitely, you know.'

'You know we love having you here! I do wish you'd reconsider accompanying me to some of our meetings, or come with us to dine with—'

'No, no,' Olivia said, holding up a hand. 'Nothing about my circumstances has changed. I must still seek a new situation, so there's no point picking up any of the threads of my former life.'

'You know your friends would love to see you. Especially Lady Lyndlington and the other ladies from the Committee.'

'That is kind of them, but I don't mean to remain in London much longer. I've decided to journey to Laversby Hall as soon as I can make suitable arrangements.'

'You are missing your former charges.'

She smiled. 'Yes. I promised Elizabeth I would bring their gowns as soon as I finished them. It's going on three weeks already since they left Somers Abbey—a very long time for a six-year-old!'

'Sometimes a very long time for grown people as well! I wouldn't want you to break your promise to Elizabeth, so I won't try to detain you, but I did learn today about a situation I wanted to speak to you about. Something

I hope you will seriously consider when you return to London.'

Though Olivia was increasingly convinced her path lay elsewhere, she couldn't help but be a little intrigued. 'What sort of situation?'

'You remember the Dowager Marchioness of Trent? She's worked with Lady Lyndlington on the Committee since its inception, but has been less active the last few years.'

Olivia scanned her memory, coming up with a tall, thin lady with a ready smile and an infectious laugh. 'Yes, I think so. I don't believe I've seen her at meetings above once or twice.'

'No. She took a fall while riding two years ago and has had a very slow, painful recovery. She still has difficulty walking and lifting her arms to get a book from a high shelf, or pull a shawl from the top of her armoire, is a misery. When Lady Lyndlington called on her recently, she said she regretted that she hadn't been able to attend many meetings. Lady Maggie suggested that she might find a companion—not a servant, more a friend, who could converse with her, help her to the dinners or balls she wishes to attend, take her to the Committee meetings and assist her with her letter writing. She said she would consider it. When Lady Maggie related this story at the Committee meeting today, I told her I thought you would be perfect for the position.'

'Me?' Olivia said dubiously. 'Recall that I'm not very good at taking orders, or running and fetching.'

'Oh, but she isn't like that! Lady Maggie likes her very much and you know she doesn't care at all for officious people who are puffed up with their own consequence. Only think, Olivia! You would be able to live in London in a lovely town house, attend balls and dinners, bring Lady Trent to meetings you'd want to attend anyway and even be paid a salary in addition to your room and board! Surely that would be more attractive than seeking another governess position.'

To remain in London, being paid for light duties while being able to throw herself into the work of the Committee, keeping her finger on the pulse of reform legislation as it evolved... Six weeks ago, before she'd first set out for Somers Abbey, she would have leapt at the opportunity.

Picturing Sophie's shy smile, Elizabeth's infectious giggle, such an opportunity no longer seemed quite so appealing.

'Sara, I'm not sure that I will return to London. If I can find a way to stay on at Laversby, I will.'

'Stay on at Laversby?' Sara echoed. After studying Olivia's face for a moment, she said quietly, 'You love those girls that much?'

Olivia sighed. 'I'm afraid I do.'

Sara nodded. 'If being with them will make you happy, then you must stay at Laversby.' She paused, then continued, 'I don't mean to tease you to talk if you don't wish to, but it seems to me that you've been deeply *un-*happy since you left Somers Abbey. And I don't think it's just because you miss your charges.'

Olivia smiled faintly. 'Ah, Sara, don't ever be foolish enough to fall in love!'

'The Colonel?'

Olivia nodded.

'Reading between the lines of your letters, it seemed to me that you had an ever-growing regard for him. He... did not return your affection?'

'He does…care for me. But if it weren't enough that he lost his son to a fever in India, his wife was so distraught after the child's death, she left him. She died in an accident while running away with another man. So he…he doesn't really believe that love can last.'

'How awful for him! No wonder he shies away from risking his heart again. Still, if he doesn't realise what an excellent, superior lady you are, one who, if he were fortunate to win her love, would cherish it for ever, then he doesn't deserve you!'

'Thank you, my dear advocate. But there the situation remains and, frankly, I don't think it will change.'

Sara pulled her into a hug. 'I'm so sorry,' she whispered against Olivia's shoulder. 'So, your journey to Laversby. When do you propose to leave?'

'As soon as I can make arrangements. The day after tomorrow, if possible.'

'That soon! Then I must make the most of the time I have left with you. I'll tell Aunt Patterson I cannot dine out with her tonight. I'll stay here and we'll have a comfortable coze, just as we used to do at school.'

Olivia smiled sadly. 'As we'd hoped to do, all three of us, at Judd Street.'

'We mustn't mourn what can't be changed,' Sara said briskly.

'Are you sure you want to cancel your plans? I wouldn't want you to distress your Aunt Patterson.'

'I'll have plenty of time to appease her after you've left for Laversby.'

'Then I would love to share the evening with you. You can tell me all about the latest projects of the Committee.'

'Excellent! I'll just go tell Cook we will both be dining in.' After pressing her hand, that concerned look still on her face, Sara walked out.

Olivia added the green material and her sewing box to the trunk with the newly made dresses. Hopefully she would be at Laversby Hall long enough to sew new gowns using that material, too.

She smiled wryly. Had anyone predicted two months ago that she would be willing to give up her work on the reform Committee to live in the countryside caring for two little girls, she would have laughed at them.

And laughed even harder had someone suggested in a tall, aloof, world-weary Colonel, she would have found—and lost—the love of her life.

A week later, Hugh Glendenning rode up the carriage drive to the large, imposing mansion that was Laversby Hall. As the miles had gone by, from Somers Abbey to London and out to Kent, he had become more and more convinced of the rightness of it. Perhaps it was just as well that he'd missed Olivia in London. She was here now—all the ladies he loved were here together. And if he were persuasive enough, he would be taking all of them back to Somers Abbey.

Rather than ride up to the entrance, he took the side path to the stables and turned his horse over to a groom. It had been many years since he'd visited his great-aunt's estate, but he remembered it well from his childhood visits. Walking from the stables through the formal walled garden to the manor would give him time to rehearse again what he meant to say to his great-aunt, the children and, assuming he could get her to agree to see him, Olivia.

The second of his objectives came abruptly to the

forefront as he walked through the gardens—and almost literally stumbled over Sophie as he turned the corner to a rose allée, where she was bending over, smelling one of the fragrant blooms.

'Whoa, sweeting, careful!' he said, gently steadying her before she could fall. Kneeling down to address her at her eye level, he said, 'Are you all right?'

Her eyes going wide, she stared at him. Then, throwing herself into his arms, she said, 'You came back for us?'

No first words spoken could ever have been sweeter. Clutching her tighter, feeling tears at the corners of his eyes, he said, 'Yes, I've come back for you.'

It seemed so natural to hold her, to cradle her small body against his. He would never stop aching for the little boy he'd once sheltered as he now sheltered her, but he'd found his heart could survive many hurts and was stout enough to bear the risk of more. If he'd ever doubted that, the perfect peace he felt at this moment was all the proof he needed.

'Sophie, where are you?'

He heard Elizabeth's voice before she rounded the corner—and saw them.

'Colonel?' she breathed, stopping short. Then she, too, ran to his arms. As he added her to the embrace, he felt deep within the rightness of it.

'You came back, just like you promised!' Elizabeth said against his coat. 'We've missed you so! Please say you're going to take us home!'

For a few minutes, he revelled in their innocent embrace. Then, releasing them, he took one small hand in each of his large ones and led them to a nearby bench.

'Haven't you liked being at Lady Laversby's house? It's had all the nice things I promised you it would, hasn't it?'

'Oh, yes, she has ever so many pretty things,' Elizabeth said. 'Dolls and blankets and puzzles and lots of dresses and two maids to bring us anything we like. But we're ready to go home now. Does Pierre miss us?'

'Everyone at Somers Abbey misses you.'

'Good. I miss them, too. I have so many words I want to teach Pierre! And Sophie promised she would talk to Pierre, too, didn't you, Sophie?'

The little girl nodded solemnly. 'I talk to Pierre, too.'

'When are we leaving, Colonel?' Elizabeth asked.

'It wouldn't be polite for me to leave so soon after arriving. I must speak with Lady Laversby... And I need to talk to Miss Overton. But if we're all going home together, "Colonel" sounds a little too formal. Do you think you could call me "Uncle Hugh"?'

Elizabeth angled her head at him, considering, then nodded. 'I like that. Will you talk with Lady Laversby right now, Uncle Hugh?'

'First, I'd like to speak to your governess. Do you know where Miss Overton is?'

'She reads to Lady Laversby in the afternoons, while she rests on her sofa, and Sally takes us to play in the garden. Lady Laversby says she has the most soothing voice.'

'She does indeed, doesn't she? You two go back to playing and I'll go find her. I'll see you later then, when you come back inside.'

Dropping a kiss on each girl's head, he let them go. Giggling, Elizabeth seized her sister's hand and began skipping her down the pathway. 'We're going home, we're going home!' she sang. Just before he walked away, grinning, Elizabeth halted and blew him a kiss. 'I love you, Uncle Hugh!'

He blew it back. 'I love you too, sweeting.'

His heart lighter than it had been in months, he took the path back to the manor. If only his interview with their governess would end so delightfully.

The vision he saw as he reached the next cross path stopped him in mid-stride. Strolling down a parallel path, her attention on the book she carried, was Olivia.

For a moment he simply stood and drank in the welcome sight of her. The graceful walk. The fringe of curls that shadowed those expressive brown eyes. The well-rounded figure that set his senses ablaze even as his heart swelled until his chest ached and he felt tears sting his eyes.

Murmuring a prayer for God to grant him eloquence, he walked over to intercept her.

Chapter Twenty-One

Idly browsing the book she'd been reading to her hostess, Olivia only vaguely noticed movement on the path parallel to the one she was taking to find the girls and bring them in for their nap. Until something about the height and stride and presence of the man, some subtle stirring in her senses, made her halt abruptly and look up.

Hugh.

Delight and trepidation spiralling within her, she barely choked back a gasp. She'd known if she stayed with the girls, she'd probably encounter him at Laversby Hall at some point—but she hadn't expected to see him today. Now.

Not while she was unprepared, unarmoured against the love that burst from her longing heart in effervescent waves and made her want to throw down the book and run to his arms.

She had to grit her teeth, clutch the book and curl her toes in her half-boots to keep herself from doing just that. And frantically tried to use the few minutes' grace she had while he approached to recover her façade of serenity.

When he reached her, she gave a curtsy to his bow. 'Colonel, I didn't realise you were visiting,' she said, proud of how calm her voice sounded. 'Have you met the girls yet? They will be so happy to see you.'

'Yes, I just spoke with them. How glad *I* was to see *them*! Much as I initially tried to resist them, those two little minxes have carved a place in my heart. And that's not all I have missed. Nor is seeing them the main reason I came here.'

Though her heartbeat leapt at that, she made herself reply coolly, 'Indeed?'

'Yes. Would you sit on this bench with me? I have a few things I'd like to say.'

Praying it was what she wanted to hear, and not more apologies or explanations, she said, 'I suppose I can spare a few minutes.'

As they took their seats, curiosity compelled her to ask, 'Did you know I'd be here?' At his nod, she added, 'How?'

'I've already been to London and called on your friend, Miss Standish. She told me you'd come to Laversby.'

'And…you wanted to see me about…?' she probed. With her stomach in knots and her emotions jumping from agonised hope to steely resignation, she needed to discover his reason for seeking her out as quickly as possible.

His eyes roved over her face with a tenderness that made her breath hitch. 'First, though you may well tell me it is none of my business, I wanted to know if…if you have accepted the offer Stephen Saulter told me he intended to make you. Although what I want most in the world is your happiness, I can't bear the thought of you risking yourself, going out to India.'

He was worried about her, she realised. Compassion and a sympathetic sadness filled her. Given his experiences, she could understand why the prospect of having any child or female he cared for taking a ship for foreign lands would fill him with trepidation.

'It's…kind of you to be concerned—' *though kindness is not what I want from you!* '—but you needn't have worried. Mr Saulter did call on me right before I left London. But I politely let him know that I could not encourage his suit.'

'Thank heaven,' he muttered, such an intensity of relief in his voice she had to hide a smile.

'Miss Standish also told me she didn't think you'd be returning to London. That you'd turned down a position there so you might come here and be with the girls.'

'I love them,' she said simply. 'I spoke frankly with Lady Laversby about my feelings for them and my…circumstances, offering to remain here in any capacity she would allow, even unpaid, as long as I might stay with them. She's agreed to hire me as her companion.'

'So you love them more than your political causes? You'd be happy to spend your life with them?'

Suddenly exasperated, she burst out, 'If there is some point to this interrogation, I wish you would reach it! If what you mean to discover is what would make me happiest, I suspect you already know the answer to that. After all, I've already all but thrown myself at your feet with a lack of feminine modesty that would have made my mother swoon! And all you had to offer me back was…*money.*'

Unable to keep the hurt and disappointment from her voice, she rose from the bench. 'If you'll excuse me, I need to find the girls.'

'Wait!' he said, catching her hand. 'That isn't…all I would offer you. But before I say any more, you need to know the truth, all of it. Please, won't you listen?'

She could hardly refuse that plea. Trying to keep her battered emotions, which had already swung several times from the heights of hope to the valleys of disappointment, from rising again, she sat down. 'I'm listening.'

Despite his avowed eagerness, he remained silent for several minutes before beginning. Whatever he felt compelled to say must be difficult for him, she realised.

'You know my wife died shortly after Drew,' he said at last. 'But she didn't expire of a fever or a broken heart. At least, not directly. She was killed in an accident while trying to return to England…with another man.'

Despite all her attempts to armour herself against him, her heart ached anew. 'I know,' she said softly.

'You know?' he repeated. 'But how—? Ah. Stephen.'

'You mustn't think he was breaking a confidence! I'd told him earlier that I knew all about what had happened in India, so he assumed I knew that, too. He didn't realise no one in England had heard the full story. It…must have been so dreadful for you.'

Gazing into the distance, he took her hand, absently rubbing his thumb over her wrist. She knew she should pull away, but she didn't, instead closing her eyes to savour his touch.

'I was so distraught over Drew I was hardly aware of the gossip.' He sighed. 'I… I still don't know why or how things changed between us. I'd known Lydia since we were children. She had such an adventurous spirit, such a zest for life! When I came back from university to find she'd turned into a beauty, I was…dazzled. With her spirit and enthusiasm, I thought she would be a perfect wife for an army officer in India.'

He shook his head. 'But the India that fascinated me…frightened her. Of course, while we were courting, I'd brought her gifts and flowers and made her pretty speeches. I didn't realise for many months after our marriage that she still expected those tributes. By the time I did, there were plenty of other men eager to offer them. So I let them. And when it seemed that, rather than looking forward to my company, when I came home she had nothing to offer but complaints, I…started delaying my return. I hoped having Drew would bring us back together, but it only seemed to make her more anxious. She wanted to take him and return to England. God forgive me, I wouldn't hear of it. If I had…'

Her heart weeping for his pain, Olivia said, 'You couldn't have known what would happen. And what if they had taken passage back to England? With storms and shipwrecks and pirates, there's no guarantee they would have returned safely.'

He swallowed hard, obviously forcing himself to continue. 'As I told you before, when we…we lost Drew, she blamed me, as I blamed myself. Wrapped up in my own grief, I didn't realise how truly desperate she'd become, until it was too late. She was my wife, my responsibility to care for and protect. I failed her completely.'

'My dear Hugh,' she said softly, squeezing his hand, 'I can't speak for your wife, but it's past time for you to stop thinking of women as delicate, brainless little beings who must be protected, incapable of making decisions or taking action on their own. We have hearts and minds and the will and courage to act for ourselves, and, yes, to bear the responsibility for our choices and actions.

Or, in a loving partnership, to share them. I think you take too much on yourself, to assume you should have been able to decipher the mind and heart of someone else, even someone you loved. The reaching out must come from both sides.'

He gave her the shadow of a smile. 'Trying to aid and succour, as always.'

'So,' she said slowly, 'it isn't that you don't trust me to be faithful?'

Obviously surprised by the question, he said, 'Not at all! Of course I trust you—as much as one can trust anyone, knowing that hearts and minds may change. It was always my abilities as a husband that I questioned. But in spite of that, now that you know everything, I still feel compelled to ask if you'll…take a chance on me. I had to let you know how much I love you. How much I desire you. How much I need you in my life. And how ardently I will do all in my power to make you happy.'

Shaking her head to make sure she'd heard him correctly, unable to check the hope now soaring again in her heart, she said, 'Hugh Glendenning, are you asking me to marry you—again?'

He gave her a slight smile. 'Yes, I suppose I am.'

'Without orders or recommendations or making the choice for me? You will let *me* decide? Knowing what happens afterward is as much *my* responsibility as it is yours?'

His smile broadened, some of the anxiety leaving his eyes. 'As I recall, you are a managing woman, rather difficult to guide.'

'So I am. Nor am I one to sit about, expecting to be pampered and waited on. Or to demand flowers and speeches and costly gifts and grand gestures. If I am unhappy about something, I will definitely let you know it.'

'You'll rake me over coals?'

'Most certainly.'

'Then are you saying—you *will* marry me?'

Almost giddy with elation at having what she'd lost all hope for come true after all, she said, 'I suppose I'll consider it—if you ask me properly.'

In an instant, he went down on one knee and seized her hands. 'Olivia Overton, my saviour and my angel, will you accept the hand of this rough old soldier? And make him happier than he ever thought or deserved to be again in this life?'

Joy making her feel illumined from within, she nodded. 'I will.'

With an exultant cry, he sprang up and seized her hands, yanked her to her feet and wrapped her in his arms. Then he was kissing her, deep, desperate, passionate kisses that showed more than words the strength of his need and the depth of his love.

She was melting in delight, ravenous for more, when suddenly he pulled away. 'Enough,' he said, gasping. 'Not until after the ceremony.'

'After?' she squeaked in protest. 'If you stop kissing me now, I… I'll withdraw my acceptance!'

'So I'm to ravish you right here in the garden? I'm afraid we'll scandalise my great-aunt.'

'Unladylike language, screaming in gardens, brazenly proposing to recalcitrant men? Haven't you realised yet that I'm a scandalous woman?'

Grinning, he pulled her close again. 'I'm so glad,' he murmured and took her mouth again.

Approving of that action wholeheartedly, she threw

her arms around him. Her lesson in passionate kissing was going quite well—until she dimly noticed what seemed to be a tug at her skirts.

'Uncle Hugh, why are you kissing Miss Overton?'

Chuckling, the joy on his face so radiant she felt her own heart leap, he tucked his arm in hers, pulled her to sit back beside him on the bench, then lifted Elizabeth, and Sophie who'd followed her, on to his lap.

'Well, you see, Miss Overton just agreed to marry me. Gentlemen are allowed to kiss ladies after they agree to marry them. So she won't be your governess any more.'

Elizabeth frowned. 'But I want her to be our governess! And I want all of us to go back to Somers Abbey and teach Pierre more words. Dogs are lovely, but I like my parrot.'

'Oh, we will go back. And I'll still be your Uncle Hugh. But Miss Overton will be your mama.'

Sophie giggled. 'Mama!' she said, giving Olivia a hug.

Elizabeth's grin was huge. 'Oh, yes! I like that even better.'

Two weeks later, nervous anticipation swirling in her stomach, Olivia stood beside Sara in the small salon off the grand receiving room of Lady Laversby's imposing mansion in Grosvenor Square. 'I'm sorry Emma and Lord Theo won't be here to witness this, but Hugh didn't want to wait another four months for the ceremony—and neither did I.'

'Of course not,' Sara said with a fond glance. 'He's such a tall, forceful, commanding man, I expect one just naturally wants to follow whatever he recommends.'

Olivia chuckled. 'Not exactly. He's a bit too ready to

take everything on his shoulders. I have to force him to share the load.'

'Well, you are good at managing.'

'You must all come visit at Somers Abbey when Emma and Theo get back from their grand tour.'

Sara brightened. 'Emma writes that Lord Theo is doing some wonderful portraits. You should commission him to do one of the girls. One of you, too. I'm sure your new husband would appreciate it.'

Olivia smiled, peeking through the partly opened door to where Hugh stood in the next room with the Reverend, taking in the erect military figure, the strong jaw and broad shoulders. Just for her, he'd worn his regimentals.

'I can't wait to be "appreciated". But I do wish I didn't feel quite so much like I am…abandoning you. Silly, I know, when I would have had to leave you if I continued in service, but—'

'Nonsense,' Sara said, shaking her head at Olivia. 'I couldn't be happier for you—or for Emma. How differently everything has worked out from what we'd planned! Emma's purpose now is helping Lord Theo pursue his art, while you'll be working with the Colonel to restore his estate. Maybe I'll take that post as companion to Lady Trent, as an alternative to our Judd Street plans. I'd be able to help us both remain fully involved in the Committee and the reform group legislation.'

'And be freed from Aunt Patterson's attempts to drag you into marriage,' Olivia noted. 'But only if the Marchioness is pleasant to be around and intelligent enough to appreciate what an excellent, superior lady *you* are.'

After peeping through the door to slide a glance at Hugh, Sara sighed. 'It's so romantic, though, isn't it?

Both you and Emma swept off your feet by handsome princes neither of you ever expected to find.'

Olivia pressed her friend's hand. 'I feel sure there must be a prince out there for you, too. A true prince—not just the conventional boring aristocrat your Aunt Patterson wants you to marry.'

Sara laughed. 'If there is truly someone for me, he will certainly not be that. But, look, the girls have just come down. It's time now.'

With joy, anticipation, and more than a little awe at her marvellous good fortune, Olivia squeezed Sara's hand, then walked with her into the reception room where Elizabeth and Sophie, garbed in the blue gowns she'd made them that Elizabeth had insisted they wear, had just been escorted by Lady Laversby to stand beside Hugh. Taking each girl by the hand, he leaned down and whispered something that made them giggle.

Then he looked up and saw her, and she couldn't look away. His gaze the magnet that drew her, she walked over to stand beside him. Knowing his love would be the lifeline to comfort and delight, exasperate and bedevil, pleasure and rescue her for a lifetime. As hers would be for him.

With the coterie of friends and family surrounding them—Lady Lyndlington and her husband, Sara's Aunt Patterson, Hugh's great-aunt and the girls—they stood before the Reverend, reciting the ancient vows and pledging hand, heart and lives together.

The short service ended, their well-wishers surrounded them with hugs and congratulations, and Lady Laversby invited the group to the wedding breakfast set out in the next room. The girls beside them, Hugh took her hand and led her in.

'The ballroom in this house is where you will make your debuts when you grow up and are ready to be married,' his great-aunt was telling the girls. 'It's large enough to host everyone who is anyone in London!'

'I'm more looking forward to the large, private bedchamber we'll be sharing tonight,' Hugh murmured to her.

'As am I,' she whispered back. 'As you'll recall, my sensual education was rudely interrupted.'

'No more interruptions,' he said, his voice rough and his eyes gleaming with erotic intent. 'Tonight and every night, here and at Somers Abbey, for the rest of our lives.'

'Only at night?'

Hugh chuckled. 'Ah, you are a scandalous woman, aren't you?'

The kiss he leaned down to give her was as sweet as it was rich with his promise for the future.

* * * * *

*If you enjoyed this story, check out the first book in
The Cinderella Spinsters miniseries*

The Awakening of Miss Henley

and look for the next one in the series, coming soon!

*And whilst you're waiting for the next book,
be sure to read the Sisters of Scandal miniseries
by Julia Justiss*

A Most Unsuitable Match
The Earl's Inconvenient Wife